The Bygone Dagger

Joseph R. Lallo

ISBN: 978-1951240066

Table of Contents

ACKNOWLEDGMENTS

I would like to thank Nick Deligaris for his excellent cover illustration. I would also like to thank Tammy Salyer for going above and beyond to help make this story comprehensible. And most importantly, I would like to thank the readers for giving this first story of a new series a chance! Thanks for all your support!

Chapter 1

This was it. This would be his big win.

Fel Masker adjusted the flimsy wooden divider in front of him for the fifth time. The other players were all friends, people he'd squandered many a night with, drinking and telling the same stories. But this was a game of grum, and there was easily a month's pay sitting in a heap on the table. He wouldn't trust his own mother to keep her eyes on her own tiles at a time like this.

The smoke of a cheap cigar burned his eyes. He squinted in the dim light of the back room. Anxious fingers shuffled the little black, white, and blue tiles, arranging them and rearranging them as though he might somehow find a better combination if he iterated enough. The game was all about bidding for tiles to build the strongest run. He had a *very* strong run already, but a single tile in the middle would make it virtually unbeatable. His buddy Tem must have known it, because for the last five minutes the game had reduced to the two of them raising their bids on that tile, trying to secure it for their own run.

Fel sipped his ale. He glanced at the meager pile of coins he had left, and the mound in the middle of the table. He swept up his money. "What's the bid at?" he asked, jangling his coins in his hand.

"Twenty-five duots. Same as it was the last time you asked," said Tem, half a smile on his face. "Look, you're the last one with any money left. Either outbid me or show your run."

Fel narrowed his eyes. He didn't like that face. That was the face of a confident grum player. But it was also the face of Tem, a man he'd seen slip in the same pile of harpy flop three times in the same day. He was a fool. And he'd soon see just how foolish he was. Fel finished his ale.

"I bid thirty duots," he said, tossing six piles of coins into the pot. After a moment he shrugged and tossed in his last two coins. "Make it thirty-two. May as well be tidy."

"Take it," Tem said.

He snatched the tile and slotted it into his run. It was glorious. He'd not had a grum run like this in months.

"Ready to reveal?" Tem asked.

"We better be. There's no money left to bid," Fel said. "Left to right, what've we got? Lou?"

The portly and highly inebriated fellow to his left pushed down his divider. "Three plowmen in a row, and a milkmaid," he said. "Trash."

"Hah!" Fel slapped down his divider. "I've got a queen's run! Blue and black!"

"You lucky scoundrel," grumbled Mel, to his right. "All I've got is four falconers and a milkmaid."

"You had the other milkmaid?" Lou said. "So I was never going to get it?"

"It was the first tile I bid on!" Mel said.

"… Was it?" Lou said.

"You've got to pay attention, Lou," Fel said. "Or better yet, don't. Because I'm going to *love* spending your money once Tem shows me whatever run I just beat."

"Oh, well then you're going to be waiting a while." His friend flicked his divider and revealed his tiles. "A king's run, all red."

Fel's face dropped. There were only three runs that could beat his. That was one of them. He scrutinized the run of tiles and glanced at the neat stack of unused ones behind it. "What was with you bidding on plowmen and carpenters for the last five rounds?" he said. "You must've had us all beat after the third bid!"

"They're called tactics, Fel. Learn them and maybe you'll win a game or two."

Just like that, Fel was left angrily sipping the last of his ale as Tem gathered a week's pay from each of the players into his sack.

"Thanks for the contributions, all," Tem said with frustrating swagger. "I'll buy a round before I go. I'd hate for you all to go thirsty on account of me."

"Keep your charity," Fel grumbled. "You just wait until next week. No man stays lucky forever."

"No, but skill sticks around," Tem said.

Fel shoved his chair aside, left the table, and pushed open the heavy door to the rest of the tavern. He squinted at the light of the midafternoon sun as it shined through the expensive glass windows.

"Cleaned out?" said Allie the barmaid, her voice insultingly chipper.

"Luck wasn't with me," he said, dropping heavily into a seat at the bar.

He set his tankard down. She snatched it and lingered on the other side, swinging it from a finger.

"You didn't even last until sundown. I'm starting to think you and luck aren't on speaking terms."

"Quit rubbing it in and fill that up, would you. I'm half-drunk already, I may as well finish the job. In fact, skip the ale. Give me a bottle of that rum I like."

She tapped the bar. "No bottles on tabs, Fel. You know the rules."

He leaned forward. "Allie. Darling, sweet Allie. Light of my life. I work like a gnoll all through the night to earn a pittance." He hiked a thumb over his shoulder at Tem as he left the room. "And I lost a week's worth of it because this so-called friend of mine ran up the cost of the good tiles when he'd already won."

Tem clicked his tongue and smiled on the way out the door. "Tactics!"

"Surely you can see your way to giving me a bottle of the good stuff to ease my suffering. It's medicinal!"

"If I gave you a bottle of rum every time you lost a game of grum, we'd *both* be begging for our next meal. But tell you what." She reached behind the bar and set a nearly full bottle with a crooked label on the wood top. "We had a merchant come through here and sell us a case of these and we can't even give them away."

He grabbed the bottle and popped the cork. "If you can't give them away, it's because you haven't been offering to your buddy Fel." He took a swig, fought it down his gullet, and wiped a tear from his eye. "Smooth as honey," he croaked.

#

A young man marched up to the side of a coach house in a small town near the center of Thayn. He was disheveled, but there was a softness and delicacy to his appearance that suggested he'd spent the greater part of his life sheltered and primped. This messy lifestyle was plainly a recent phenomenon. He carried a wooden case, far heavier and more ungainly than anything an experienced traveler would choose to haul from place to place without a wagon to stow it in.

The coach house had a weathered map posted on the wall. He smiled as he spotted it and set down his heavy case to investigate. His journey hadn't been going precisely as he'd hoped. The going was slow, but that much he could have supposed. He had no horse and wagon of his own, so he was beholden to the charity of other travelers to make his way from town to town. Alternately, he could hire a driver, but his budget would not bear that particular expense at the moment. Not after his rather substantial purchase at the alchemist shop at the edge of town.

"Let me see, now..." he mused.

He held his hand up to the legend at the bottom corner of the map and spaced his fingers as a makeshift compass to walk off the distance from his current location to the next likely stops.

"Any way I slice it, I'll be on the road for another full day once I leave this place. Best to find myself somewhere to sleep and get myself a proper meal. But maps are hard to come by. Particularly maps of this level of detail."

He rubbed his hands together and paced to the edge of the map. Row by row he ran his finger along the grids. There were hundreds of towns and villages listed on the map. He had to imagine it was comprehensive. If there was a place worth spending his time in Thayn, it was somewhere on this map. The circles of each town corresponded to their size. This town, with maybe two dozen residents, was little more than a flyspeck. Teskal, the capital, had been marked with a fully rendered town seal the size of an apple. Tempting as it was to head there, he'd need to amass a bit more of a fortune if he hoped to last more than a few days in Teskal.

"What would be a good intermediate stop? Somewhere sizable but small enough to have an avenue for an up-and-comer like myself..."

Three or four likely places had turned up in the top three rows of the map, but he was a long way from the northern edge of the kingdom. In a move that would have been obvious to a more seasoned traveler, he abandoned the systematic top-to-bottom search in favor of tracing his way along the roads. The biggest town that he could reach in a reasonable amount of time was a thumbprint-sized city called Beffshire. It had the benefit of serving as a bit of a crossroads as well. Plenty of options when he chose to move on.

"Beffshire it is," he said with a nod.

He reached into his pocket. The entirety of his fortune had dwindled to three duots. That wasn't enough to get much of anywhere. He grappled with his conscience for a few moments, but the battle was doomed from the start. He reached into a pocket in his coat and produced a small folio of handwritten slips. He selected one and slipped it out. A small general store, something that was thankfully a part of any given town, was just across the way. He hauled his case to it and glanced inside. Within the store, a counter had been set aside from the rest. An elderly woman sat there stirring a pot of warm stew. A stack of rolls had been carefully arranged beside the stew pot.

He nodded and deftly folded both of the coins into the sheet of paper. Once he'd formed a neat packet, he held it up, tore the top, and placed it in his palm. The edges of the page darkened. They flaked away and wafted into the air as though they were burning, though there was no flame. When the last of the page fluttered away, what remained in his hand was a pair of dodecots, each worth twenty duots rather than one.

He stepped inside. "Hello, ma'am!" he said. "I'd like to make some purchases, if I may, but I am in a considerable hurry."

A few minutes later he stepped out of the store with some fresh paper, a pot of normal ink, a passable quill, and a loaf of bread. The whole purchase had only cost him fifteen duots, leaving him with five duots change. Somewhere in that shopkeeper's coffers, the illusory dodecot was losing its brief enchantment and shifting back to its proper appearance. With any luck, the end-of-day or end-of-week accounting would chalk up the difference to a simple accumulation of mathematical errors. However, just to be certain, it was best to be on his way without further delay.

#

The next hour or so put a fair dent into the awful liquor and, with it, the lingering remnants of Fel's sobriety. As tended to occur whenever he was far enough into a drinking session, he turned to gaze out the window and focused on the spot of pink visible near the end of Broad Lane.

"What do you think she's doing?" he mumbled, sloshing the bottle.

"Who, Mariss?" Allie asked, toting a tray of empty tankards back to the bar. "Probably selling pastries, what with her being a baker. Or the daughter of one, at least."

"She's a baker," he said with certainty. "She makes all the cream-filled buns and cakes. And she makes those little… what do you call them… rosettes on top of the fancy stuff. She's talented."

It was telling, and for some it would be a bit worrisome, that he managed to remain articulate after so much cheap booze. That was the sort of thing that took practice.

"She better be, for the prices they charge at that place. You could have a night of fun for the cost of one cake from Divinity's Oven."

"They're worth it. It's the best bakery in Beffshire. Heh, probably the best in all of Thayn. She's high class…" he said dreamily. "What do you think it'd take to catch the eye of a woman like that?"

"Whatever it is, you're probably not going to find it in the back room of a bar or the bottom of a bottle of cheap booze."

"See, that's where you're wrong, Allie. It's like I said, class. Class just means money, basically. And I already work myself ragged to barely afford a decent drink, so working isn't the way to get where I need to be for her to give me the kind of look I want her to give me. So I have to get creative. Gambling's a way to do it, and what's more, it's the only way I've got."

"The fact that you had to sweet talk me into giving you a bottle of bottom-shelf hooch would suggest otherwise."

"I just haven't had the luck yet."

She started wiping down the mugs. "Fel, you're twenty-seven years old and you drink and mope like Burnt-out Benny over there. He's twice our age. If this is where you've gotten heading in the direction you think you should be heading, maybe it's time for a change."

He sighed and slapped the cork back in the bottle. "Tell that to my parents. Masker's Antiquities has been there since before there *was* a Beffshire. Tradition is like a sandbag around my neck. I'm sure they'd be happy if I just forgot about my place in the world and just focused on taking over the shop.

5

I'd probably be happier if I accepted my job and settled down with a woman like you."

She snorted. "Fel, you'd be settling *up* with a girl like me. I've seen how much you drink and how little you win at grum."

He gave her a sideways glance and handed her back the bottle. "Set that aside for me, would you? Like the bottles of brandy you hold for the high-rollers." He dug into his pocket and tossed two of the coins he'd separated from his gambling money onto the bar. "This is for the excellent service, and this"—he pressed his finger to the top of one of the coins and slid it back into his pocket—"is for the critique."

She shrugged and took the other coin. "Worth the price. See you tomorrow?"

"Unless I find something better to do with my life…"

Chapter 2

Fel took his time walking home. The family shop, and thus his home, was near the south gate of town, a fair distance from the tavern. The Fox and Log wasn't the closest tavern to Masker's Antiquities, which was one of the many appeals of the place. A little distance from a disapproving mother was never a bad thing. The walk home gave him time to sober up a tad as well.

"Go!" squawked a voice. "Get out! Rat bird!"

He looked to the rooftops. A quartet of wild-eyed, blunt-beaked lesser harpies lined the peak of a tailor's shop. They looked like cat-sized ravens with curiously upright postures and skinny necks. One had a button in its beak. The others wanted it and were seeking to separate it from its current owner with what passed for negotiation among lesser harpies—flapping wings, making grabs with hand-like talons, and croaking the words they'd learned from the townsfolk.

"Give it back, you stinking flying rat monkey!" screeched the smallest one.

Fel laughed. "We've got a scholar among us."

He scraped the toe of his boot between the cobblestones. The birds had been gathering around the tailor's ever since an apprentice had dropped a box of buttons and the pea-brained birds had become enamored with the shiny black disks. A bit of digging with his boot turned up three more buttons. He fished them up and buffed them on his pants.

"Hey!" he called. "A couple more for you! Maybe now you'll move along."

Fel knew it wasn't true. You give them what they're after and they'll keep coming back. But the antics were funny, and he didn't mind if they lingered… so long as it wasn't on the roof of the antiquities shop. He tossed the buttons up. The three harpies that hadn't gotten ahold of a treasure of their own hopped into the air and snatched them nimbly.

"That'll teach ya, ya weasel bird!" screeched one.

"The blasted thing's got my boot!" croaked another.

Fel snickered. "I'd like to hear the story behind that one."

The family shop was just ahead. A carefully carved sign with faded gold paint in the lettering swung over the door. A garishly painted mask had been attached to the sign with some twists of wire. An empty space beside it with some splintering revealed where a matching mask had been stolen years ago. He reached up and tapped the chin of the remaining mask, a good-luck ritual that he'd been doing for so long that the chin was beginning to shine with whatever cheap metal was beneath the paint.

He opened the door, producing the pleasant little tinkle of the brass bell that hung above it. The shop was a smallish square room lined with shelves. The front of the shop was dominated by twin glass windows. Shutters jutted in at the points where the windows met, allowing them to lock up the shop for the handful of hours they weren't actively doing business each day. A thick, attractive rug lay in the very center of the shop floor. Each of the display shelves had a carefully curated assortment of wares that were seemingly random to everyone but his mother, who was staring disapprovingly from her station behind a counter at the far side of the room.

Vivian Masker was at once the perfect match for and mirror opposite of his father, Martin. Like the patriarch, Vivian would rather work than sleep. Every waking moment was spent in service of the shop.

"Fel! You're early, lovely. I've got deliveries. The Gellner and the Tallby family silver is polished up and ready."

"Is it wrapped up?" he said.

"No. Still needs wrapping," she said, motioning with her head to the crate of silverware behind the counter with her. "Been drinking, I see."

"What else is new?" he muttered, hefting the crate onto the counter.

He mechanically worked his way through wrapping and layering the precious silverware with cheesecloth.

"You'll be dropping these off, then doing the north-end circuit. There's bound to be more silver that needs polishing and jewelry that needs repairing."

"Refresh my memory, Mom. Are we an antiquities shop or a silver-polishing shop?"

"We're whatever we need to be to keep a roof over our heads. Now hush up. After the north circuit, but before dinner, I want you to swing by the watchhouse. They have a few of those alarm contraptions your father made that need to be picked up and reset."

He nodded dully. She flipped through a ledger and crossed off some items.

"Did you lose a whole week's pay this time?" she asked.

"Not a whole week. I held back enough for breakfast tomorrow."

"And to get drunk, I see."

"Getting drunk was part of the gambling budget," he said.

She shook her head. "You know, I don't mind the drinking. My father drank. So did my mother. Martin's father was a tea-drinker, but his mother drank enough for both of them. You come from a line of drinkers, but I wish you'd learn to handle money better. You might have to run this place when your father and I are gone, you know."

"I think we both know that's going to be Fanny, not me," he said. "And isn't she supposed to be here already?"

"Your sister Epiphany can't run a shop by herself. So if you're not going to learn to stop squandering your money on grum and rum—your breath reeks of the latter, by the way—then either she's going to have to marry someone good with devices, or you're going to have to marry someone good with numbers. And since neither of you seem too keen on either, the two of you are going to have to work together."

"Fine, then I'll handle the devices and she'll handle the numbers, problem solved," he said. "The silver is packed for delivery. Should I head out now?"

"Not just yet. Your father has something to show you in the workshop."

He gave her a sideways glance. "Should I be worried?"

"It's harmless. *This* time."

"Is it something we're going to be able to sell?"

She shook her head slowly.

"May as well head down and take a look before the assayers come and take it then."

He stepped to the back corner of the shop and opened what folks these days called a "Beffshire Door." This was one of the older buildings still in use in the town, and like the other holdovers from the olden days, they preferred to dig down instead of build up. Most buildings weren't more than one or two stories tall, but the shop had a basement and five sub-basements. Access to these lower levels usually came in the form of a combination doorway and floor hatch. The door was about half the height of a standard door, and the hatch could be raised to reveal steps leading down. The reason they'd used such awkward doors in favor of a normal staircase or a ladder was, like the makers and intentions of the contraptions his father worked on, lost to antiquity.

The level below the shop was home to the kitchen and dining room. Below that was his parents' bedroom. Then three more bedrooms including his own. A general-purpose floor, which was perpetually in a state of disorder, a storage floor, and finally his father's workshop on the lowest level. Fel shivered as he reached the workshop level. Thayn had very hot summers and mild winters, but go much below the second level and it managed to remain positively chilly throughout the year. He knocked on the door.

"Come in!" shouted his father, a tad more loudly than was necessary.

Fel opened the door to the glorious balance of fastidiousness and chaos that was his father's shop. He was a ruthless organizer. The workshop was the same size and nearly the same layout as the top-level shop. Whereas the display shelves upstairs were designed to intrigue and allure would-be customers, the workshop was his father's best attempt to externalize the contents of his mind. Bins of every shape and size, mostly cobbled together out of larger crates, held parts and tools. A single wall was kept clear. The stone of that wall still held the tool marks of the men and women who built this town. It had been blackened, chipped, and in one particularly unsettling place, turned bright blue and glassy. This was the testing bench, the place where his father activated the contraptions he'd endeavored to repair.

"Ah-ha! Fel, my boy! Come on! Quickly, did your mother tell you? Did she spoil the surprise?" he said.

"She just said you wanted to see me."

The patriarch of the family had a pair of compound lenses perched on his face, and at first glance, he seemed to be wearing gloves along with his usual shop apron. Upon closer inspection, his fingernails were visible, meaning his hands were simply pitch-black.

Fel's father busied himself screwing a small black box to the top of an odd, spindly stand. Fel buttoned the top button of his shirt and shivered again. There was a stiff breeze coming down through the dumbwaiter beside the wood-fired stove in the corner. Fel pressed the door to the waiter shut and held his hands in front of the stove. It was barely warm.

"Dad, for as long as I can remember, you've kept this fire burning in this stove, but you never actually stoke it enough to be warm," he said, pulling the door open and tossing in a few sticks from the kindling box.

"I don't need it warm, I just need it workable." He paused and sniffed. "Are you drunk?"

"Not *very*."

"What time is it?"

"Just past tea."

"Ah…" He raised his eyebrows and clapped his hands. "Well, wait until you see this. Stand over there. Just there. I've marked the floor."

"Dad, I get nervous when you have me standing on marks…" Fel said, eying a hasty ink mark on the ground warily. "Remember the thing with the net?"

"There's no net. I've tested this twice. Trust me. Just stand there and look presentable."

"Presentable?"

Fel stood on the mark and wrangled his hair a bit. His father poured some ink into a canister and set it beside the device. He stood back, eyed the arrangement, and adjusted the position slightly. The device itself was relatively simple, as contraptions go. A box with smooth black sides; tiny, intricate screws clustered about the corners; and an open top with a missing panel. All manner of tiny pieces were visible within, and the front face of the box had an opaque blue bead in the center.

Mr. Masker looked at Fel one last time, nodded, and plucked a pair of tongs from a pocket on the front of the apron. He used them to position a square of paper beneath the stand. He used a smaller set of tongs to pull an orange bead from a velvet-lined case and delicately slot it into a small receptacle in the top of the device.

Wheels and governors started to spin and rock in the exposed insides. A needle clattered down from the bottom of the device and dangled midway between the box and the paper. It flicked aside and jabbed down into the inkwell, then darted back and started to scratch at the page. There was no string, no complex linkage connecting the needle to the box. It simply moved of its own accord. After a few tentative lines, the motion became faster, oscillating between the ink and the page in a blur. Little spatters of ink peppered the top of the shop bench, and drops blobbed around the edge of the page, but the center stayed mostly clear of blemishes. After fifteen seconds of buzzing and clicking needle motion, the shard of metal receded back into the box.

Mr. Masker took a fresh pair of tongs and slid the paper from beneath the contraption. He handed it to Fel. "Be careful, it's still wet. Hold it by the edges," he said.

Fel held the page to the light of the lamp. It was a drawing of Fel. A rather flattering one at that. The rendering was a far cry from the unkempt and bleary-eyed young man who had just gambled away his earnings. It was idealized, but still unmistakably Fel himself.

"Impressive, no? I've been restoring it for weeks, trying to get it to operate again. The real breakthrough was when I realized there was something that wanted to come out of the bottom of it when it was activated."

"A contraption that can make images in seconds… This would be worth a fortune," Fel said without an ounce of excitement in his voice. He knew the eventual fate for anything that passed through this shop and was actually worth decent money.

"Yes! Oh, absolutely. The assayer will be along to take it soon. Standard fee. Seventy-five duots. This is far too high-level a contraption for them to let us sell it ourselves. But they only come through once a week, and I figure before then we can use it to get a nice family picture once your sister arrives."

Fel waved the picture, eyes fixed on the middle distance.

"We could charge people five duots for a picture… We could rent it out to the wealthy to have drawings made for their parties."

"Fine ideas if not for the assayer," Mr. Masker said. "It isn't as though the assayer's office wouldn't notice an enterprise like that."

He started to pack up the contraption. Fel clenched his teeth.

"Then we could sell it!" he said. "At least then we could have fifty or sixty cenots instead of a few lousy duots."

"And then the assayers would come and shut us down. Must we go through this every time, Fel? It isn't worth the risk. Not to the shop when doing it wrong will end something we've been doing for generations, and not for the world. Do you remember that contraption last month? The one that could simply unlock any lock you placed it near? What if that fell into the wrong hands?"

"A magic lockpick and a magic image maker are hardly the same, Dad! And who is to say the assayer's office are the right hands? They're buying one-of-a-kind, world-changing devices for pocket change. I'd call that robbery, and what's the sense of giving a lockpicker to a bunch of robbers?"

"We're not discussing it," Mr. Masker said.

"I'm just saying it's unfair that their definition for an unsafe contraption boils down to 'any contraption worth having.'"

"They let us fix and sell the door alarms. Those have been a real boon. And the music boxes, too."

Satisfied it was dry enough, Fel slipped the picture into his pocket and marched to one of the many carefully sorted sets of bins. These bins were far larger than the rest, and it was fair to say they were the three bins that had dominated his father's life for as long as he could remember.

The first was labeled "To Be Fixed." A half-filled crate of dirt-caked and tarnished doodads and gewgaws. They ranged from oddly complex jewelry to heavy, dented boxes to rusted-out wrecks too beaten up to discern their original shapes. Some of them had been purchased from people who came into the shop looking to make a quick profit. The contraptions had a way of turning up everywhere, provided the dusty corner or forgotten basement was old enough. People uncovered them in attics, they unearthed them when plowing fields. But as often as people came to sell them things, the vast majority of them had been gathered by Fel himself. A few times a year he'd be sent to this place or that, on what his father called "expeditions." They were dangerous and dirty, but tended to fill the to-be-fixed box to the brim with broken contraptions.

Judging by their ubiquity, there was a time when contraptions were a part of everyday life. That time was long gone and mostly forgotten. Now they were just relics, nonfunctional and worthless to the average citizen. But Martin Masker had a knack for fixing them. It was equal parts experience and intuition, but sifting through spare parts salvaged from other machines and replacing pieces with similar ones had a way of breathing life into the gadgets. Mr. Masker's passion was slow, laborious investigation and restoration.

The second bin was nearly empty, and bore the label "To Be Appraised." Martin placed the picture contraption inside beside what Fel already knew to be a "dancing acrobat box," a harmless toy that they'd likely be allowed to sell, and a box that produced bright light and terrible noise when opened. That one the assayer would take. Then there was the final box, the "Scrap Box." This is where the lost causes ended up. Contraptions that he had given up on or parts that were too mangled to be salvaged. It was mostly filled with snapped-in-half cogwheels, bits of wire that were too short to use, and tarnished or worn plates that had been replaced. But something caught Fel's eye.

He fished out a clamshell case. His father had clearly done some work on it, because the milky-green tarnish had been cleared away from any of the mechanical components. The hinge was clear and oiled. The clasps operated without difficulty. When he opened it, the inside looked to be an ornate compass protected by a thick dome of glass. It lacked any sort of directional markings, though, and the needle didn't do much more than jiggle regardless of the orientation.

Fel held it up. "This is scrap? It looks like one of those complexity compasses we keep in the tool kit."

"I've swapped out any parts that are even lightly corroded for fresh ones. It *should* work. But the needle doesn't even budge when I place it next to the picture contraption, which is complex enough to turn the needle of even the weakest compass in our collection. It doesn't have any other parts I can service. I've got plenty of better-quality pieces than can be found inside of it, and it doesn't seem to serve a purpose, so it's scrap."

"Did Mom see it yet?"

"Not yet."

"Can I have it?"

"Take it. But if you're going to sell it, don't tell your mother or your sister."

"Trust me, Dad, I know."

"Oh! And another thing. I'd nearly forgotten. That strange little sack of flanges you brought back from the Wellspring Coast last month? You'll never believe what I was able to use them for."

He pulled a step stool out from beneath one of his benches and stood on it to fetch something from a top shelf. The item he presented was a familiar one: one-half of a pair of artifacts that they'd inherited from Martin's father. It was a strikingly beautiful lantern. It had a pill-shaped, brightly polished metal housing containing an oval door with a glass window. It was a perfect match to a lantern sitting on the edge of the workbench.

"I am going to be able to get the second sentry lantern working!" he said. "For the first time, Wick will be able to travel properly! It will take a bit of care, the flanges need to be etched and there's some fit and finish, but by this time tomorrow we can start sending Wick with you or Epiphany when you venture out of town."

"I see. That's… great, Dad."

The lack of enthusiasm in his voice, like most social subtleties, flitted by his father without raising any pesky concerns or follow-up questions. Which was good. He really didn't feel like informing his father of his reasons for disliking that particular family relic. At best it would lead to his father admonishing him for holding a grudge about being tattled on in his youth, and at worst it would suggest Fel had plans that he'd rather keep secret.

"But I've kept you long enough. I'm sure your mother has things for you to do. See you at dinner, son!"

"See you then, Dad."

#

Epiphany rode in a coach across a stretch of increasingly familiar road. The door opened, and the man who had been sharing the ride with her stood to leave.

"It has been a joy to ride with you, Miss Masker," the man said.

"I've quite enjoyed the ride as well. And remember, if you're concerned about that shop of yours, send a message to Masker's Antiquities in Beffshire for an alarm box. A handful of duots is small price to pay for peace of mind," she said.

"I will, I will. Have a good trip."

He shut the door, pulled his bag from the roof, and went on his way. Now Epiphany was the only passenger. In the past, she'd treated long rides like this as a training ground for her tactics of persuasion. Even in family businesses, sending a woman to be the face of the business for the purposes of trade and the like was rather rare. While she was the second Masker woman in a row to hold the position of designated traveling merchant, the chances were very good that for anyone she dealt with on the road, she was the first woman to handle finances at her level without at least a partner or escort. Not because ladies weren't seen as business savvy. Again, if it *was* a family business, chances were if a man was off doing the road business, his wife was dealing with the business at home. The issue was that the road was a fair bit less safe for a woman traveling alone than a man. As it happened, the large and rather cruel set of brass knuckles in her purse served to restore the manners of anyone who neglected to treat her like a gentleman. And if they were particularly persistent, she kept a blade in the heel of her boot. So far it hadn't come to that.

One of the reasons the blade remained pristine was the aforementioned practice she liked to focus on during lengthy rides. Someone could not be on the offensive if they were on the defensive. And anyone who felt they were being sold to had a strong tendency to raise their defenses. After the literal weeks she'd spent cooped up with unwilling partners in her conversational sparring training, she'd become something of a master of riding the very edge of keeping someone on the defensive, such that at any moment she could give the conversation a nudge and regardless of who was talking to her and what their intentions were, they would abandon it all to avoid being talked out of a large sum of money. Most important, she'd learned to do this all without resorting to flirting. As a sales tactic, flirting was enormously effective, but poor calibration would have, at the very least, led to a lot more time cleaning her boot knife.

This ride hadn't been her best performance. If this had been the ride north, she would have been going over her tactics to determine how they could be improved. None of that had happened on the ride home. She was far too preoccupied with the contents of the folio on her lap. And now that she was alone, she was free to slip it open and marvel at it again.

As tended to happen when someone was in possession of something truly valuable, the tendency was to concoct elaborate, anxiety-inducing scenarios in which the item mysteriously vanishes while unobserved. She leafed through the records of her sale and located the item in question. It wasn't much to look at. Quite old, clearly hand-rendered. It was a map surrounded by some ancient writing. But what it represented was… everything. It was freedom from the yoke of financial burden. It was the key to a door to new wealth and prosperity. It was a source of discovery. It was a source of power. She flipped past it to a second slip of paper, one she'd written herself. Though written in a modern tongue, the message she'd recorded was no less cryptic.

Bazaar. Mr. Badgerweed. Purple, spices. Dull Dagger, Chain Pack, Mask.

And under it all, written large and underlined twice:

DON'T TELL MOM AND DAD.

She carefully separated this page from the rest and folded it, then slipped it into her bag. As marvelous an opportunity as this all was, there were obstacles. Some of them, her brother would have to overcome. Others were hers to clear. But if they could do it, it would change everything.

It would change *everything*.

#

Hours later, Fel trudged down the stairs to the little floor that had been sectioned off into three smaller rooms. One was his sister Epiphany's. The second had belonged to his sister Euphoria before she'd married out of the family. The last was his own.

He rubbed his belly and searched his pocket until he found his sparker— a contraption that he remained astounded the assayer hadn't confiscated. A flick of the lever at the top produced a spray of sparks, which helpfully found their way to the charred wick of an oil lamp. It slowly flared to life and cast light on his little corner of the world.

Fel's room was modest, to say the least. A bed that was barely long enough for his strapping frame occupied one corner. Another corner held a sloppily kept wardrobe and half-packed bit of luggage from his last expedition. He had a shelf of contraptions and keepsakes, and in the remaining corner, his own workbench.

As poorly as he fit into the family business, the apple hadn't *entirely* rolled down the hill when it fell from the tree. Now that he'd had half a day to let his drunkenness ease into a dull ache in his head, his hands were steady and sure enough to put his limited tinkering skills to work.

Fel moved the lamp a little closer and adjusted the polished reflector. He placed the compass from the scrap bin on the leather working pad and selected a rag and some polishing paste. Slow, measured strokes and a tremendous amount of patience stripped away the decades, or perhaps centuries, of tarnish. The first thing he noticed was a very finely engraved set of symbols on the front of the clamshell. They had been completely hidden beneath the tarnish, and thus had been missed by his father. That much wasn't a surprise. It wouldn't have occurred to him to clean the tarnish away until he knew the device was salvageable. It wasn't that Martin lacked reverence for fine detail and artful presentation. He appreciated form, but he appreciated function much more. More to the point, he had a tremendous amount of work to do and had thus developed a rigid triage system that had rejected this device long before it could be beautified.

The shape of the large central symbol was difficult to describe. It looked roughly as though someone had taken a traditional twin-hook anchor of the sort he'd seen dangle from the fronts of ships down at the Wellspring Coast and affixed a crooked rectangle to the top. Or perhaps it was a winding key for a clockwork device? He supposed it didn't matter. He carefully re-etched the symbol with a graver and returned to polishing.

When the outside was gleaming, he opened the compass and picked a different, thicker polish for the glass. It was marred in just a few places by scratches, but he took the time to buff the entire surface until nary a whisper of the defect remained.

Work like this was a departure for him. Fel knew his value, and it lay mostly in his size. He was a brute of a man. Took after his mother's side of the family. A head taller than either of his parents, broad in shoulder and thick through the trunk. When he needed to earn extra money, and he often did, he loaned his back and his hands to local shops to tote crates and load wagons. Work like this was nearly too delicate for the ham hocks he called hands. And the meticulous nature was a test for a mind that was better suited to bar fights and bawdy drinking songs. But there was a peacefulness in working this way. And if he was lucky, he might even have some use for what came of such work.

When he was through, the broken compass looked good as new. The metal was a rosy, coppery color he couldn't quite place. Perhaps some sort of high-quality bronze. The needle still didn't give any useful information, but it was a lovely bright blue, some sort of iridescent metal that caught the light in dazzling ways. He snapped the piece shut and fastened a comparatively dull bit of jewelry chain to the sturdy little loop on its back. Just one more thing.

He pulled the drawing from his pocket. Steady work with a knife cut it as precisely as he could manage to a shape that would match the inner curve of the clamshell lid. A bit of melted resin affixed the drawing. Just as his eyes were beginning to droop and he could hear his bed calling his name, he raised the finished piece to admire it. What had once been an ugly and useless piece of forgotten technology was now a pretty—if somewhat large—improvised locket. He wrapped it in a piece of cloth, tucked it in his coat pocket, and crawled into bed.

Joseph R. Lallo

Chapter 3

Fel woke a bit earlier than his body would have liked him to. The rum Allie had provided may have been cheap and harsh, but what it lacked in flavor it more than made up for in duration. A full night of sleep had failed to fully wipe away the general sourness in his stomach and throb in his temples. But he'd been trained since birth to associate that first jangle of the door's bell with the beginning of a day. Even filtered through three floors of his house, the tinkle of the bell could stir him from sleep. And it just so happened, this morning he had someplace to be. He freshened up, got dressed, and hurried out the front door before his mother could assign him any chores.

He turned the corner at The Fox and Log and continued up the street, eyes set on the gay pink sign in the distance. A reed basket swung in one hand. He'd thrust the other hand into his pocket to count through the fistful of coins he'd set aside before yesterday's ill-fated game of grum. It should be enough for what he had in mind.

When he reached the bakery, Mariss was just setting out the cakes for display in the window. He smiled at the sight of her. She was dressed in bright yellow, a plump, sunny little ball of joy pleasantly arranging trays of cookies and artfully constructed cakes that would dance through the dreams of every child who walked past. She noticed him through the window and waved. The smile she shined in his direction was the same one she offered to every customer, but Fel liked to imagine it was just a bit brighter for him.

She hurried aside and pulled the door open. "There's my favorite customer. I've got sweet buns ready for you, fresh from the oven," she said. "Just give me a moment to get them in a basket for you."

"I brought the old one back," he said, presenting it like a teacher's pet.

"Lovely! That's a free yeast roll for you," she said.

She took the basket and replaced it with a new one to start loading with buns. Fel took a moment to enjoy the sweet, spicy scent of the bakery.

"So, I…" He cleared his throat. "My sister will be in town today."

"Oh? That's nice," Mariss said absentmindedly. "Has she been away long?"

"Two months," he said. "She headed up through Quarr, got as far as the border of Shalia."

"Oh? They've been having that problem with the disease in Shalia, haven't they?"

"So they say. It's why she didn't cross the border."

"Nice to have her home then. Safe and sound."

"Right, right. So, I…" He reached into his pocket and found the cloth-wrapped compass. "You know I'm a Masker, right? Masker's Antiquities?"

"Mm-hmm," she said without looking up.

"I go on these… my dad calls them expeditions. They're these trips to places where he hopes I'll find contraptions. They're… I don't know… they're kind of dangerous."

His heart was pounding in his chest. He didn't know what it was. Maybe it was that he really didn't belong in such a high-class place. Maybe it was that this bakery was a place he'd always wished he could shop when he was a child, and being here dragged him back to the little boy with empty pockets and a sweet tooth. But when he came here, when he talked to Mariss, his heart fluttered, his cheeks burned, and his tongue tied itself in knots.

"Be safe," Mariss said. "Here you are. That will be thirty duots!"

"Right, right." He dropped the coins into her hand. "But, um… I found this, a while back, and I thought… maybe I thought you'd like it?" He gave her the cloth-wrapped compass.

"For me?" Mariss said, more puzzled than excited.

"If you like. You don't have to take it."

She clicked it open. "Oh! This is you! Did you draw this?"

"No, no. It was a contraption my dad fixed."

"Oh. Well, it's lovely. Thanks!"

"You're welcome," he said with the dopey smile of a child who'd gotten a pat on the head from his grandpa.

She dropped it into her apron and handed him the basket. "Here you go! Don't forget your yeast roll!"

"Thanks! I'll see you next month!" he said, grabbing the treats and hurrying out the door.

The very instant the sugary scent of the bakery was replaced by the crisp morning air, his mind helpfully replayed the entire transaction, following it up with a hot sting of embarrassment.

"What is *wrong* with you, Fel?" he grumbled to himself. "When you found that compass, you were in Mallowmire Swamp, and you'd just knocked a thorn-lizard's teeth out with a club. That's an exciting anecdote. One of your best! Why can't you talk to Mariss without your head filling with fuzz…"

He glanced through the window, taking the utmost of care to ensure he wouldn't make eye contact when he did so, and saw her pat the pocket with the compass and smile to herself. The flutter rushed over him again like a fever. He turned on his heel and scurried away before whatever strange power she had over him leeched what remained of his intelligence.

Without the looming prospect of a chat with the girl of his dreams to give him pause, the trip home was much faster. He kept a heavy cloth draped over the sweet buns, both to keep them warm and to keep them safe from the *other* staple of his trips to the bakery.

"Go!" croaked a lesser harpy from the tailor's roof.

"Greedy rat pig!!" cackled another.

"Yeah, yeah," Fel said.

He pulled out the yeast roll and crumbled it up into the street. The birds descended on the offering, each happily snatching the largest piece they could manage and returning to the roof.

"I'll wring your neck if you don't get out!" said the orator of the group, its tone conveying gratitude even if its words didn't.

"Don't get used to it. I can only afford so many trips to the bakery on what I earn."

When he reached Masker's Antiquities, he could see through the window that his sister had arrived. She'd yet to drop her pack, and his parents were already enthusiastically going through one of the three crates she'd brought. He tapped the mask on the sign and shoved the door open.

"Hey, Fanny!" Fel said as the bell signaled his arrival.

"Fel! There you are!" She pointed at the basket. "Let me guess, Divinity's Oven?"

"To celebrate your return."

She scoffed. "I'm sure that's the only reason you bought them."

He set the basket on the counter. She eagerly pulled the cloth from the top and grabbed a bun.

"Still *warm*," she purred, indulging in the sweet treat.

"Let's see the ledger," their mother said. "I want to see how the sales went."

Epiphany swung her pack around and slipped a sturdy leather-bound journal from an outside pocket to present to her mother. The born and bred businesswoman dug into the dense pages of accounting with the same zeal as Epiphany ate her breakfast.

"Good, good. Oh, that's a *lovely* price. Mmm… Could have done better there. The folks up north like the music boxes, I see."

"Oh, yes. I've got at least three reservations I sold for the next ones we complete. And four people interested in commissioning a song. … We can do that, right?"

Her mother glanced at the ledger and smiled. "For five hundred and fifty duots per song, your father can darn well learn how. Make a note of it, dear. Take those music boxes off the shelf and keep them in storage until the next time Fanny heads north."

"In a moment, dear," Martin said, elbow-deep in crate of contraptions Epiphany purchased. "Are you certain none of these work?"

"None of them. I bought the whole lot for fifty-three duots."

"A steal, a *steal*!" He held up a badly damaged contraption the size of a picnic basket. "The wheels and axles in this piece alone will be enough to repair three alarm bells, a couple of dancers, and still have some to spare. You have an eye for value, Fanny."

"I learned from the best." She finished her bun and pulled a kerchief from her pocket to wipe her sticky fingers clean. "But the best of it all is right here."

She pulled a carefully rolled page from her pack and smoothed it out on the table. It was old, the sort of high-quality vellum that was a dead giveaway for contraption-era documents. A few small blocks of text were scattered irregularly around the page, but the rest was dominated by a carefully rendered map. It told the tale of a much older world. The coastlines made it clear it was a depiction of the southeast portion of the continent. Dotted lines broke it into grids, and tick marks along a top and left axis divided it further.

"That map cost me nearly a hundred duots. But I have a feeling it'll be worth it. I don't know half of the words on there, but *that* one you taught me, Dad."

She tapped one of the words in the block of text. Fel blinked at it blankly. Martin practically jumped out of his boots.

"Vault! Fanny, if this is a map to a vault, you may have made this family's year."

For most people in the world, collecting antiquities or contraptions simply meant paying regular visits to shops run by people like the Maskers. But for the proprietors of those shops, inventory was a bit more difficult to acquire. Lesser merchants made do with items sold by customers or items offered by traveling merchants. The truly enterprising, which included Fel and Martin, sought out new items to repair, restore, and sell. The absolute best place to find intact antiques and functioning contraptions were vaults. They were heavily fortified chambers, often found in ruins or buried deep underground. Near-impenetrable walls and deadly traps made investigating them a terrible risk, but the rewards were such that every known vault had eventually been breached picked clean, often with more than a few casualties. A new one? Previously unknown? It would be the find of a decade.

"That's what I thought," she said.

"They wouldn't grid this map out so finely if there wasn't something on this page that would need to be identified. Fine work, *fine* work, Fanny. Fel, my boy, I have a feeling you'll need to get your hiking boots on. If I can work this out, you'll have a trip ahead of you."

Fel munched on a bun of his own. "Suits me. Even if Fanny gets to go to all the fancy places, at least a trip'll keep me away from Tem and his 'tactics.'"

"Oh! Speaking of that, Fel, I wanted to have a word with you. Let's get somewhere where we won't disturb Mother and Father."

Fel motioned toward Martin and Vivian. "Look at them. You'd have to smack them with a plank to get their attention at this point."

Epiphany leaned forward and whispered, "I really think you and I need to discuss this alone."

Fel raised his eyebrows. "Downstairs then?"

#

The smallish floors and the vertical layout of the house meant that the Masker clan were no strangers to climbing a flight of stairs to get some privacy, but normally just one floor would do. Epiphany didn't even slow down as she passed through the dining room and bedrooms. She went clear to their father's workshop, the bottom floor, before she spoke again.

"Right. Wick? Where's Wick?"

"The lit lamp is upstairs in the shop, like it always is during the mornings."

"The *lit* lamp."

"Dad finished another sentry lamp," Fel pointed. "It's not lit yet."

"Right, fine. That's fine. Now listen close. I want to get this out quick in case Mother or Father comes this direction. I found a buyer."

"You were on a trade trip. I should hope you found at least one, or else what were you doing up there?"

"No, no." She leaned closer, looking him dead in the eye. "I found a *buyer*."

"A buyer… a raw buyer? A buyer willing to buy without an appraisal?" he said with escalating excitement. "A buyer who'll pay what something is worth instead of sacrificing it to the assayer? *That* kind of buyer?"

"Shh, shh, shh," she urged, wincing as if he were going to cause an avalanche. "Yes. Yes *that* kind of buyer. He's the one who sold me the map. He's part of the traveling bazaar that will come through Beffshire next month. The man is extremely wealthy. I have been cautious about approaching him, as this is precisely the way the assayer's office tries to catch people who would break the rules. But he's legitimate. He's probably been doing business like this all over the continent for years. I doubt he would have ever approached us, save for the fact that the specific dialect on that map page is one of Dad's specialties, and this fellow hasn't been able to find anyone else who can translate it."

"You know we're never going to be able to persuade Mom and Dad to sell to someone without going through the assayer. They're too nervous about getting the shop shut down."

"I know, which is why I'm talking to *you* and not to *them*. This isn't a blanket offer to purchase contraptions. Not yet anyway. This man has three items in mind. Three specific items, though the descriptions are a bit vague. I have a feeling they're a sort of test."

She counted on her fingers as she named the items. "He wants 'the heavy pack, filled with chain,' he wants 'the dull dagger, blunt and black,' and he wants 'the fearsome mask, ready to mount.' That's all he has for us, in terms of description. He seemed confident that those items will be located within the vault on the map and they will be evident when you see them. These are the *only* items he is interested in purchasing, but he is willing to pay twenty-five thousand duots each."

"Twenty-five thousand…" Fel said.

"He has every coin of it, I'm sure of it. And he'll be here with the traveling bazaar in twenty days. With any luck, if we do what he wants, he'll be open to a more general trade agreement."

"Depending on where the vault is and how hard it is to find these things, it might be difficult to get back in time to make the sale."

"I think the reward is worth the risk and the rush."

"Agreed. That much money all at once…"

"It would change things," she said. "But no word of this, not a *word* of it, reaches Mom and Dad. Not just because they wouldn't let us go through with it, but because they have good reason not to let us go through with it. If this goes wrong, it goes wrong on you and me. Mom and Dad can't be touched."

"Absolutely. And if it goes right?"

Epiphany grinned. "If it goes *right*, then I think dumping seventy-five thousand duots on the table in front of Mom will weaken her resolve, and once she falls, Dad won't last long. But it is crucially important that… wait…"

Thumping footsteps approached from above. The pair kept quiet. After a moment, their father burst through the door, holding the map.

"Ah! There you two are. Lost track of you for a moment," he said, hurrying to the workbench.

"Did you decipher the map?" Epiphany asked.

"Not just yet, but the location should be fairly simple. There's different cipher on the individual values than there is on the text. The value cipher is one I'm familiar with, and that ought to get us an answer in no time. The rest of the information will be more stubborn. But it looks like this will be quite an impressive cache of goods."

"Great! What brings you down here, though?" Fel said, fidgeting a bit at having perhaps the most important meeting of his life interrupted.

"I don't want to mark up the map. It's a relic! So I'd started transcribing it, but then I remembered the new contraption that might be able to make a duplicate far more quickly."

"What's this now?" Epiphany said.

"Oh, wait until you see it! It is *grand*. Shame we'll be losing it in a few days."

As Martin raved about the picture device and prepared it to duplicate the map, Epiphany gave Fel a meaningful glance. He nodded and excused himself. One way or another, he was going to be heading out for another expedition. Best to be prepared.

#

Upstairs in the shop, Vivian looked up to find an unfamiliar customer eying up the establishment with an uncertain look on his face. She took great care to keep her expression neutral as he finally pushed at the door. She knew that look.

"Excuse me, ma'am?" the man said, removing his hat.

"Vivian Masker. Welcome to Masker's Antiquities. How may I help you?"

He walked carefully toward the counter, keeping to the center of the floor lest he stray too near to the shelves.

"I am a friend of Victor DeWaltz," he said.

"Oh, yes. Mr. DeWaltz. A fine collection of Bygone Era silver and goldware. One of Thayn's finest collections of jewelry from the era, if memory serves."

"Right. That's him. He recommended this place to me. And naturally I trust his recommendation given his expertise. But he'd neglected to mention that this was a *contraption* dealer."

"We are an antiquities shop, sir. Contraptions are by their very nature antiquities."

"They aren't... *dangerous*, are they?"

"Any antiquities that are even remotely dangerous are handed over to the officials in Teskal. Those that remain are quite harmless."

"Mmm... I'm sure you'd like your neighbors to *think* that," he muttered, not quite low enough under his breath to escape her notice.

"I take it that you have some jewelry you'd like polished or repaired?" Vivian said, her expression still as impassive as she could manage.

"Repaired. You don't... use the same tools on the contraptions as the jewelry, do you?" he said.

Vivian shut her eyes. This was always how the first business with a new customer went. To the average person, a contraption shop was like a den of sin or a pit of disease. For some reason it was simple enough for people to keep a music box or tinker with a puzzle box and not worry, but the thought of people actually *turning the screws* and *greasing the gears* of such things gave the whole shop and anyone in it a tainted, poisonous feel. Eventually, if they worked with the Maskers for any measurable amount of time, they would invariably come to the conclusion that Masker's was the rare "decent" sort of contraption shop, or at the very least that the Maskers themselves were harmless enough. But it always added an extra level of friction to the first sale. It was fortunate that nowhere else in town was even *half* as good as Martin when it came to jewelry repair, and Fel's trips to the field ensured that they had a constantly refreshed stock. Few antique dealers could come close to their selection. If someone took their jewelry seriously, they came to Masker's, even if they had to hold their noses to do it.

"My husband keeps not only a separate tool set, but a separate workbench specifically for jewelry repair," she said. "Would you like to see some examples of his restoration work?"

"I think that would be prudent."

She pulled a key from a chain on her belt and unlocked a small chest behind the counter. From within, she pulled out a flat case and placed it on the counter.

"What we have here," she said, opening the case and beginning a speech she'd given at least once a week for the last decade, "is perhaps the finest example of a Bygone jade-and-gold-compound earring pair that isn't currently on display in a museum or private collection. You'll note the chain is not a single row of links, but a *plait* of links. At their smallest, the wires forming these links are scarcely thicker than a hair. The chains themselves are braided utilizing five strands of three different-gauge chain, but the links of said chains are actually *cross-linked* between neighboring chains at regular intervals. This not only adds to the strength and durability of the piece, but it also allows it to keep its shape and prevent tangling, which ensures that the chain will remain as gorgeous in another two hundred years as it looks today. Provided it is polished and maintained by someone as skilled as my husband. Because, as you will see here, the earring's twin has been kept in the condition of its discovery."

Vivian moved a bit of velvet aside to reveal the nearly unrecognizable counterpart to the restored earring. The man leaned forward to inspect. Vivian produced a magnifying lens for him to more thoroughly investigate the claims and the handiwork. In the past, she'd continued to add further description and further compliments of her husband's handiwork, but over the years she'd learned that his skill with jewelry spoke for itself.

"Astounding... I can't imagine anyone managing something of such fine detail. Not now and not then."

"As you might imagine, the same hands that delve into the hearts of contraptions—devices which, you'll recall, can misbehave in catastrophic ways if mishandled—acquire a level of steadiness and precision that non-contraptioneers can't hope to achieve. It is for this reason that Masker's

Antiquities cannot be matched with regard to not only our selection of jewelry, but our expertise in its care."

This was one of the rare benefits of the absurd level of distrust most people had for contraptions. Vivian could depend upon their own certainty that the devices were vile, capricious, and eager to destroy any who came near them to assign a nearly supernatural level of prowess to her husband for surviving their wrath.

"Mmm…" the man said, tapping his chin. "Provided you *only* use the jewelry tools, I would be willing to entrust my wife's brooch to you. How quickly can you have it done and what is your fee?"

"All jewelry left before noon is done by midnight, all jewelry after noon is done by noon the following day. The fee is twenty duots per piece, with a five-duot surcharge for large pieces. Payment upon completion. If you provide payment up front, I can have the finished piece delivered to you as soon as it is complete."

"Delivery won't be necessary. I will pick it up tomorrow."

He handed over the piece, which was comparatively crude, and hurried out the door like he'd been holding his breath the whole time and was desperate to reach the surface. Vivian dropped the piece in a small cloth bag and opened the dumbwaiter behind her.

"Martin! Another polish piece. Due tomorrow," she called, down the shaft. She placed the piece inside.

"Lovely, darling. Would you mind coming down for a moment?"

"Then send Epiphany up to work the counter."

"This requires the entire family. It will take two minutes, I assure you."

Vivian huffed in frustration. She glanced to a small lantern, which at this time of day seemed superfluous given the amount of light coming through the window. The flame was bright and rigidly still within the lantern. She nodded and turned to the hatch leading downstairs.

"Make it quick, and if I hear the bell, someone is heading up to do business."

She made her way down to the dining room where her children were standing, somewhat awkwardly, to one side of the room. The floor had been cleared by pushing the table and chairs clear. Martin was tinkering with the picture-making device.

"Ah! Good, good, stand right there! With the kids. I want to have a drawing made."

Vivian gave him an uncertain look. "This isn't going to fire a net, is it? I recall treating the rope burns on Fel," she said.

"It's fine, Mom. It just draws a picture," Fel said.

"Honestly, you accidentally activate *one* net-launching contraption and no one will let you forget it," Martin said.

"How long will this take?" Vivian asked.

"It took less than a minute for the picture it drew of me," Fel said.

She brushed some wrinkles out of her outfit and stood rather awkwardly beside her children.

"Did I hear someone fretting over the dangers of having jewelry polished by a contraption shop up there?" Epiphany said.

"You did. He was a particularly skittish one. I had to go through the whole braided-chain speech."

Epiphany shook her head. "You'd think we regularly killed our neighbors."

"Complaining about stubbornly ignorant people is like complaining about the weather. No sense to it, it won't change anything. Stupidity is a fact of the world, and we simply find ways to allow for it."

Martin dashed over to the rest of the family as the contraption started to click.

"Hold still, everyone, and look how you'd like to look in a drawing!"

Epiphany and Martin smiled. Vivian and Fel didn't bother adjusting their expressions. The device scribbled and scratched at the carefully positioned bit of paper until a lovely family portrait was completed. The moment the motion stopped, Martin dashed over and snagged the drawing with tongs.

"Lovely! Lovely. A shame to part with this thing. Careful. The ink is still wet."

The family gathered around and admired the image. As before, it wasn't a perfect rendering. The smudges of ink and soot that perpetually speckled Martin during work hours had been left out. Despite the lack of a smile on Fel and Vivian, their expressions had been subtly adjusted to be a bit more pleasant and content.

"It's curious how it 'adjusts' drawings of people, but the drawing of the map and the text was a precise copy," Martin said.

"Yes. Curious. Have that thing do some more drawings of assorted interesting objects before we lose it. We can use them in some of those old frames to help sell them," Vivian said.

"Wonderful idea, my love."

"I'll be at the counter. Measure that drawing. I'll mat it and select a frame for it as well," she said, turning to the stairs.

#

A few hours later, Fel filled his bowl with some of his father's stew. The men of the family had always done most of the cooking, as his mother had started grooming his sisters to work the counter and do the day-to-day business practically from birth. Fel and his father's jobs were equally indispensable to keeping the enterprise running, but it was far more reasonable to set down the tinkering to chop onions. His mother couldn't very well leave the shop empty.

One would imagine that such a division of labor would lead Martin and Fel to develop a general aptitude for cooking, but unfortunately the Maskers tended to specialize. Martin took the time to learn to make one brilliantly delicious meal and then had served some variation of it nearly every night since. The hearty, thick concoction was composed of whatever vegetables were available paired with whatever meat was available, and rendered sumptuous by a mix of spices that had been iteratively refined over thousands of meals. Dinner was so consistent, the family had unofficially renamed the evening meal "stew."

"Epiphany!" Vivian shouted. "Come get your stew before your brother eats all the dumplings. And Martin, you pulled yourself away from the map long enough to make dinner, the least you can do is get a bowl in your belly."

Martin waved irritably and continued scratching at the page.

Vivian and Epiphany passed each other on the stairs, mother with bowl in hand on the way up to relieve her daughter of shop duties. Epiphany plopped down in her mother's seat and scooped out a bowl of stew and three fat dumplings.

"You know, Dad, you don't always have to drown the meat and veggies in gravy. They serve them separately up north."

"But then it isn't *stew*," he said.

"Yeah, Fanny," Fel said. "If there was no gravy, what would you sop up with your bread, or cook the dumplings in?"

She shook her head with a half grin. "As usual, the logic on display in this household is dazzling. How goes the mapmaking, Dad? Any progress from the one you brought up to me a few hours ago?"

"Mmm?" said Martin. "Oh, *yes*. I was way off. A full twenty-five ticks too far south. I've got the vault pinpointed now. Quite confident. And also, there is this bit." He slid the second copy of the map toward her. He'd just finished populating a circular pattern with a series of dots and crosses.

"What am I looking at?" Epiphany said.

"See, this is what you lose by going off and doing the easy stuff like negotiating prices and finding buyers and sellers. That's one of those… spinny things. With the dots. For opening doors," Fel said.

Epiphany gave him a level look. "Forgive me for not sharing your insight."

"Vault doors have spinny locks," Fel said. "That's how you open this one. And that looks like it's a complete solution."

"Oh, yes. That's complete," Martin said. "I'm not sure about the rest of the text, but that's the combination to the main door. No doubt."

"So… I can go?" Fel said.

"I'm trying to work out if it's worth the risk," Martin replied.

"That's for me to decide, Dad. And if you know where it is and how to get in, it's worth the risk."

"It'll take me another day or so, but there's a particularly large encoded text block yet I'm still working on. It might be the inventory for that place, or other relevant information. If I decode that and we see what's inside, then we'll know if it would be a waste of time sending you down there. It's a good week or so of travel due south, and it takes you right to the edge of the Greater Lands."

"Does it?" Epiphany said with a flicker of concern.

"Let me see that," Fel said. He snatched the map and gazed at it. His father had helpfully sketched the modern borders onto this copy. "It's right on the border. It's not like it's *inside* the border. It'll be fine."

"Fel, not that I don't have faith in your skills, but it's the Greater Lands we're talking about. Home of the Greater Mystics. These aren't lesser harpies that you feed bread to—don't think I haven't noticed that bad habit, by the way. It's the greater harpies with claws that can tear out intestines. Greater Fae with their charms and greater dragons with their fiery breath."

"There's no greater Fae left and you know it. And when's the last time someone saw a greater dragon?"

"I *think* there are no greater Fae, but I don't know it. And it isn't as though you've been blessed with good luck. If there's a dragon out there, you'll find it."

"I've been that close to the Greater Lands plenty of times. And again, it's *on* the border, not within the border."

"I don't think Greater Mystics are obliged to honor the line the surveyors lay down."

"Probably not, but that big wall down there is probably a pretty good motivation to stay in."

"Wings beat walls, Fel."

"I'm a grown man, Dad. I'm more than capable of deciding if it's worth the risk. And I've already decided that it is."

"Just give me some time and we'll be able to draw a more informed conclusion."

"Dad, when you play grum, you learn to trust your gut."

"I thought you lost your last game of grum. I thought you lose *most* of your grum games."

"That's beside the point. For all we know, that hunk of text is the name of the people who drew the map and decoding it would be a waste of time."

"What's the rush?"

"That's a week south! Another week back, that leaves just a few days to search and gather before I'd end up missing the traveling bazaar to sell whatever we might find."

"The bazaar comes through twice a year. If we miss this one, we'll catch the next."

"They are on the verge of closing the border with Shalia, Dad," Epiphany said. "The disease is ravaging that place. If that happens, this might be the last time the bazaar comes through for the foreseeable future. It's the Shalians who pay the drivers, let's not forget."

Fel gulped down a dumpling. "The point is, if I move now, if I leave *today*, then we won't have to worry about it, because I'll be back with time to spare."

"You seem to be in a terrible rush, Fel."

"It's an opportunity, Dad!" he said. "When's the last time we had one of those? Most of the expeditions you send me out on are old mines or the odd well-looted temple. I haven't been to a vault in two years, and to this *day* half of the stuff Mom's got on the shelves came from there. That was after it had already been cleaned out, too. We've been living off the picked-clean bones of a vault. This one might be untouched. It's near the Greater Lands, so it isn't as though someone would just stumble upon it. Uncharted territory, Dad."

"It's on a map, son. It is, by definition, charted."

Fel glanced at Epiphany. "Help me out here, Fanny."

"Virgin. Unspoiled. Fertile."

"Right. All of those things." Fel said. "Think of the *contraptions*, Dad."

"Well… we should ask your mother."

Epiphany leaned back and raised her voice. "Mom! Fel wants to go on an expedition to the Greater Lands to clean out a new vault."

"Do it," she called back from above.

Fel and Epiphany looked at their father. He scratched his head.

"It appears I have been outvoted. Fine, fine. Go with my blessings."

Fel drained the rest of his stew in one half-choking gulp and sprang from his chair.

"*But!*" Martin said.

Fel winced. His father's conditions tended to be legendary in their capacity to hamstring an otherwise simple plan.

"You take Bluebelle and the cart. If you do find an abundance of goods, I want you to be able to bring plenty back with you."

"Of course."

"And I want you to present your expedition contraptions to me so I can be sure they're in proper operation."

"I'll get them right now."

"And you're taking Wick."

"… What?" Fel said, casting a subtle glance at Epiphany.

"I've finished the second sentry lantern. Now we can afford to send Wick with you as well as keeping him here."

Epiphany tried to hide the dismay at the suggestion.

"Dad, you *just* managed to get the second sentry lantern repaired. Like you said, this could be a dangerous trip. Are you sure you want to risk it?"

"I'm sending my son along, what sort of father would I be if I was willing to risk *you* but not the lantern. Besides! Wick can answer questions, and he can deliver messages over even that sort of distance in minutes instead of days. It worked brilliantly when we sent him along with Epiphany even *without* a lantern, until it blew out. The lantern will make it even more convenient. No pesky tending to a flame day in, day out. It isn't negotiable. If you're heading anywhere near the Greater Lands, you're taking Wick."

He finished the last morsel of his meal and gathered up the pages. "I shall make some duplicates to educate Wick with, and then I'll light the lantern and we'll start outfitting you for your trip. You two clean up the table, will you?"

Martin marched down the steps. Fel and Epiphany took a moment to exchange a frustrated glare before gathering the dishes.

"Just how am I supposed to keep this from Mom and Dad if I'll have Wick spying on me?" Fel whispered.

"I don't know! I didn't know he had the second lantern working. I thought when the flame 'accidentally' went out on the last trip it would be enough to convince him not to send Wick around on any trips. Maybe it won't be a problem. *I'm* the one who has to make the sale."

"But I'm the one who has to find the goods, and if he sees them, he's going to tell Dad."

"And if you don't use Wick as your light during the expedition, Dad might get suspicious. … I can't help you here, Fel. You're going to have to figure it out."

"I'm not the one who figures things out! I'm the one who carries heavy things and trudges through swamps and tundra to find things to fix and sell. I do the back-breaking stuff, and in exchange I get to get drunk when I'm off duty. You do the stuff that requires being clever, and in exchange you don't have to learn what a greater pixie bite feels like. That was the deal!"

"Sometimes if you want to make the big score, you have to step up your game."

"… This guy better come through with the money, Fanny."

"You do your part and I'll do mine."

Chapter 4

The Masker family wagon was a bit of a relic, like most of the goods they sold. It was a two-wheeled affair, wide enough to crowd two into the seat, and with a cargo shelf in the back with room for one large chest. Their horse Bluebelle was old and didn't share Fel's sense of urgency for the trip. As a result, six long hours of riding, taking him well past midnight, had yet to bring him past the next town on the southern road.

He glanced at the sentry lantern dangling from the hook on one side of the stiff canvas shade mounted over the seat. It was the very one his father had shown him, though now there was a bright orange flame flickering inside. It lit the road ahead nicely, but that didn't stop Fel from feeling what might have seemed like a foolish amount of resentment toward a simple light source. But the fact that the light source was not simple was precisely why he resented it. It was a sentry flame, and it had a name.

"Not so chatty, at least," he muttered.

"I only speak if spoken to, Fel Masker, son of Vivian and Martin Masker," the flame replied.

It had no face, not even a mouth. But it had a voice. The voice was deep and articulate, with a crisp precision that brought to mind a professor. Wick had been a part of the Masker collection for at least two generations, and he represented the sole exception his mother and father made to the rule of presenting all contraptions to the assayer. It just so happened that sentry flames were so rare and obscure that the assayer had no reason to suspect that a well-crafted but otherwise visually unremarkable lantern might have so deep a secret to keep.

"Did you require something?" Wick asked eagerly.

"I absolutely did not," Fel said.

"Your father likes to dictate his day's agenda to me each morning so that, if asked, I can remind him of remaining tasks. It is a very pleasant and fulfilling service to provide, and I would happily provide it to you as well."

"Right now my plan is to keep riding until I see a place to get a drink and sleep until sunup. I don't need help remembering that."

"Your memory is to be a praised, then. Your father is really quite forgetful when it comes to minor tasks."

"He's not forgetful. He just picks and chooses the details he likes to focus on. Little things like eating or sleeping aren't even on the list."

"An insightful observation!"

"He's my father. I know him," Fel said.

"Observation is my specialty," Wick said.

They rattled along in silence for a second or two.

"Do you still enjoy bouncing balls off crowded shelves?"

"… What?"

"When last we had a conversation, it was when I warned you that bouncing a ball in your father's workshop might knock things down. You then bounced a ball and knocked things down."

Fel twisted his head aside, trying to make sense of the statement. "That was twenty years ago."

"Was it? How swiftly time goes by when one has pleasant and fulfilling services to provide."

"Why did you go back and pick something from when I was seven years old as the topic to chat about?"

"It was the last time we discussed anything at length. You were, in fact, quite vigorously opposed to further conversation after I informed your father of your ball-bouncing."

"Oh, right. I called you a rat for telling on me and said never to speak to me again."

"I do endeavor to serve faithfully!" Wick said brightly.

Fel sighed. It was clear this thing had an ironclad memory and a sharp eye for detail. He couldn't rely upon it simply overlooking what he was up to or what he'd found. If he was going to find a way around having Wick tattle on him to his dad, he'd need to learn more.

"So what's your deal?"

"To what deal are you referring?"

"To me, you've always just been that thing that hangs in Dad's workshop or in the store and keeps an eye on things."

"That is the primary role of a sentry lantern!"

"But how do you do it?"

"I can see anything my light falls upon. I can hear anything that is presently under the influence of my heat, and if I choose, I can be heard by one or all the individuals influenced by my heat as well."

"So can Dad hear what you're saying right now, back in the other lantern?"

"No! My ability to observe is limited by proximity. The flames need to be near each other for me to observe through more than one of them simultaneously. Otherwise I need to travel between them."

"So if you're here, you're not with Dad and the other way around?"

"That is correct."

"So how do I know if you're here or not?"

"Ask for me to answer and, if I am present, I will."

"Right, but is there a way I can tell by just looking?"

"When I am observing a flame, it is still. When I am not, it is subject to the whims of the wind."

He nodded and smiled. "That's good to know. Useful."

"My absence is the least useful of my many services."

"Yeah, well, that depends…" Fel muttered under his breath.

"Pardon me?"

"Nothing, nothing. So do you just pop back and forth between flames?"

"There is something akin to travel time, though much compressed. At present it would take me just a few seconds to pay a visit to your father. We are headed to the Greater Lands, are we not?"

"We are. Or pretty near, anyway."

"At that distance, it will take me between one quarter and one half of an hour to reach your father's lantern."

Fel nodded. The cracks were beginning to show in his chaperone's defenses. With some well-timed messages to his father, he could arrange for some privacy.

"Anything else I should know about you?"

"A service your father has used to great effect is my capacity to remember anything that is consumed by my flame."

"So… a bunch of wood and lamp oil?"

"Yes, though those rather uninteresting fuel sources are not the most valuable of the records I keep. Your father likes to transcribe his texts and notes, then burn the pages, providing me with a record of their contents so that I can serve as reference."

Fel shrugged. "Yeah, that sounds like a Dad thing."

"Furthermore, thanks to your father's efforts, if this flame is extinguished, it can be relit and I will be able to return. If I set to light something that is *outside* of a sentry lantern, I can only observe through it while it burns continuously. If it is extinguished, my link is lost. This occurred during your sister's last trip when she carelessly left the mundane lantern lit by my flame outdoors on a windy evening."

The cart rumbled around a turn, the cloud-shrouded moon leaving only Wick's light to keep them on the narrow road.

"I am very interested in expanding my knowledge, so that I may provide still greater amounts of fulfilling service."

"That's great, Wick."

"What do you know about the Greater Lands?" Wick asked.

"It's big, it's dangerous, and there's loads of contraptions there."

"That is very approximate information. Do you have more precise information?"

"Not really. See, you like to know everything about a thing, I guess. I'm more of a 'just enough to get the job done' sort of person."

"Efficient. A laudable aim."

"If you say so."

He squinted at a point of light in the distance. "Oh, thank goodness. The tavern. I need a drink and a bed. Keep quiet while we're in there. I don't need people figuring out you're a contraption."

"I am well aware of the value of secrecy. I shall hold my tongue. If you'll pardon the levity."

Fel glanced at the lantern.

"Wordplay," Wick said.

Fel's expression was unchanged.

"Tongues of flame."

"Oh."

"Humorous banter is also a pleasant and fulfilling service I provide."

"You might want to work on that."

"Thank you! I look forward to practicing with you!"

Fel winced. "No, I didn't mean… you know what, let's start by practicing being quiet, all right?"

#

Back in the shop, Vivian had finally barred the door, closed the shutters, and begun working on the ledgers for the day.

"It's good to have you here, Fanny," she said, sliding the lamp a little closer and running her finger down the page. "There is always so much to do after a long day."

Epiphany yawned and pulled out the stepladder to start arranging the shelves for the following morning. They'd sold a few of the lesser contraptions, some antique silverware, and a few pieces of jewelry. Now it was time to replace those items with things that had been otherwise gathering dust outside the eyeline of the average customer.

"It seems we are selling a good deal more mundane antiquities than contraptions."

"Don't I know it," Vivian said. "The contraptions still bring in more money than the rest combined, but the worthwhile ones are getting fewer and farther between. Not quite as far between as the shelves would indicate, but that's the assayer's guild for you."

"They've been sticklers lately, have they?"

"I had to argue with the new representative from the guild for two hours to be permitted to continue selling the dancer's boxes. He said something about 'autolocomotion' being a prohibited function of a simple contraption. We've been selling these since your father's father owned the shop. But now we've got to twist their arms to get them to let us continue."

"Terrible."

"I wouldn't mind it if they'd just make up their minds. But one month an assayer will let you put a drill up for sale, and the next it'll be considered a deadly weapon. How can I plan a sales season if they won't be consistent?"

Epiphany carefully positioned a silver soup tureen and made herself look busy arranging some pewter mugs. "You know, when I head north, now and then I hear tell of contraption restorers partnering directly with buyers."

"We've got plenty of regulars, dear. You know that."

"Yes, but I mean they give the collectors right of first refusal. Offer up full slates of contraptions to buy as a lot, before they're even assessed."

"Wouldn't I love to have access to a buyer like that."

Epiphany raised an eyebrow. "Would you?"

"Sure. Someone foolish enough to buy a lot of goods before the assayer came in to cherry-pick the best ones? It'd take the money out of his pocket instead of ours."

"Oh, right. But, you know, I've heard that *some* of the buyers take their goods and go without the assayer being any the wiser. I mean, if a seller doesn't present goods for appraisal, there isn't *really* any way they will find out."

"They'll find out. They always do. Anyone who tries to get around them gets the lords and the watch after them before long. Anyone brash enough to tempt the ire of the assayer's guild deserves what they get. The assayers may as well be thieves, but we knew the cost of doing business when we got started. Somewhere they've got a fortune waiting to be sold, and they're just sitting on it because it's too 'complex' and 'might be misused.' Knowing they're too stubborn to make money off what they stole from us takes a little of the sting of having them harvest their pick of our finds. But it's all worth it to keep this place open. We're generations old at this shop. I mean to keep it alive long enough for you to take over."

"I've seen the ledger, Mom. We won't last much longer if we keep going the way we're going."

"So we do more. We work harder. You don't risk something like this, something with this legacy, for a few bags of duots."

Epiphany slouched a bit and tested a music contraption. "No. I suppose you don't."

#

Fel shook off the chill of the night as he stepped into the tavern. There was something about the stink of bad pipe smoke and stale ale that made him smile. He'd had some good times in places like this. The Fox and Log was leaps and bounds better than this place in every way but one: he wasn't a regular here, so he didn't have to worry about stories of his exploits reaching his family. That is, assuming he didn't do anything *too* notable.

He scanned the dimly lit establishment. The place was nearly empty. That wasn't a surprise. There were only three other horses in the stable besides his own. A wide smile crossed his face as he realized that the only thing of any note going on was a game of grum being played at one of the back tables. Three of the men in the game had the size and disposition of either roadside thugs or heavy laborers—not that those two careers were mutually exclusive. The smallest of them was a match for Fel's weight, if not quite his stature, and the largest looked like he would have trouble fitting through doorways. The remaining fellow in the game was another thing entirely. He was perhaps half a head shorter than Fel and rail thin, though he did try to hide it with a well-worn billowy blue robe. His hair was long and wild, and his face was a scraggly unshaved mess. He had a large pile of duots beside his set of tiles and seemed a bit lost as he stared at them.

"A question, sirs," the blue-robed player said with a thick accent Fel couldn't place. "The plowman square. This is a good one to have?"

"It's a good one, yeah," said the hulk at the end of the table, stifling a chuckle.

"And to have just one is better? Or is three better?"

Fel's eyes widened. This was a man with a heap of money who didn't even know the *rules* of grum. He practically leaped over a chair to make his way to the table.

"What's the buy-in?" he said breathlessly.

#

At The Fox and Log, Allie rubbed her eyes and splashed some water on her face. She'd lost track of which shift she was supposed to be on. At this point, if she walked in the door, regardless of what day it was or what time it was, every other employee left the barroom for at least the next four hours. It worked out well for her coin purse. She probably doubled her salary from scattered coins here and there from appreciative patrons, but it was beginning to drain her. At times like this, she liked to pick a project to latch on to. In the past she'd decided the bar needed a new top and spent a few weeks maneuvering a carpenter who frequented the place to offer his services. Before that she'd gotten a mural painted on the back wall. Having some larger task to focus on in addition to the near-mindless work of tending to patrons gave some structure to the week. She'd have to keep her eyes open for it, especially now that Fel was off on one of his trips and she wouldn't have him to chat with. Of all the

38

regulars, he was the one who remained tolerable regardless of the amount of booze he swilled. Anyone could be a gentleman while sober, but find a man who keeps his manners even when drunk and you've got someone special.

As if to act as a counterpoint, the door swung open and two men tumbled inside like wild animals. Each of them wore the canvas under-armor that came with a tour of duty on the city watch, but they were a little too steady on their feet—and it was a little too early in the day—for them to be drunk already. They were just rowdy by default.

Maybe not *anyone* could be a gentleman while sober.

"Boys, boys, boys!" she said, getting their attention and swinging around to the front of the bar. "Easy, easy. You've got the whole night ahead of you. Pace yourselves. Now what's the occasion that's got you two worked up?"

"Finished our rotation on the watch!" said the first man.

"Talk about a *boring* job. Nothing ever happens here. We barely even get to thump heads," said the second.

"Nice to be out of it, then," she said. "What'll you have?"

"Something cheap, and a *lot* of it," said the first man.

"Yeah. Tonight, I'm in it for the quantity," said his friend.

"Ale it is." She popped behind the bar and grabbed two tankards. "So. How many positions cycled out this time?" she asked.

"Just us."

"So we're going to be getting two new watchmen? Have they been chosen?"

"Yeah. Two military-types from Toyl's Crossing."

"What are their names?"

"Eh. I was just calling them Fresh Meat 1 and Fresh Meat 2. What's it matter? We're all doing the same job."

She set the drinks in front of them as they helped themselves to a bowl of crickets.

"We're heading back up north tomorrow," said the first former watchman. "Wait'll I tell them I got hooked on *crickets* as a snack."

"They're salty, they're crunchy, and they're free if you know how to catch them. What's not to like?"

"Yeah, well, outside of Thayn, people don't eat bugs."

"They're missing out. Just remember, boys. If you're off the watch, no more free drinks."

"Yeah, yeah," grumbled the second former watchman.

Allie made a mental note of the first drink on each of their sure-to-be-significant tabs. She also made a point to keep an eye out for the new watchmen. It usually paid to be on their good side.

#

Two hours later, Fel was pleasantly floating on a sea of cheap ale and snacking on roasted crickets. The fifty-duot buy-in, representing two thirds of the money he'd brought for the entire trip, had swelled to a hundred, mostly at the expense of the foreigner, who was sweating a bit as his once-towering mound of coins had been reduced to a single stack.

"It is not the night for me, eh, sirs?" the foreigner said, scratching his beard.

"Just play the game, stranger," rumbled the hulk.

"Now... I am not so sure..." he said.

Fel crunched a salty cricket. "Fella, you know, I didn't ask your name."

"I am called Tome!" he said, as though he was genuinely proud of the fact.

"Well, Tome, you're starting to fall behind. Take it from me, you might be tempted to cut your losses. But people who cut their losses? They never win big. You cut your losses today, you're down however much you're down. You cut your losses tomorrow, you're down even more. Down, down, down. But if you go for it, if you have the confidence in your run of tiles and you *go* for it, then maybe you win big. And a big win is worth a dozen losses."

"It is?"

"Look at all these coins on the table. You play your tiles properly and they could all be in your pockets. You could walk out of this place like a king!"

"Yes! Yes, sirs! I will bid. I will bid *this* many!" Tome said, tossing down a stack of duots. "For you to give to me that milkmaid."

The other players gave Fel a subtle nod. He leaned back and raised his ale. He might not have Tem's "tactics," but he could keep a man at the table. A few more games and they'd have fleeced this sheep good and proper.

"Tell me, sirs?" Tome said. "Do you mind if I smoke?"

"I don't care if you burn," the hulk rumbled.

The rest of the players laughed diplomatically.

Tome took a small, stiff case from his pocket and pulled out a hand-rolled cigar.

"Here, let me," Fel said, fishing out his sparker.

"Oh, such wondrous devices!" Tome said, as the spark crackled to the tip of the roll-up.

The paper burned with an odd smell. Certainly not tobacco. Tome perched it in the corner of his mouth and swept his hands over his tiles, rearranging them.

"Are there any more bids? Or can I take the tile I need?" Tome asked.

"Well, I can't make it *easy* for you." Fel said, tossing in a stack to match.

The bids worked their way around, slowly driving up the price of a tile that all but Tome seemed to know was worthless. Two more rounds of tiles and bets left nearly everything Fel had—and for that matter nearly every coin in the game—in a heap in the middle of the table. In just a few minutes the game went from a fairly even fleecing of a player who didn't know better to a single winner-take-all flip of the screens.

Any other time, this would have rubbed Fel wrong. He'd spent enough time playing to know that someone with a lot of money and no apparent skill was a red flag. No one that bad at grum would be playing it with that big a stack. Nine times out of ten, it would be a grift. A scam. And if it *was* a scam, this would surely be the time to reveal it. But Fel had *the* best run of tiles he'd ever had. Kings and Cooks, they called it. And all black. He even had a plowman hanging off the end for good measure. If this stranger *was* running a scam, he'd botched it, because this game was Fel's, once the money was in his pocket, that'd be that.

"I am out of the coins," Tome said. "Time to show the towels, yes?"

"Tiles," Fel said.

"Oh! Ho-ho, yes. The tiles. I drop the screen?"

"I'll start," the hulk said. "Milk in blue and plow in black."

The next blinder fell. Garbage.

Same for the next. Then it was Fel's turn. He didn't even bother announcing the win. He just flopped the blinder down and stood to collect his winnings. His hands were still hovering over the pot when Tome spoke.

"Oh, look at that!" he said. "We are the same. Except I have a queen instead of a plowman."

Fel's eye twitched. It was one of only two runs that could have beat him. And at no point did the man called Tome bid on any of those tiles. He had to have been *dealt* that run. Everything else had been for show.

"You lucky rat…" the hulk growled.

"Is this a win? Oh ho! I am so lucky indeed! And I have you to thank, Mr. Fel, for convincing me to keep playing."

"But… how can you…" Fel's eyes fixed on the queen. "Wait…"

Tome reached to collect his winnings, but Fel slapped his hand aside. He tipped the basket of unclaimed tiles onto the table and started flipping them. He uncovered kings, several of which were already in Tome's hand. Then he found the precise queen Tome had used to beat him. Not another queen of the same type. The same precise tile. The same chipped corner. The same bloodstain.

"What in muck is going on?" the hulk fumed. He clapped his meaty mitt over the tile in Tome's run. When he lifted it and opened his hand, it was the milkmaid tile he'd bid for… and the queen remained on the table, looking a bit hazy and translucent. "Trickery…" he rumbled.

He slapped Tome's face. The cigar flew from his lips and struck the wall. It unraveled to reveal a smattering of cheap tobacco and some indecipherable runes scrawled on the paper.

"He's a paper mage," shouted one of the smaller players.

The brute grabbed Tome by the neck and pulled him from his chair.

"Now, now, boys, it was all in good fun. I wasn't going to actually take the pot, honest," Tome stammered, suddenly with a far firmer grasp of the language.

"That's right you weren't, because I'm going make all those fingers bend backward. See if you can write any of your grum cheat spells *then*."

The others made their way around to join in what was sure to be an epic beating. Fel, angry as he was, didn't feel the need to put fists to face, but he wasn't opposed to watching it happen from a safe distance. Tome hastily stammered his way through some excuses and promises. Fel crossed his arms and waited. But a notion fought its way through the thin fog of ale clouding his mind. The winnings were still on the table, and no one was watching them.

He opened his coin purse and scooped handfuls of coins inside. This night was going to work out well for him after all. As he flicked the grum tiles out of the remaining heap of winnings, one of the smaller men caught him by the wrist.

"Just what do you think *you're* doing?"

"What? His run was faked. My run won. This is my pot, fair and square."

"We're playing it over."

"No! *He's* the cheater. Why should I lose my win because *he* cheated?"

"We're playing the run over, or do you have a problem with that?"

"Oh, I'm taking my winnings, and if you think you can stop me—"

The man abandoned diplomacy before Fel could finish his sentence, but he'd been in enough bar fights to see what was coming. He dodged the swinging fist and ducked down to drive a shoulder into the other player's gut. Fel's back and legs had earned him most of his booze money by running around town and lifting boxes other people didn't want to lift. That sort of thing day in, day out had a wonderful way of making short work of relatively light loads like raging drunks. He burst forward, hefting the man off his feet, and sent him tumbling onto one of the empty tables. Another man dove on his back, but Fel ducked down and turned in a tight circle to toss him off.

That, it turned out, was a tactical error. Spinning in circles had a way of upgrading one's status from tipsy to dizzy. He stumbled but kept his feet. At least, until one of the other men came and tackled him to the ground. He endured a few kicks to the ribs before he was able to haul himself up and shed the angry gamblers. He grabbed a chair and swung it twice. It didn't make contact, but it gave him some space. Tome stumbled away from the hulk. One eye was almost swollen shut already, but judging from the dazzling cloud of sparkles around his head, the mage had been able to deploy some manner of enchantment to slip free.

Tome took refuge behind Fel.

"What are you doing? Get over there. With you over here, it's three on two. I like three on one better, with me running away," Fel said. "If I didn't have them to worry about, I'd put this chair through your head for starting this."

"Hey. They want to pummel the both of us. That puts us on the same team, doesn't it?"

"No!"

"Do you have a way out of here? A cart or a horse?"

"Yeah, if I can get to them."

"If I help you get to them, will you take me? I hitched a ride with one of those fellows, and I doubt they'll be receptive to taking me all the way to Beffshire."

"You're the reason I'm *in* this mess."

"And by me extricating you, it shall even it out."

He reached into his pocket and revealed a small folio of handwritten pages. While Fel kept the jilted gamblers at bay, he selected one, tore its end, and tossed it to the ground.

It fluttered to the feet of the angry drunks and began belching a strangely cold, odorless purple smoke. Fel took full advantage of the startling distraction to use the chair to shove the men against the table. It flipped, sending tiles and what few coins Fel hadn't claimed clattering to the floor.

Fel bolted, with Tome hot on his heels. The fleeing pair made it to Fel's cart. Tome pulled a heavy wooden travel case from where it was hidden in the hay. He hefted it into the back of the cart and jumped into the seat. Fel heaved the cart up to connect to Bluebelle. The angry gamblers tried to make it through the tavern door at the same time as Tome snapped the reins and the horse surged to the brisk walking pace that was as fast as it was ever likely to move.

"This isn't going to make for a very successful getaway," Tome said as Fel hopped aboard and crammed himself into the seat beside him.

"I wasn't planning on having to make an escape," Fel growled.

The mage handed over the reins. "I hate to burn this on so trivial a threat, but desperate times make desperate demands, don't they?" He reached into another pocket in his billowy shirt and revealed a veritable scroll. He unfurled it and held it firmly with both hands raised over his head. "When I tell you to, turn off into the field."

"Once this horse gets off the road, it takes her a while to get back on," Fel warned.

"Shouldn't be a problem. Ready… *now.*"

Fel tugged the reins. Tome tore the scroll. Sparkles and glimmers traced the hard edges of the carriage, and for a moment, the world became blurry. As he rattled off the road and nearly toppled the cart, a duplicate of the cart resolved itself. It had the same vague translucency as the false tile the mage had nearly won the game with.

The duplicate cart turned and followed the road behind them in the opposite direction. Blinded by lingering smoke, a night of drinking, and the red haze of anger, all three of the angry gamblers piled onto their horses and made chase. The illusory cart helpfully stayed *just* far enough ahead of them to keep from being revealed for what it was. After a few minutes, Fel and Tome were out of danger and free to slowly work their way back onto the road.

#

Tome had kept his attention glued to the road behind them as they rumbled forward.

"So, is Tome your real name?" Fel asked.

"It is. Tome Inkbrand. Fifth of my name."

"Mmm. Fel Masker. First, as far as I know."

The mage leaned aside and squinted in the distance.

"Not confident in your illusion's ability to fool them for good?" Fel asked, his eyes on the road ahead.

"I am not certain how long it will last."

"Didn't you *create* it?"

"I did, but… it's a bit complicated to explain to someone unversed."

"Complicated nothing. It's magic. You can make impossible things happen. The only mystery is why you're wasting your time bilking drunks in a tavern instead of… whatever sort of things a magician *ought* to get up to."

Tome turned to him, satisfied they were safe for the moment. "I'll have you know that I *cannot* make impossible things happen, a fact that should be made plain by the fact that I've made them happen, thus rendering them not only possible but inevitable. And I am not a magician. I am a mage, a wizard. There are worlds of difference."

"Not to me."

"Then you don't understand nuance. A magician is a performer, a mage is a practitioner. A mage harnesses the *art* of the word, constructing and composing—as necessary—phrasings concise and potent or sprawling and complex. A magician is a charlatan who pretends to achieve through trickery what a proper mage achieves through equal parts improvisation and memorization."

"So you're not a charlatan."

"Anything but."

"Then what was that with the cheating at the grum game?"

"*That*, my burly inquisitor, was evidence that the world lacks balance and equity. Someone who can unravel the mysteries of the metaphysical has no direct means to translate that raw, mystic know-how into financial compensation."

"That's crazy. You should be able to just charge into wherever you like and do whatever you want, if you've got magic power."

"Flattering though it is to hear such an assessment of my capabilities, they are not without limits. My focus is chiefly on illusion and enhancement. I can, after a fashion, heal or empower someone. I can conjure images. But any and all of those things require that I put pen to page. And on that point…"

He reached back to fetch his wooden case. Flicking open the clasp revealed a change of clothes, a few pots of ink, and a sheaf of blank pages. He took an ink bottle, the quill, and a sheet of paper from inside. The ink bottle fit snugly into a small recess in the top of the case. He spread the paper and began to jot down an enchantment with all the casualness of a shopping list. That the carriage was rattling along an uneven road seemed to make little difference. He wrote quite legibly despite the bumps.

"A small general spell requires a few hundred runes. A powerful or specific one requires thousands. Then there are the variables of the ink, the page, the quill, all of which require adjustments that are not immediately clear to the novice. And most frustrating of all, the most potent of spells, those possible only with high-quality ink, specially treated paper, and *volumes* of writing, do not maintain their potency. They are *so* specific and sensitive that the location and the timing of their creation and their execution are so precise in their calibration that the greater the separation in both space and time from the point of creation, the weaker the effect. That little carriage trick took me the better part of three days to concoct. I would wager if I'd waited another day or two, the spell wouldn't have had the fidelity or duration necessary to fool even those drunkards."

He finished filling about half the page. A fold and tear removed the blank portion of the page to stow in his bag once more, along with the sealed ink and quill. Once the gear was tucked safely away, he tore the edge of the spell, right through the middle of the first word, and slapped it against his swollen eye. The edges shimmered with light. In a slow, smoldering wave the light consumed the page and left it fluttering into the wind as feathery white ash. By the time the leaflet had burned away, his eye had greatly improved. It was still bruised and puffy, but he could open it.

"This question would have been more appropriate to ask prior to joining you on this leg of the journey, but where precisely are we headed? I notice we are heading *away* from Beffshire, which was my intended destination."

"I'm headed to the Greater Lands. I don't know where you're headed."

"Certainly not there. I don't suppose you could see your way clear to turning about and taking me to Beffshire before you head to that forsaken place of beasts and misfortune?"

"I don't have the time. And you wouldn't want to go to Beffshire anyway."

"Oh?"

"You used your real name when cheating at grum. You pull that stunt more than once in Beffshire and you'll be sent packing, with or without use of your legs. We don't suffer fools."

"Ah, a local, I take."

"Born and bred. So start thinking about where you want to get dropped off. And maybe plan for a different place if you're looking for marks."

"Duly noted. As it happens, I imagine south is as good as north. The important thing to me is that I don't head back west."

"Oh?"

"The entire purpose of this journey is to seek new lands and new fortunes. I was born far west of here, and have come a long way to escape it. It is fair to say the journey has inspired more than a few groups similar to those three gentlemen who would greatly relish the opportunity to extract some recompense from my hide."

"Can't imagine why," Fel muttered.

Chapter 5

Back in Beffshire a few days later, Allie was nearing the end of a rather typical day at The Fox and Log. A few of the regulars were at their usual seats, still covered with the grime of their jobs in the fields. She passed them a few complementary baskets of roasted crickets. The fieldworkers had it tough, especially at this time of the year. Long workdays, hot fields. The ale was as much medicinal as it was recreational, washing down the layer of dirt that accumulated in their mouths over the course of a day.

The door swung open. She turned to greet the newcomers. "Hello! Oh, new in town?"

She needn't have asked. The Fox and Log wasn't the only tavern in Beffshire, and it was a rather large city, so there was every possibility that there were locals she didn't know. But even a glance at these two made it clear that if they were locals, she would have remembered them. The pair were nearly identical. Two men on the short, stocky side, with dark hair, stubbly beards, and intense scowls. The only thing that differentiated them from each other were the positions of the major scars on their faces. One fellow had one across his left cheek. The other had one on his right temple.

"You own the place?" said Temple Scar.

"If I owned the place, I wouldn't be working closing," Allie said.

"A bottle of brandy," said Temple.

"A bottle of rye," said Cheek.

"Not that I don't trust you two, but that'll be thirty-five and twenty duots respectively."

They reached into their pockets in a synchronized motion and produced gleaming brass badges. Allie gave them a look.

"Officials from Teskal?" she said. "Well, have a seat. Officials drink free." She slipped behind the bar and selected two bottles from the low end of their stock and two pewter shot glasses. "So, what brings you two to Beffshire? We don't get officials down from Teskal unless it's something important," she said, pouring out a shot for each of them and leaving the bottle.

"Looking for a place called Masker's."

"Masker's Antiquities?" Allie shifted smoothly from small talk to gossip mode with the grace of a lifelong professional. "What's up with Masker's?"

"It doesn't matter what's up," said Cheek.

"We just need to speak with them," said Temple.

"Do you know where they are?" asked Cheek.

"I know where the shop is, sure. Clear across town, though."

"Travel isn't a problem," Temple said.

"Even so. You boys just started a bottle. And you look like you've been on the road a while."

"Not on the road, but in the saddle," Cheek said.

Allie tipped her head. "You boys got hippogriffs, do you?"

"We do," said Temple after knocking back his shot. "So why don't you head back to the bar and swap this for something worth drinking?"

"Absolutely. My apologies. We don't usually attract folks with such a discerning palate." She glanced at the regulars. "No offense."

The locals raised their mugs and gave very little impression to suggest they even heard what she'd said. She snagged the brandy.

"You want the next one up too, friend?" she said to the man with the scar on his cheek.

"It's good enough. Rye is rye," he said.

Allie nodded and trotted over to the bar. She stowed the one bottle and made a show of digging for another one under the counter.

"Davie?" she shouted. "Would you lend a hand?"

A diminutive fellow of the gnomish persuasion trotted out from the back room. He was what the owners called a "town runner." Keeping a tavern running and keeping its patrons happy often produced unexpected needs that had to be met quickly. Sometimes they would run out of this booze or that ingredient at an inconvenient time. Occasionally a patron would need to deliver a message. They couldn't keep making money off someone who left to deliver that message, so it paid to deliver it for them. But they couldn't very well send out one of their servers. Thus, each tavern kept someone on hand to do the running. Lately it was Davie, a waist-high gnome who had retired from carpentry to work at the tavern to keep busy and get a free drink now and again.

Allie crouched behind the bar and pointed. "I need that bottle of brandy back there," she said, loudly enough for the newcomers to hear.

"For the young lady, anything," he said, as though he'd been asked to mount his horse and ride in defense of the kingdom.

As he reached past the bottles, Allie lowered her voice.

"I also need you to run down to Masker's Antiquities and tell them there's a couple of hippogriff riders who say they're from Teskal. I could be wrong, but I've seen enough Teskal officials to know they wouldn't hire anyone who'd stop at the tavern before doing their rounds, and those badges didn't look right to me. Something might be up. They should be on their toes."

Davie handed her the bottle and crisply saluted. He dashed around the bar and out the door. Allie stepped up to the table and poured a fresh shot of brandy.

"So… hippogriffs. I've heard some stories about them. Supposedly it's a walk in the park to fly those things. They've received expert training, and the Greater Mystics are *always* smarter, so they pick up training quicker, right?"

"Whoever told you that doesn't know the first thing about hippogriffs. You want to keep one of those in the air? Going where you want to go? You need force of will," Temple said.

"Force of will and nerves of steel," said Cheek.

"Oh, really. Tell me all about it," Allie said.

The pair launched into an alternating serenade of boasts. Allie couldn't care less about what they were saying. The plan was to give Davie time to get the message delivered, and there were few better ways to get rugged men like this talking than to give them a reason to defend their ruggedness.

#

A few minutes later, Vivian leaned over the counter, gazing down at Davie as the breathless gnome finished the message.

"… and she was secretive about it, so I think she wanted the make sure the boys on the hawk horses won't know you know," he said.

"I see…" Vivian said. "And here I was thinking I should close up because there wouldn't be any more business this late at night. Excitement at all hours in the antiquities, it seems. Thank you, Davie. And send Allie my thanks."

She tossed him a duot, and he trotted out the door. Vivian slid open the dumbwaiter and stuck her head into the shaft. "Martin! Seems like there was something in the goods Epiphany brought home that's got someone interested. We're having visitors."

"Do you want me up there for it?" Martin called back.

"No, no. Just bar the doors. I'll tell you when the coast is clear."

The soft thumps of braces dropping into place signaled the beginning of a time-tested procedure. Vivian supposed other shops that dealt strictly in things like silver and porcelain—the precious and pointless knickknacks that filled a wealthy person's house—didn't have to worry about moments like these. Yes, there would likely be the occasional thief hoping to make a big score, but those thieves were at least *conventional*. The Maskers dealt in contraptions. As precious as a gold serving set might be, it wasn't likely that a rival government would arrive and attempt to claim it. There was no limit to what a contraption might be capable of, and thus the Maskers didn't simply

49

have to ward off thieves, they had to be mindful of foreign agents who might want to acquire high-value contraptions before the local assayer could spirit them away to be secured. As much as she wasn't fond of having her own kingdom lay claim to a contraption for a pittance, she certainly didn't want a rival kingdom to get it. Not for free, anyway.

She rolled a large display case behind the counter onto the hatch leading to the rest of their home. A quick tug of a curtain hid the door portion of the hatch, and a rattle of a feather duster sprinkled them both with enough dust to make it seem like they'd been there for ages. The crate of goods Epiphany had brought back had already been sorted and brought to Martin's shop for repair and restoration, but if these people were coming because they knew a shipment had arrived, it was probably best to provide one. She hefted a crate onto the countertop and slid a rolling ladder around. One by one she plucked up the contraptions and antiquities that had spent the most time on the shelves without being bought and stowed them in the box, then shifted the other items around to disguise the empty spaces.

Just as she rolled the ladder back to its spot in the front corner of the shop, the door rattled open and Temple and Cheek shoved their way inside.

"Master's Antiquities?" Cheek said.

"Masker's actually. How may I help you, gentlemen?" Vivian asked in her best serving-the-customer voice.

They each dug out their badge. Vivian gave them a look. After decades of sorting out genuine antiques from forgeries, it didn't take more than a glance to see that these badges were fakes. The lettering was too crisp. These were handmade, not pressed or cast. The spacing between the letters and the crest was all wrong. They were forgeries, but expensive ones. The sort of things made by people who overestimated just how cheap the officials of Teskal were.

Vivian smiled and did her best to keep her expression even. "How may I help you, gentlemen?" she asked again. "You aren't our usual assayers."

"We came direct from the office in Teskal," said Cheek.

"Something was sold recently, up north. It is a potential risk. We came directly. Very dangerous. Your daughter may have purchased it."

"Well, sirs, if you'd like to look over our recent acquisitions, I would be happy to offer them. I had just pulled them out to assess. It has been terribly busy, and I simply haven't had the time."

They marched forward, coming just short of pushing her aside. Cheek clattered the goods around in the box. There was nothing even remotely official about their behavior. He wasn't inspecting. He was searching. These men had something in mind. And that was a problem.

"Trash," Cheek said. "All of it."

"Not every bulk purchase has treasures."

"Is this everything?" Temple asked. The question carried the weight of a threat.

"I've done *some* organizing. Perhaps there are some other items. Are you searching for something in particular?"

"A booklet, maybe," Cheek said.

"Perhaps a sheaf of pages?" Temple suggested.

Vivian's eyebrow raised a fraction. They were after the map. That was potentially problematic. They clearly knew more than they were letting on.

"There may have been something like that. Let me go through the records," she said.

She pulled the ledgers from the last few months and plopped them on the counter one after another. Five thick volumes of pages, she hoped, would give her a plausible enough delay to think up a means to send them on their way.

Temple snatched one of the books and roughly flipped through it. "These are all handwritten by you," he said.

"Yes, sir. They are records."

"I want the pages, woman. The pages. Ancient. Precious. You sell antiquities, you know what I want."

Cheek shoved her aside and started rummaging around behind the counter, throwing her other books aside.

"Sirs, please. If this persists, I will have no choice but to call the watch."

"Teskal officials don't answer to a simple city watch," Temple barked, pulling open another book.

As the pair manhandled her records, they were briefly distracted enough for her to cast a quick glance around the room for something to persuade them to leave. There was the bludgeon she kept hidden in the corner, but she doubted she could best two men, even with surprise on her side. She glanced at the wastebasket beside the counter. All of the new goods had filled her days such that she'd not emptied it in a week. Crumpled in the bottom was one of the discarded sheets from when Martin had been deciphering the map. A plan started to form in her mind.

"Nothing old here," Cheek said, leaving Vivian's filing system in a complete shambles. "We're looking for something old."

"You want the map," she said, raising her voice a bit louder than she needed to. "You won't leave until you find the map. I realize that. But it isn't here."

"What's that, woman? Sounds to me like that's a struck dog howling." Temple squinted at the back wall. "This is an old place, lady," he said. "You know what they say about the old places in Beffshire, don't you?"

"They're cramped, drafty holes in the ground?" Cheek said.

"Right. Holes in the ground." He stomped his boot. "Start looking for a way down. There's more to this place."

The door opened. Both men turned to it, hands instinctively going to their belts, where both daggers and crossbows hung, ready to deploy. It was Epiphany. With Fel on an expedition and Martin hard at work restoring the *actual* contents of her recent purchase, Epiphany was left with the drudgery of jobs that normally fell to her younger brother.

She looked wary as she entered the shop. "Who are you two?" she asked. "And do those hippogriffs belong to you?"

"Yeah. Officials from Teskal," said Temple. "Who are you?"

"I'm Epiphany Masker. I help run this place."

Temple grinned. "So you're the one who went and got all this stuff. You're the one we're after, then."

"They want the map. I told them it isn't here," Vivian said.

"Of course it isn't here," Epiphany said, without even a pause to prepare herself for the deception. "Ancient documents with the earmarks of local or regional navigation aids are to be given directly to the assayer's office for assessment. It's the seventh imperative in the Teskal assayer's office oath of obedience. You of all people should know that."

Cheek rubbed his chin. "Of course we know that. But just because you're *obliged* to do something doesn't mean you'd do it."

"We're here to *enforce* the oath," Temple said.

Vivian had to stifle a grin. No word of her daughter's claim was true, but without even taking a glimpse at their forged credentials, she'd coaxed them into revealing their status as impostors.

Epiphany crossed her arms. "Normally I would assume you'd have checked with the assayer's office directly before coming here to harass us, but I know you haven't because if you *had*, you'd know that they have the map, not us."

Temple stalked toward her. "You *bought* the thing. You had to have *seen* the thing to buy it. Who would be dumb enough to buy something only to surrender it to the assayer?" he said.

"It's called civic duty," she said.

"Civic duty doesn't keep a shop open," Cheek said. "You're lying."

"*You* are the ones who are lying," Epiphany said, standing her ground. "I spend *weeks* in Teskal every year doing business. I've seen their hippogriff riders." She pointed out the door. "Those aren't the right saddles. You're not from Teskal. Those look like Delleyde saddles to me."

Again, in unison, their hands went to their belts. This time, though, they actually drew their daggers.

"The map. Now," Temple demanded.

A soft rattle shook the door of the dumbwaiter in the back of the room.

It was subtle. It took a practiced ear to even notice it. But it was precisely what Vivian had been waiting for. She threw her back against the dumbwaiter and spread her arms against the wall, barricading it shut.

"I tell you there is no map here. Hurting us won't solve anything," Vivian said.

Temple looked to Cheek. "What do I always tell you? One little flash of steel and it gets people making mistakes."

He charged up and threw her out of the way. A single rough yank shattered the meager latch of the dumbwaiter. The moment it was open, a fist-sized piece of gadgetry sitting in the center of the dumbwaiter hinged open. A high-pitched trilling sound and a dazzling rush of swirling lights belched forth from the dumbwaiter. Vivian took full advantage of the startling distraction to deploy the cudgel. She delivered a solid blow to Temple, knocking him to the ground. Cheek rushed in, but Epiphany tackled him from behind. A short, desperate struggle followed, but even getting the drop on them wasn't enough for an elderly woman and her untrained daughter to get the best of what were certainly two trained mercenaries. Cheek forced the women back and kept a knife drawn. Temple tossed the glaring contraption aside and pulled a leather folio from inside. He flipped it open.

"We have it," he barked.

"Decoded?" Cheek asked.

"Location marked." He flipped it over and back again. "Nothing else."

"It's good enough. Let's finish these two and…" He trailed off as he caught the sound of a distant commotion. "The contraption must have been loud enough to stir the neighbors," Cheek said.

"Everyone knows what that sound means in this town," Vivian said. "You'll have the watch and half the town to deal with in a moment."

"Leave them. They're not worth the trouble."

The two men backed their way out of the shop, weapons held ready. Once they were outside, the flap of wings and clatter of hooves signaled their departure.

Vivian took a breath and slouched a bit, hand to her chest. "A bit of excitement, eh?" she said.

Epiphany grasped her by the shoulders. "Are you all right?"

"Fine, fine."

The floor rattled as Martin reached the top of the stairs. Heads began to peek in the front door.

"Go tell them we're fine, dear. I'll see to your father."

Epiphany nodded and hurried to the door. Vivian cleared the hatch and pulled it open. Martin burst from below, clutching a club, which seemed an awfully straightforward weapon for such a meticulous man.

"Where are they? What have they done?" he said.

"They've gone. It's fine. No harm no damage." Vivian gazed at the mess of her records. "Just some cleaning to do."

Martin lowered the weapon and crouched to start gathering the ledgers. They worked silently until Epiphany finished convincing the neighbors that all was well. The moment the door was shut and bolted, Martin spoke again.

"They were after the map. That means something," he said.

"It means there's some good stuff in that vault is what it means," Vivian said. "Or at least someone thinks there is. What did you give them?"

"I had to act fast, and I didn't know how much they knew about the map. The only map I had handy was the one I was marking up during the early stages of decoding."

"So it was the *real* map?" Vivian said.

"Yes, but I'd blotted out two of the blocks of text, and the position I marked was incorrect. It may as well be a random mark."

Vivian rubbed her face. "Not the perfect outcome, but the best we could manage, I suppose. They certainly wouldn't have left without getting a map. Remind me, dear. If we get a document like this again, prepare a false one for occasions such as this."

Epiphany looked up and swept the shelves until she spotted Wick's lantern. "Is it here? Is Wick present?" she said.

Martin gazed at the lantern with a practiced eye. "No, with Fel, or on the way there or back."

"We should send a message to Fel. If those people found their way here, they're able trackers. They could cross paths with him."

"Right. Good thinking."

Epiphany stared at the disorder, her expression complex.

"Something bothering you?" Martin asked.

She gave him a sideways glance.

"… Aside from the obvious."

Epiphany shook her head. "It's just that… I take care when I make my purchases. I vet my sources. I take greater care in acquiring the things I buy than most of the people I purchase them from took in finding them. Nothing should have led anyone here. Certainly not with knowledge of something as specific as a map. And it is *all* they wanted."

"These things happen. When your mother was the one doing the sales trips, she brought home what turned out to be a stolen light-focuser. That's what taught us that we needed to have a plan for this sort of thing."

"I know, but…" Epiphany knelt to pick up more of the books. "I can't shake the feeling that this is different. And if those two ever work out that they've been fooled, they'll be back."

Vivian straightened a corner of a page that had been dog-eared during the search. "If they make that mistake, we'll make sure they don't make another. A Masker with a plan is someone you don't want to meet."

#

Fel kept his eyes on the road ahead. For the last three hours, he'd been blessedly free of conversation. Of all the things he thought might complicate this trip, he'd not anticipated a chatty, vaguely smug wizard talking his hear off for days. The only peace he got was when one of them was sleeping or when Tome was busy scratching away at one of his spells.

"You waste a great deal of lamp oil," Tome muttered.

Fel blinked his eyes and shook his head, reluctantly pulling his brain from whatever pleasant doldrums it had settled into in order to once again engage in unwanted socialization. "What's that?"

"It's struck me, you never snuff this lantern. Even during the day you burn it."

"It's the middle of the night."

"My point stands. At noon it was burning."

"Don't worry about it. It isn't your concern."

"At the moment our fates are linked, since you are my means of conveyance, so I feel as though a word of advice is only fair."

Fel pointed at the road. "You see that fork up there?" he said.

Tome squinted. "I don't."

"That part there where this road veers to the west and the bumpy stone bit continues. Do you see that?"

"That's not a fork, that's a well-maintained road butting up against something that might once have been called a road."

"Well, that's where our fates stop being linked, because the thing that used to be a road is still a road, and that road leads to the edge of the Greater Lands. So unless you are coming with me, this is where you get off."

"You aren't going to drop me off at the nearest tavern or stable?"

"I dropped you off at every stable we passed. You kept getting back on. This is the end of the line. From here, the shadows in the clouds and the footprints on the ground start getting bigger."

"How far is it to the next town?" Tome asked.

"On foot? Eighteen hours if you're dedicated. But if you're halfway decent at hitching, you'll catch a ride by morning. This is a main road, after all."

"Surely you can just take a quick trot along the road, drop me off, and double back."

"You tried to trick me and a bunch of other guys into losing our money to you in a fixed game of grum. The only reason I didn't thump you in the head and leave you in their path is because you had a way to get me away safely. That earned you three days of talking my ear off and a nice long ride. That's Bramf down that road. Catch a ride and this time tomorrow you'll be

55

swindling a nice fresh group of grum players.”

“I most certainly will not!” Tome crossed his arms. “In Bramf the big money game is sixes.”

“Great, not even my game. Go get them. I’ll be heading into the Greater Lands.” He brought the cart to a stop where the roads diverged and turned a level gaze toward Tome.

“You know these roads are a haven for thieves and scoundrels,” Tome said. “Especially at night.”

“Oh, I know. There’s about to be one more. Off you go.”

“You will be risking my *life*, sir.”

“You are a wizard. I am not concerned. Off.”

Tome grumbled and gathered up his things. “If our paths ever cross again, I’ll remember your positively unneighborly conduct.”

“If our paths ever cross again, I’ll already be having a terrible day, I can tell you that.”

Tome hopped down. “Wizards have long memories, Fel.”

“Yeah, well, lucky for me I don’t, because I’m looking forward to forgetting about you,” Fel said.

He gave the reins a snap. Bluebelle rattled his little wagon over the edge of the road and onto the ancient trail. Fel tipped his head back and grinned as Tome stood sourly at the edge of the road receding into the distance behind him.

“Finally. Company is all well and good when you want it. But I’m ready to be left alone for a while.”

“Then I am afraid the present timing is unfortunate,” said Wick.

“For the love of…” Fel snapped. “What is it, Wick?”

“There has been an incident at Masker’s Antiquities.”

He shot a severe look in the direction of the lamp. “What happened? When?”

“A pair of individuals posing as Teskal officials came seeking the map. There was a physical altercation. No one was hurt, but they are now in possession of a flawed and incomplete copy of the map.”

“You’re sure no one was hurt?” Fel said, fists clenched about the reins.

“No injury. Minor disorder to your mother’s records. But there is some concern that the individuals have the wit and resources to track you and/or the vault down in time.”

“When did this happen?”

“A few hours ago.”

He scoffed. “If they were in Beffshire a few hours ago, time is on my side. Even with a perfect map, I’ve got a three-day head start, going on four.”

“They are hippogriff riders,” Wick said.

Fel shut his eyes and flared his nostrils. After a huff of frustration, he snapped the reins again. “Nothing is ever easy, Wick…”

Chapter 6

Epiphany knocked at the door of the north-side watchhouse. It was one of two watchhouses in Beffshire, which seemed horribly extravagant considering the size of the watch seldom exceeded a dozen members. If she'd had her druthers, she would have gone to the watch immediately after the two mercenaries had made their appearance, but her mother had been quite insistent that business came first, so days had passed before she was able to make time. Her mother had also expressed her doubt that the watch would be of any use. Her precise words had been, "Those dolts didn't do any good when it was happening, what good will they be now that it's over?" But Epiphany had inherited the stubbornness of her mother and the doggedness of her father. She wasn't one to leave well enough alone, and this was far from well enough in her eyes.

"Yeah! Yeah, coming," came a sharp and frazzled voice.

The door opened and the watch captain stood before her. It was a man named Captain Boltt. He was the sort of man that everyone, including his children, referred to by either his rank or his surname, so it wasn't clear to Epiphany if he even *had* a given name. He wore the official uniform of the watch. It was a sturdy canvas outfit that likely had been dyed the mustard color that someone, somewhere had decided should be used to represent city officials. The reason this was "likely" and not "definitely" a dye job was that the stoutness of the cloth meant the current captain was probably the second or third person to inherit the outfit. Years of sweat, toil, and half-hearted washing had left it more of a tea color.

The captain himself wore the outfit well. He was fit for a man his age, but in his late forties his days of personally chasing brigands and ne'er-do-wells were mostly behind him. A crosshatch of scars on his hands and face told the tale of a long and storied career keeping the peace in Beffshire.

"That's… Fanny, isn't it? Fanny Masker?"

"Yes, sir. May I come inside?" she asked.

"Come on. Come on. I've just put some water on, if you're a tea drinker."

"Thank you for the offer, but I'll pass. I'm here for business."

He tromped through the watchhouse, which like the uniform was rather overused and undermaintained but still held up well. It was mostly empty, including a few tables, some racks of weapons, and one of the older members of the watch leaning precariously back in a chair.

"Terrible thing that happened with those 'griff riders. Terrible thing. I'm glad no one was hurt," he said.

"That's what I'm here to discuss."

"I thought it might be. That's certainly the most excitement we've had here in some time. Certainly since the drunk fights after the half-year celebration."

"I'd say this was a bit more 'excitement' than some drunks getting into a shouting match, Captain."

"Certainly, certainly," he said. "What would you like to discuss?"

"I'd like to discuss what you're going to do about it."

"… It's done, isn't it?" he said. "They've come and gone."

"Yes, naturally, but shouldn't we be trying to find out who they were?"

"They were some hippogriff-riding mercs. That's as deep as I thought we needed to go."

"But who sent them?"

"That's a fine question," he said.

"It is. Which is why I'm wondering what's being done to answer it."

Boltt scratched his head. "Er… Nothing. They're not from Beffshire, so that's as far as I can go."

"I'm afraid that's not good enough for me. What if they come back?"

"If they come back, call the watch and we'll do what we can."

"Forgive the bluntness but 'what you can' wasn't very much last time."

"They had hippogriffs. I've got me and nine volunteers. We keep bad folks out, and if they get in, we kick them out. But we're just men."

"You didn't keep the 'griff riders out *or* kick them out."

"True, true. But they flew in. The town council saw fit to give us the gear to enforce the law at the wall. You fly over the wall, that's more than we can handle. And, again, we're working with volunteers. The stipend I pay these boys isn't enough to convince them to do battle with a greater hippogriff. I've got to get on their case to get them to deal with the lesser harpies when they get nippy. Truth be told, if I didn't get a few new boys cycled in from the fort at Toyl's Crossing every month or so, the watch'd be down to me and Leonard back there."

The mentioned watchman snorted, overbalanced his chair, and slammed to the ground. After a moment of bewildered confusion, he assessed his situation, found it to be acceptable, and continued his nap.

"It's a testament to the good people of this city that we haven't dissolved into chaos as it is. Nice to know that Beffshire doesn't tend toward violence and crime. Good people in this town."

"These people impersonated officials from Teskal. Surely that is worthy of investigation."

"I asked around town, no one knew them. I'd like to do more, but that wall isn't just the limit of what I'm supposed to protect, it's the limit of where I'm *allowed* to protect people."

"Have you communicated with Teskal? Asked if they've had badges or other emblems of office stolen?"

"As a matter of fact, I did. Dropped the letter in with the city's dispatches that very evening. Should get there in a day or two, where I imagine the Teskal watch will... well, ignore it."

"They'll just *ignore it*?"

"His job's the same as mine," Boltt said. "Protect his city. If they're not there, his job is done."

"It seems like this is the sort of thing that would call for some coordination. Maybe the officials in Teskal would like to know that they're being impersonated? Maybe *they* will investigate?"

"I wrote it all up in the message. If they want to look into it, they will, I'm sure. I did what I can do, Fanny. Sorry it can't be more."

She rubbed her forehead. "Do we know for certain those two 'griff riders were the *only* ones involved?"

"I think if there were more 'griff riders, we'd have seen them."

"They could be working with *other* people who are still in the city. Had you considered that?"

He scratched his head. "Hadn't. Hadn't considered that. Why, you have any more trouble?" He stood and grabbed a truncheon. "If you've got more trouble down at the shop, I'll sort it out right quick."

"No, no. I mean there could be people here in secret."

"Oh... Could be, I suppose. But how would we know that was so?"

"I would think that would be something you'd be accustomed to handling. These would be foreign agents operating within the wall."

"The city's full of foreign agents operating within the wall. People come from all around to do business."

"But some of them could be here with ill will in mind."

"Sure, sure. And if they do it"—he slapped his palm with the truncheon—"we'll oblige them to stop. Otherwise, I just don't know how we're supposed to know what they're planning. I wish I could do more. I really do. But it is what it is."

Epiphany released a sigh that she hoped disguised her frustration well, but not *too* well. "Thank you, Captain Boltt. As much as I'd prefer something proactive to keep my family safe, I'll try to be quick to alert you when we're threatened next, so that you can at least react quickly."

"We'll react good and quick, Fanny. Good and quick."

She glanced at the snoring man on the floor on her way out the door. "Give Leonard my regards."

#

"So you're one of them magic-types? Eh-heh-hee-haha," cackled the man at the reins of the latest wagon Tome had persuaded to pick him up.

Tome wasn't sure if it was the cargo on the wagon, or the man himself, but there was a stench that was positively eye-watering. All in all, having driven with the surly but tolerable Fel for so long had spoiled him for the realities of hitching rides through the more rural parts of Thayn. Ever since parting ways with Fel, things had gotten steeply worse in his journey toward a city large enough to make his mark. The irritable brute was downright cordial compared to this last batch. The first had been a man driving a hay wagon at an agonizingly slow pace. At the lightest suggestion that he might speed up a bit, he'd threatened violence upon Tome in an explosive display of temper. The second had been a woman who expected to be *paid* for the ride. Worse, she only made the demand after she'd carried him far enough to extort a few duots out of him. Now he was coping with a man who might be the single smelliest human Tome had ever encountered. That was an achievement, given the summer heat.

At first, the smell had been acceptable, but after he'd been taken through a country village and a fair distance beyond, the sun and heat had baked the stench into something downright otherworldly. And it wasn't as though the driver's personality was a saving grace. The man used a thick, unhealthily moist cackle as a sort of all-purpose punctuation.

"I am a paper mage, sir. It is a nuanced and—"

"Eh-hah-hah-hah. So you just write something you want to happen and it happens. Eh-hah!"

"No, as I say, it is a nuanced field. My abilities are limited by—"

"If I learned to write, could I get myself a big heap of gold? Eh-heh-heh."

"I feel comfortable in saying without fear of contradiction that it would be well beyond your capability. As it stands, if I wanted to conjure even a single gold coin from nothing, I would need to write many *volumes* of magic text, all carefully worded to be executed at the same moment, all using exquisitely expensive ink and paper, and then activate the spell. It would be a net loss."

"But gold from nothing! Eh-heh-heh-*hack*!" The man lurched and spat a glob of something unspeakable onto the flank of his horse.

"Right here is fine," Tome said with a twitch of his eye.

"You sure? Eh-heh-hah. We're a long ways from anyplace. Heh-*hah*!"

Tome pulled his travel case from the back. "It's fine, it's fine. Thank you for the ride sir," he said quickly.

He practically dove from the wagon and retreated to the side of the road. The wagon rattled along, though the scent lingered for so long enough after it vanished into the distance that Tome was worried he'd been stained with it somehow.

He set himself up on an old stump and watched the road. Surely someone else would be along soon. Someone who didn't appear to be decomposing.

#

Two more days of travel, and Fel was still on the road, though not for much longer. Navigation should have been getting more difficult. He was deep into the no-man's-land at the fringe of the border between the Greater Lands and the rest of the world. The old road he'd been following had abruptly ended with a worrisome gouge into the soil, and Bluebelle was left hauling the wagon without any road at all. As it happened, he'd spent only half a day or so traveling across rough, overgrown fields and sun-parched land that was suffering through a bit of a drought before he came upon a grand, ancient byway. It was unkempt, but like most of the remnants from the Bygone Era, it held up a good deal better than what had come to replace it. Precisely cut stones traced a long, level road toward the heart of the Greater Lands. Freezes, thaws, and rainy seasons had heaved and shifted some of the stones, but all in all this road, which hadn't seen maintenance in generations, lay in roughly the same state of repair as the main street through Beffshire.

The one thing he knew for sure about the Bygone Era, its people knew how to build things.

Perhaps no greater example of that existed than what lay ahead of him now. A long, squat wall followed the landscape ahead of him. It was only perhaps two stories tall, but it was at least as thick, and baffling both in how long it was and how intact. The Greater Lands Wall extended in a shore-to-shore sickle shape that separated the Greater Lands from the rest of the world. No one was certain just how long the wall was, because it didn't stop at the shore. At both ends it continued beneath the waves. For all anyone knew, it traced a loop that encompassed half the Gleaming Sea. Mapmakers these days treated the Greater Lands as simply separate from the proper world. It showed up on regional maps as a kingdom-sized bite taken out of the continent. Those pressed to provide some sort of label to the area offshore resorted to the time-honored, and in this case highly accurate, tradition of claiming "here there be dragons."

Early in his trip farther toward the wall, he'd relayed information back and forth with his parents and Epiphany via Wick. He learned the specifics, learned what these hippogriff-riding mercenaries looked like, and discussed what to do. All were in agreement. Get while the getting was good.

This was the third time Fel had been this far into the Greater Lands. Anyone who dealt in contraptions was inevitably going to pay a visit to the wall eventually. Vaults and caches of Bygone artifacts popped up everywhere, but they were usually scavenged as soon as they were discovered. The closer one got to the Greater Lands, the more likely would-be raiders had lost their nerve. In theory, the greatest treasures could be found on the other side of the wall, within the borders of the Greater Lands. Ambitious and foolhardy as Fel was, even he wasn't willing to scale the wall. He'd heard tell of at least seven hunters or raiders climbing over the wall for an expedition. He'd never heard any tales of anyone climbing back.

The closer he got to the wall, the more important it was to listen. And he wasn't just listening for *something*. The far more important thing was to listen for *nothing*. And that was precisely what he was hearing.

"Wick, you there?" he asked.

"I am."

"Keep an eye out for anything dangerous. The birds have gone quiet. Something might be lurking about."

"Something? Do you have any more details you can provide?"

Fel's eyes lingered on something by the roadside. It was the size of his overstuffed pack. Judging from the smell, and the flecks of bone, it was the droppings of a particularly large carnivore.

"Something big and hungry…" he said.

"I shall remain vigilant until told otherwise. I am a sentry, after all. My vision is not quite as acute in bright light, however. I am intended for night use."

"We're looking for—"

"There is a shadow, sir, to your left."

Fel turned to see a black patch of ground slide by. Whatever was flying overhead was large enough to blot out the sun over a stretch of field larger than the shop. He didn't waste time looking up. There was nothing a glance could teach him about an enormous, winged creature flying overhead that would change the tactics he intended to employ. Seek cover, and seek it fast.

He snapped the reins. From the speed his rickety old horse managed to produce, the nag had caught a whiff of the threat as well.

"Can you see it, Wick? What is it doing?"

"I can only see the shadow. It is turning about. I believe you have been spotted."

Fel scanned his surroundings. Trees dotted the field, but they were low, wispy things. Nothing that would serve to protect him from something so large. The only protection was the wall itself. It had been his intention to keep his distance a bit longer. The point on the map seemed to be right on the wall, but self-preservation had persuaded him to stay away from the heart of the

Greater Lands until the last moment. Self-preservation had swiftly reversed course with the appearance of whatever had decided he and Bluebelle were a likely meal.

At this speed, it would take a few minutes to reach the wall. He was already close enough to see the low alcoves built in at regular intervals along its face. This close to the final destination, it was difficult to be sure if and when he'd reached the labeled mark on his father's map. Scrutinizing the finer points of a chart was not the sort of thing that could be done reliably while fleeing a predator. But there could now be no doubt the vault *was* in the wall, and thus the alcove ahead was the best bet. If the horse could keep this pace for a few minutes more…

The sound of flapping wings made it clear that his survival would be measured in seconds rather than minutes if he didn't do something fast.

"Let's hope this works, Dad," he said.

He reached up to the wooden crosspiece to which the sunshade had been mounted. Behind him, he could hear the faint hiss of panting breath from above. He pulled down a contraption that had been passed over by the assayers mostly because the man they'd sent to assess it couldn't work out how to activate it. The thing looked like a walking stick or scepter with a fist-size ball on the top and a small opening on the bottom. Fel gave the bottom a twist, revealing a chain with a weighted bead at the end. He angled the device toward the sky and pulled the bead. The ball spun to a terrifying speed and produced an ear-splitting whistle. It split open like a flower and produced a ball of wobbling blue light that burst skyward. As it flew, it grew. The thing approaching from above released a startled screech. It had grown so close that the howl of fear rattled the cloth of the shade.

Whether it was out of anger or hunger was not clear, but the beast pursued the screeching ball that hurtled into the sky. Fel gave the chain a second pull, but there was no screech, and when the end split, no new ball. Like most contraptions of any active value, it only worked when used sparingly. He would be lucky if the thing would do its little trick again inside of a week. But it had done its job for now. And there were other options.

The screech died away. Fel stood as best he could without being thrown from the seat and levered the bench open. Inside were some of the tools of the trade and another item that had barely escaped being snatched by the assayers. This one was officially a toy, a little gadget that would roll about on little wheels. They'd dismissed it as a worthless distraction, but they'd not realized what his father had in store for it. He gave the top a slap, activating whatever supernatural motivation gave these devices life, and heaved it onto the road behind them. Martin had swapped in wheels three times the size of those that were on the thing when Fel had first discovered it. All it did was make it faster, but Martin was clever enough to come up with interesting things to use that extra speed for.

As soon as its spinning wheels got traction, it streaked in the opposite direction of the wagon. A long brown bundle of cloth unfurled behind it. It skipped, bounced, and finally billowed as it caught the air. The brown cloth swelled to a crudely rendered bear-shaped windsock that moved along in a floaty, bouncing path behind the contraption. The intention for such a device was to scare away small creatures, akin to a scarecrow. Fortunately, when things slide far enough to the other side of the size spectrum, a misshapen bear ceases being a threat and starts being bait.

The shadow swept by again, this time continuing toward the rolling contraption. Fel spurred the horse harder. The wall was just ahead now. The alcove cut deep into its face and sloped downward. A rusted metal fence and gate separated the notch in the wall from the rest of the field. He hauled back on the reins, barely bringing the near-panicked horse to a stop before it would have run headlong into the gate.

The gate was barred and chained, but the chain was badly corroded. It and the fence both lacked the sturdiness and artfulness of the road and the wall. They were likely both added well after the construction of the wall, but that fact may well have saved Fel's life. Two sharp blows with his cudgel were enough to bash the chain to pieces. He pulled it apart and reached through the gate to unlatch it. In the distance, the shadow had turned about again and was approaching. He yanked the gate open and led the horse and wagon through. They both worked their way as far into the alcove as they could. It would be deep enough, he hoped, to be out of reach of whatever it was that had chosen to hunt him.

He crouched behind his horse and watched the landscape. The creature was too high to be seen, but he could just make out the shadow racing toward him again. With nothing else to do, he held his cudgel tight and waited. He could hear the wings whistling and rustling with the force of its dive. Closer. Again the heaving breath of the unseen beast echoed into the alcove. As the shadow blotted out the sun over the wall, he swore he could smell the stink of rotting meat on its breath. Then, the sunlight returned. The sounds of the wings receded into the distance. Fel allowed himself to take a breath of relief.

An earsplitting clank fairly stopped his heart and caused the horse to rear. He barely managed to calm it. When both his and Bluebelle's nerves had settled, he crept forward to find the decoy contraption spinning in place on one wheel. The decoy itself had been sheered away from the cord, and the whole mess was glistening with some sort of thick goop, the origins of which Fel chose not to dwell upon. He shook out a rag from his pack and picked up the contraption to deactivate it.

"I've got to give it to Dad," he said. "He does a fine job fixing up these contraptions…"

#

Fel took a few minutes to resecure the gate with a lock and chain he'd brought along. His father's collection of locks and keys was practically inexhaustible. They were simple enough mechanisms that he had little difficulty repairing them and fashioning keys, or even simply creating them from scratch. They were also the sort of thing that was always in demand, particularly in a city. Fel had learned the hard way on his first expedition that gathering artifacts was only the first step. Getting them safely home was the next step, and it was sometimes just as difficult. A few extra chains and decent locks wouldn't be enough to turn away a truly dedicated thief, but it would usually be enough to convince them to go after lower-hanging fruit, which was just as good.

He chained the gate shut and finally turned his attention to the alcove. Now that he wasn't in immediate danger of being attacked by some of the "greater" versions of the creatures he'd come to dismiss in his hometown, his mind was clear enough to make sense of this little hollow in the wall. The first thing he noticed was that it wasn't so different from the entryway of Beffshire. Dry winds had mounded the finer details with dust, but as he kicked and brushed away the fine powder, he found what he was certain was a trough and a hitch for horses. An odd little spigot emerged from the wall, attached to a mechanism with some shreds of rotten, splintered wood sticking out of a metal sleeve. He cleared away the shreds of wood with his knife and stuck the end of his cudgel in the metal sleeve. A bit of rough levering managed to rotate the sleeve. A soft gurgling sound burbled from somewhere within the wall.

"It's a pump," he said with a grin.

He levered it up and down. Soon enough his efforts were rewarded with a spritz of murky water into the trough. It ran right out again through an open hole near the bottom. He continued pumping. Fetid water that had sat in the pump for longer than he could imagine drained out of the system. Crisp, clear water replaced it. He tentatively sniffed it and gave it a taste. It seemed fresh enough. He used his rag to clog the hole and filled the trough, topping off his canteen while he was at it.

"There you go, girl," he said, patting the horse on the neck. "Drink up. It's a shame there isn't a well-stocked feed bin for you. This sack I picked up at the last stable won't last long, but I can't exactly send you out to graze with that flying nightmare around."

He scooped out and dusted off a second trough and dumped the sack of feed into it. With the horse seen to, there was the matter of the map.

Fel flicked it out and paced over to where the carriage was resting. He held the map in Wick's light.

"Let's see… Dad has these marks here circled. That means there's going to be somewhere in the alcove to unlock something."

He squinted from the map to the many carved bits of stone on the wall at the rear of the alcove. The bright sun had cast the whole sheltered portion of the wall in stark shadow.

"You're coming with me, Wick. I need the light."

"Happy to be of help! Even simply illuminating is a fulfilling—"

"Service, I know. I wish I could be as happy doing anything as you are about being used for things."

"These are the reasons for my existence. Achieving them is the fulfillment of my highest calling."

"Yeah, well. It'd be nice to have such simple needs."

"I would love to hear about the needs that you have such difficulty fulfilling. Perhaps I can render aid!"

"Unless you've got a way to make the whole family independently wealthy, Wick, I don't think you can help me out." He held the lantern high and pulled a stiff brush from his pack to start clearing the dust from the carvings.

"Is the family in financial distress?"

"Not really. We'll manage. But I'm kind of getting sick of just managing. When all you can do is manage, it means you can't move forward. You're pouring everything you have into staying put. And that's no way to live."

"It is if you like where you are."

"Then what's that tell you about how I feel about where I am?"

"Beffshire is an extremely pleasant place to live, in my observation."

"The town is fine. I'm more concerned about… why am I talking to you about this? Just help me search the wall for these runes." He shook the page in front of the lantern, then held it closer to the wall.

"I believe your father made additional notations on the back of the map," Wick said.

He flipped it over. Sure enough, in addition to some key information he'd already noticed, his father's typically scatterbrained note-taking approach had spread some idle musings around the margins of the more valuable information.

"Ah. Yes, I see. 'Markings should be found on or above locked doors. These markings indicate the correct door.' You'd think that would have been a bigger point," Fel said.

There were three doors along the back of the alcove. None of them had any knobs or latches. Instead, the center of each door had a series of concentric tile rings and a large central button. Above the rings, at about eye height, was a recessed slot. It was also sealed, and if he had to guess, he'd say it was some kind of spy hatch for anyone inside who wanted to check on unexpected visitors. Fel industriously brushed around the surface of the doors until he found, carved into the keystone at the top of each arched doorway, symbols quite similar to those highlighted by his father.

"Not a match." He trotted over to the next door. "Not a match… And…"

Fel tipped his head aside. The symbols might have been a match. They weren't precisely as the page depicted, but the similarity was within the range of plausibility of poor penmanship. "Here is where things get dangerous," he said.

"How interesting! I would have thought the dangerous part would have begun when the monster was chasing you."

"No, I mean… look, what I mean to say is, you've never come along with me on one of these things, but I can tell you that the Bygone Era took its privacy and security very seriously. There will be traps and consequences if I don't do things right."

"Oh, yes. This I am quite aware of. I am, in fact, a product of that desire for privacy and security."

"… You're that old?"

"Yes! Very old indeed."

"Why didn't I know this?"

"You didn't ask! I only provide information via direct or implied request."

"Is that so… And, out of curiosity, what if you were asked *not* to tell someone something?"

"Then I would not."

He smiled. "That is good to know, Wick. And as long as I'm learning just how helpful you are, what do you think? Does this match?"

"In that the symbols have the same meaning. The symbols labeling the door are likely more angular because a slightly different glyph is used for carving in stone in order to minimize curves. It may interest you to learn—"

"That's fine, Wick. Thanks."

He looked to the back of the map. The bulk of the sheet was filled with the complex diagram that Martin had been able to derive from the blocks of text around the map. The rings of tiles were part of a complex locking mechanism. He was quite familiar with them because locks like this existed on every vault he'd ever encountered. Unlocking them required not only the rotation of the individual rings be done into specific orientations, but that those rotations be done in the correct order. There were also specific tiles that needed to be depressed, also with the proper order, and then the central button, which should only be pressed after the full procedure had been applied. While Fel was not typically one to place emphasis on precision, he had a lingering pain in his right wrist to remind him of what could happen if an error was made by the unwary in the application of an unlocking sequence.

It took a bit of brushing and lubrication from the water trough to get the rings moving freely. Then came the painstaking step-by-step sequence. He checked and double-checked each step, performed them, and when all seemed to be in readiness, he pressed the central button.

A flicker of blue light, the same shade as the screaming ball that had distracted the flying beast, shined between the tiles. Then he heard a soft click. Not from the door, but from below it.

Fel dove aside, and not a moment too soon. The stones beneath his feet dropped down, revealing themselves to be affixed to a pair of hinged doors, the instant he jumped. A set of spikes as tall as he was thrust upward from the pit they revealed. Everything about the motion was sudden, smooth, and nearly silent. The only sound was the long, slow oiled-metal ring of the spikes retracting and the floor clicking back into place. Mere seconds had passed, but once again there was no evidence of the trap beyond the suspiciously dust-free section of floor in front of the door.

"I think Dad made a mistake…" Fel said.

"This is not necessarily so," Wick said from his position on the ground just beyond the trap. "As I had attempted to explain prior to your indication that you were satisfied with my assessment, there is an alternate interpretation for the modified symbol."

Fel climbed to his feet and dusted himself off. "Does it have anything to do with pits and spikes?"

"No."

"Good. If it did, I would have thrown your lantern in the pit and done the rest of this on my own."

"In some older dialects, that glyph indicates the cardinal direction west, while the one on the page indicates the subtly different west-southwest."

Fel glared at the lantern and flipped the page over to the map side. He squinted at the page. Unsatisfied, he reached back and slipped a magnifying lens from his pack. Upon close inspection, it was entirely possible that his present position was slightly too far north to properly represent the mark his father had made. Without any landmark but the wall itself, he didn't have many options beyond trial and error to find the right door.

"I already dumped out the feed and filled the trough…" He snatched up the lantern. "We are heading south on foot to the next alcove. If you see *anything* that might kill me, you let me know."

"Again, I will be happy to act as a sentry for you."

"Yeah, I'll bet you will…"

"I am uncertain what that statement is intended to mean."

"Never mind." He fought with the lock and creaked the gate open. The dry grass crunched under his feet as he paced along the base of the wall. "So you were alive during the Bygone Era?" he said. "That's why you know this old symbol stuff?"

"I am not alive, but I was crafted during the Bygone Era. I know the symbols because of the previously indicated capacity to store any information that is burned in my flame."

"This is a lot to go through. You're not alive?"

"No. I am a high-functioning contraption. The specifics of my operation are beyond my own understanding, but I do not satisfy a rigorous application of the definition of life."

"If you say so. And that symbols thing, are you saying someone burned an alphabet book or something?"

"Yes. Something like that."

"Does Dad know this?"

"Your father is far more curious than you. He asked many questions. He is well aware, and the information available to me has been of great help to him in his repair, decoding, and translation efforts."

"Do you know things about the Bygone Era? Did you experience much of it?"

"My experiences were limited to my role as a sentry. I observed the coming and going of foot traffic in a single building for forty-eight years. My flame was extinguished for an indeterminate amount of time, and I was reignited by your grandfather."

"That's a lot of time that passed. What was it like while you were 'out'?"

"It was not like anything. I simply did not exist."

"So it was like being asleep?"

"I do not know what it is like to be asleep."

"Well… was it like the time between just didn't happen?"

"No. It was like I did not exist for a very long time and then I did again."

"I don't know what that means."

"I do not know how to articulate it further. It was not pleasant or fulfilling. However, it was not unpleasant either. It lacked the capacity for pleasantness or unpleasantness. Please turn to your left. There is a potential threat."

Fel turned, pressed his back to the wall, and raised his cudgel. The tall grass farther from the wall had a subtle but purposeful motion to it. Fel kept his eye on the ripple in the waist-high grass that was sliding along toward him and paced backward, inching toward the alcove.

"Come on… Come on, whatever you are. I *dare* you…" he said, hefting the cudgel.

The shifting grass approached the edge of the dry patch at the foot of the wall and stopped.

"That's right. Tread with care," Fel warned. "Fel Masker is not a man to be trifled with."

He hoped his performance was a convincing one, because his nerves were not as rock solid as his bravado would indicate. The grass shifted again. A form emerged. Fel relaxed only slightly when the thing showed itself.

It was a lesser unicorn. Their greater counterparts, while majestic and every bit deserving of the revered and mythic status they enjoyed, were a tremendous threat. Anyone who had ever dealt with a wild horse knew how dangerous such a beast could be. The addition of a mystical lineage and a rapier-sharp horn on its head only made them more terrifying. The lesser unicorn was not what most people would call majestic or intimidating, and this one was hardly the most impressive specimen he'd seen. The thing was the size of a goat and had the overall appearance of one. Short gray fur, a tuft of a beard, cloven hooves. Its horn was white and twisted, gleaming like mother-of-pearl and ending in a blunt, broken, and worn tip. It lashed an ox-like tail, chasing off some flies, and gave him a pitiful look with piecing, vivid eyes the color of a robin's egg.

This creature was not well. Its eyes were dewy and irritated. It looked weak. To be more specific, it looked thirsty. Critically so. The drought that had rendered the field yellow and dry had taken its toll on this beast as well.

"Go!" he said, shaking his cudgel again. "Shoo. Get out of here. There are bad things about."

It took another step forward. He stepped back, and in doing so finally realized what had attracted the beast. The canteen on his hip was sloshing. Fel grappled with the competing feelings of irritation and empathy. As tended to be the case when animals were concerned, empathy won.

"Watch extra close for *real* threats, Wick. I've got to deal with this."

"Do you? The lesser unicorn has lived for this long in the wild. It surely can handle itself."

"Just keep a look out, Wick."

He continued to back his way toward the next alcove, sloshing his canteen with each step. The unicorn took step after wobbly step after him. It took close to ten minutes of awkwardly leading it along, but eventually he reached the second alcove. It was, as he'd hoped, a perfect match for the first. He bashed open the gate, brushed out some dust, and worked the intact pump handle over this alcove's trough. The unicorn kept its distance until the trough was half full. The promise of a cool drink after too long eventually overruled any instinct that warned it to keep its distance. It tottered to the trough, climbed onto the edge, and dunked its entire head into the water.

"That was very kind of you, Fel," Wick said.

"Yeah, well. People decide to be awful sometimes. Animals never do. Don't get me wrong. Plenty of them are still awful. But they don't *decide* to be awful. They're just being animals. It makes animals better than half the people I meet, and I think that deserves some consideration." He set down the lantern and retrieved his brush. "Keep an eye on it, though. Just because I respect it doesn't mean I trust it."

"I will fulfill this service with pleasure."

He put the brush to work and soon uncovered a pair of symbols over the second door that perfectly matched the notes from his father. He cleared the locking mechanism, worked his way through the proper procedure, and stood aside before pressing the button. As before, there was a click. Unlike the last time, however, the click was not followed by an ancient architect's attempt to reach across the gulf of time to commit murder. He gingerly pressed at the door. It slipped open.

"All right, Wick," he said, fetching the lantern. "Let's see if this trip will be worth it…"

#

Tome was still sitting on a stump by the roadside. His jaw was tight, and his face was showing the rosy pink of too much sun. Abandoning the smelly man had certainly seemed like the right idea at the time. But as day had ground on and his prospects of further travel became less and less likely, he wondered if spending a few more hours beside the ripe fellow might have been preferable. Somewhere along the way he'd clearly made a critical miscalculation, as seven full hours had passed and he'd not seen another traveler.

"It is enough to convince a man to buy his own horse…" he muttered.

He gazed at the sky, which had been mercifully obscured with clouds, and wondered just how much longer he would have to wait before someone came along to give him a lift. His stomach was growling, and his mind was helpfully reminding him every few minutes that if he'd simply started walking back toward town after the smelly man had dropped him off, he would be sitting in Bramf and bilking some of the locals out of their money in a nice, shady inn right now.

Two dark forms separated themselves from the clouds. Tome stared at them curiously.

"Hippogriffs. You don't see them this far south very often."

They circled slowly and lazily at first. But after a moment both angled into a sharp dive. What started as vague interest in the rare sight in the sky quickly escalated into panic as Tome realized they were heading directly for him. While he didn't know precisely what he had to fear from them, hippogriff riders were phenomenally expensive to keep in one's employ. Thus, the sort of people who could afford to send them out were limited to government officials or the very wealthy. Given his history of skirting the law, Tome wasn't interested in being tracked down by either sort of person.

He considered pulling open his case and selecting a prepared charm to hide himself, but the only charms that might be sufficient to allow him to escape had been written weeks ago and he couldn't be certain of their potency. He was a skilled mage, but he'd had to ration his most potent inks. They were too valuable to be used on spells that he wasn't certain he would cast, and thus his contingency measures were always a bit of a gamble if they'd been sitting for more than a week or so. With time running out, he decided to rely upon his wit and his tongue to keep him safe and hope for the best.

The beasts spiraled down and spread their wings for a landing. They were a terrifying sight up close. The front half of each was like a great eagle, scaled up to a horrid size. Their piercing eyes, clutching talons, and ax-head of a beak had a way of making even the stoutest warrior feel like a field mouse in its final moments. Where the eagle's tail should be, there instead emerged the hindquarters of a mighty stallion. Nothing about the monster's body made proper sense. It should have been unbalanced and ungainly in the air, barely able to fly. But it was every bit a cunning master of the skies. Creatures of the Greater Lands had a way of ignoring petty things like logic and anatomy. It was as though they had intimidated reality itself into appeasing them.

They struck the ground, effortlessly converting the swoop into a gallop. One skidded to a stop to Tome's left, the other to his right. Both riders hopped off and gave a sharp tug of the reins.

"Beast, watch," instructed each man.

The mounts clawed at the ground and kept Tome locked in their gazes. Easily as frightening as the beasts they rode, the men who commanded the hippogriffs circled Tome where he stood, measuring him up. The only thing that tempered the raw fear Tome felt in their presence was the state of their hair. It would seem that soaring through the sky astride a mighty sky predator had a way of leaving one's coif in a state of severe disarray, and it made them a shade more difficult to take seriously.

"Matches the descriptions…" said the man with a scar on his cheek.

"Can I help you, gentlemen?" Tome said, attempting to keep his nerves from showing in his voice.

He'd been in worrisome positions like this before. The moment you let on that you were afraid, the balance of power irreversibly shifted in the favor of the aggressor. This was, perhaps, more of a way for Tome to pretend that the aggressors weren't *already* firmly in control of the situation, but it was nevertheless a crucial part of his plan in situations such as this.

"You were traveling with someone," said the man with the scar on his temple.

"Indeed I was. I have no horse or wagon of my own, so——"

"Where is he now? You were seen together in roadside stops twice over the past few days," he said.

"You'll need to be more specific about which cotraveler you're referring to. In the past few weeks I've relied upon the generosity of quite a few travelers."

"Fel Masker," Cheek said. "He's an antiquities hunter. A contraption hunter."

"Ah, yes. I know the fellow."

"Where is he now?" Temple asked again.

"I can't say for certain. He didn't share his travel plans in any detail."

Cheek rested his hand on the pommel of his dagger. "Make a guess."

"Somewhere in the fringe of the Greater Lands," Tome said quickly.

"'Somewhere' isn't good enough," Temple said.

"If I'd wanted to follow him into the Greater Lands, I would have. He split off from the main road onto an old cobblestone byway, the last intersection in the main road south before it reaches Bramf. Days ago."

Cheek nodded. "Better. Did he have a map with him?"

"I don't know. I imagine he must have. Most travelers do."

"Worthless…" Temple nodded.

"He didn't seem the sort to be on the bad side of a hippogriff rider, let alone two."

"It's not who he is, it's what he's after," Cheek said.

Temple slapped him in the back of his head. "Our business isn't *his* business. How many times do I have to tell you to think before running that mouth of yours? Or better yet, just don't run your mouth. Let me do the talking."

Cheek muttered something unrepeatable under his breath as the pair mounted up. Eagle wings spread, stallion hooves galloped, and they lofted into the sky to head roughly in the direction of the previous city.

Tome watched them go, relief washing over him. As far as he knew, nothing in his checkered past had risen to the level of infamy that fellows like those would be after him. This little run-in, and the knowledge of just how far and fast they could travel in search of their prey, was nearly enough to convince him to straighten up and fly straight before he found himself at odds with them.

Nearly.

Once they were gone and his mind was functioning beyond the focus on simple survival, the dyed-in-the-wool schemer inside him started to sift through what he'd learned. Fel was a contraption hunter. And something he was after was so significant that someone had seen fit to put *two* hippogriff riders on his tail. A map, a major manhunt… that spelled vault. And there was *always* more of value in a vault than could be gathered in a single trip. There would be prime pickings for a scavenger.

Tome watched the hippogriffs soar toward the horizon and ran some numbers in his head. Even with what he'd told them, there was a lot of land to cover. Fel must have known precisely where he was going, and the 'griff riders wouldn't. They'd have to scan huge stretches of the fringe. There was no doubt in his mind they would find Fel… but if the timing was right…

"This one will call for the good ink, I think," he said.

Tome popped open his case and pulled out a pristine piece of paper. He pulled a small key from its place on a thin chain around his neck and used it to unlock a box deep in his case. Inside, there was a bottle of ink barely a third full. It pained him to do it, but the proper spells would take every last drop of it. It was a gamble, but gambling was his trade these days. He smiled and started to carefully etch out a spell in the tiniest lettering he could manage. For something that would do what needed to be done, he was going to need every scrap of space he could manage.

#

Fel held Wick's lantern high. It would have been too easy if the door he'd unlocked had simply led to a room heaped with contraptions. Instead, it led to a massive hallway that, he quickly realized, must have run the length of the wall. The section beyond the door stretched far enough in either direction to encompass the two neighboring alcoves. It wasn't immediately clear to him what this place was supposed to be. There was a barracks aspect to it, that much was clear. Racks for lances and other equipment lined the walls on either side of most of the doorways, as well as a handful of wall mounts for the sort of sophisticated crossbows that the better-equipped representatives of the assayer's office liked to claim for themselves. The dozen or so lances and shields still present would fetch a reasonable price. If he gathered all of them and found buyers, it would probably be enough to pay for the trip and leave enough profit to make it all worthwhile. But he knew there must have been more. For his sake and Epiphany's, there had to be at least three things more.

All the exit doors were on the safe side of the wall, which was just as well. He had no interest in accessing the Greater Lands, nor did he relish the thought of accidentally stumbling onto the wrong side of the wall by getting turned around. But beyond some tables, some chairs, and a few well-preserved banners and pennants that might have had interest to a collector, he'd yet to find the mother lode that he'd expected to encounter.

"Perhaps there is nothing further to find," Wick said helpfully.

"I'm not coming this far and escaping whatever it was that was after us just for some old weapons. There's something more here. I'm sure if it. And the better they hide it, the more valuable it is. That's just logic."

"Perhaps what was of such great value isn't here anymore."

"I've seen looted vaults before. This isn't what they look like. Keep your eyes open for a hatch. This wall is at least as old as Beffshire, and Beffshire is built *down*. And a vault will be hidden."

"Bygone Era sites are dangerous, Fel."

"I know."

"The Greater Lands are dangerous."

"I know."

"This location is an example of both of those places."

"*I know*, Wick," he growled. "It feels like you're trying to talk me out of searching this place."

"You asked me to keep watch for things which might be dangerous to you."

"Fine, then from now on, warn me about things that are dangerous to me unless they'll make me rich."

"I will attempt to fulfill this service, but I am not skilled at that particular assessment. Perhaps you could help me to clarify your specific meaning. First, in the instance of the winged beast that attempted to kill you, and in doing so would have prevented you from reaching this place, would that qualify as something I should have ignored?"

"No."

"I see, and if you were to encounter…"

Fel let the words wash over him, giving vague answers when prompted, as he continued his search. Everything about the map, about the way the door was locked, about the location suggested vault. Even the fact that someone had come looking for the map suggested it was a treasure trove. There simply wasn't a chance there wasn't at least *something* worth more than what he'd already found.

He crouched down and lowered the lantern to the floor. Like so many of the things built in the Bygone Era, the precision of this place was impressive. There was barely a seam between the stones of the floor, and even laying his head on the cool blocks and eying the length of the hallway, he couldn't see any bumps or shifted stones. The only variations were in the thin carpets that crisscrossed the ground here and there.

"Of course…" he said. "Just like at the shop."

Wick continued to drone on. Fel grabbed the edge of the first rug he could find and heaved it aside. There was nothing but smooth, clean floor beneath. He moved another to find more of the same. The third one revealed what he'd been searching for, a suspiciously worn central tile with a gap far larger than those around it. He pulled his knife from his belt and slotted it into the gap. The tile lifted easily out of place to reveal a hatch… with another complex locking mechanism. It had a similar set of tile rings, but with three additional rings.

"No…"

"I am confident that attempting to open that hatch without a reliable unlocking procedure will critically endanger your life," Wick said, a sprinkling of relief in his voice as he finally came upon something with a degree of certainty.

Fel pulled out the page his father had given him. Nowhere on the front or back was there any reference to the hatch or how to unlock it.

"Shall I contact your father to see if he has uncovered additional information? There were blocks of text that he had yet to decipher fully when last I spoke to him."

"How long will that take you?"

"Twenty minutes to transfer to his lantern, twenty minutes to return, and whatever amount of time it takes to discuss the message."

Fel scratched his head. "You might as well."

"I will be happy to fulfill this service."

The only sign of the departure was in the behavior of the flame. When Wick left, the flame ceased to be rock solid and instead flickered and danced. With Wick gone, and likely to remain gone for nearly an hour, now would be a lovely time to uncover the vault, find the specific goods he was after, and stow them without the tattletale lantern ever knowing. He squinted at the hatch.

"Well… I was able to avoid the trap on the door. How bad could this one be?" He fetched one of the spears from beside the door, selecting the one with the least resale value, and flipped it around. "Let's see what we're working with…" he said.

He slid the blunt wooden end of the spear handle to the top of the hatch, turned his head aside, and depressed the switch in the center. A weak blue light flared behind the tiles. He took another step back. Having worked in the antiquity shop all his life, he was familiar with the odd, crackly sensation that came with the activation of a particularly energetic contraption. He'd never felt anything like this. The hair on his arms stood up. Dust from the floor rose and gathered into long, shifting streamers of motion. He could almost feel reality itself creaking as whatever supernatural motivation fueled the contraptions did its work. Then, just as suddenly as the reaction began, it ended. The dust settled, the air calmed… and the wooden tip of the spear handle collapsed to the surface of the hatch as though it had been loosely formed of wet sand.

Fel pulled the handle back and inspected the end. The place where the damage stopped was almost glassy smooth, far smoother than any cut he'd ever seen.

"Right. I won't be trying that without a code I'm confident of," he said. He paced around the hatch, glaring at it with the lantern in his hand. "I won't be able to break it. I broke a pickax on the last one out in the swamp."

Fel placed the lantern on the ground and scratched his head. Puzzling out solutions that didn't involve brute force, intuition, or following directions had always been more the purview of his sisters and his parents. He was willing to do the hard work and the tedious work. But if the way forward wasn't laid out for him, he tended to just plow through or go around. Neither was an option. The Bygone constructions were simply too sturdy and too well defended.

He reached down to the lantern, reluctantly planning to give up for now. Until Wick returned with word from his father, he could tote some of the more valuable weapons and gear back to the cart in the other alcove. Before he plucked the lantern from the ground, though, he noticed something odd. The flame—released from Wick's influence and free to waver—was leaning to the right. He lowered his hand and felt the faintest of breezes. With the angle of the flame to guide him, he tracked the source of the draft to a single gap between two stones near the corner of the Greater Lands side of the hallway. The edge of the gap was irregular, speckled with the telltale signs of gnawing teeth. He held his hand over the hole and felt a breeze. Dropping a pebble through rewarded him with a short clatter followed by the constrained echo of a stairwell.

"Hah! Looks like even the Bygone Era's architects couldn't account for a few hundred years of rodents."

He snatched up the spear, spun it around, and jammed the tip into the gap. It would take time and effort, but that didn't bother him. Nothing worth doing was ever easy.

Joseph R. Lallo

Chapter 7

"Perfectly preserved! Ah-haha! A chamber within the Greater Lands Wall and it is perfectly preserved," Martin Masker crowed, dancing around in his shop with the lantern in his hands.

"Yes, but the hatch, likely leading to the vault, is still sealed and needs to be opened."

"Of course, of course. There is this last block of text. I'm sure it contains the code to open it. I'd been working on the previous block because it was more substantial." He set down Wick's lantern and pulled out his notes. "Imagine what he'll find inside, Wick. Imagine. If there are weapons and other accoutrements of a barracks, perhaps this place was some sort of wartime meeting hall. No doors leading out to the Greater Lands, perhaps this was some sort of headquarters for guards patrolling the wall. And where there is a headquarters, there are *books*! Oh, do tell Fel to keep an eye out for any good, thick books."

There was a knock at the door.

"Come in, come in!" Martin called, not looking up from his work. "Wonderful news!"

The door opened. It was Epiphany.

"Oh! Fanny, dear, your brother has—"

"I know, I know. You're echoing through the whole house. Exciting!"

"So exciting. More than exciting. Oh, to be there with him when he finally opens the vault. It will be untouched, Fanny. It must be. We'll learn so much! The contraptions inside may not even need to be repaired. I can take them apart and see how they work!"

"Just so long as you can get them back together," Epiphany said. "Or better yet, maybe leave a piece out for the assayer."

"You know better than to suggest something like that. I am to present contraptions repaired to the best of my ability, and moreover, if I plan to sell them, I must present them as they are to be sold. The rules are very specific."

"The rules are very specifically crafted to ensure you don't make what the contraptions are *worth*, Dad."

"It isn't our place to argue such things. Tell me, when you acquired this page, were there more to acquire?"

"No. Why?"

"This demarcation here indicates it is page sixteen of thirty. The wealth of knowledge on this one page makes me *dream* of what the others held. And the separation of this page from the rest makes me wonder what became of them."

"I wouldn't have been able to afford them if they'd been available for offer," Epiphany said.

"Who was the man who was selling them?" Martin asked, jotting down some fresh notes.

"We spoke on condition of anonymity. It's entirely possible he didn't have permission to sell what he had." She glanced at the corner of the workbench, where the picture conjured by the now-confiscated illustration contraption was waiting beside a half-completed frame. Epiphany picked it up. "Too bad we didn't find that device while Euphoria was still here."

"It would have been nice to have an image to remember her by until she returns."

"Until she returns…" Epiphany said. "Dad, you don't really think she's coming back."

"She's family, Fanny. She's always got a place here and she knows it."

"That she knows it doesn't mean she *wants* it. She made her choice. She stole one of the masks off the family *sign,* by the high. And took half the goods from Fel's first good haul. She decided it was worth burning everything she had to start a life with that *viper* in Shalia."

"We all lose our way sometimes…"

"She didn't lose her way. She knew what she was doing and she chose to do it." She calmed herself and put the image down. "But she's still my sister. And that pandemic is supposedly spreading. The man I bought the page from said it came from up by her way, and the borders were shutting tighter and tighter. I worry."

"I worry too, but we needn't do so." He turned to the smoldering stove and tossed an extra bit of wood inside. "Your sister knows how to take care of herself."

"Mmm. Never let it be said that Euphoria didn't know how to make sure she came out on top."

"We're a family," Martin repeated. "And we've each gotten enough of the family skills to keep this shop alive. You got your mother's business acumen, and you've been an indispensable asset in keeping the flow of trade open. Your sister… well, she got more of your mother's father's business acumen."

"Grandpa Mason?"

"A brilliant trader," Martin said with a nod.

"I don't know if you're being quite as articulate as you need to be, Dad. The word is 'traitor.' He sold to both sides during the skirmish between

Thayn and Shalia."

"I didn't say he was ethical, but he *was* skillful. And then there's Fel. He got a dash of my contraptioneering and a healthy dollop of my grandfather's stubborn, nose-to-the-grindstone dedication."

"He's a bit of a bull in a china shop, Dad."

"He is precise and careful when he needs to be. I wouldn't have trusted him to go to the vault if that wasn't the case."

#

"Get… Out… Of… The… *Hole*!" Fel growled, jabbing the borrowed spear at the stone that stubbornly refused to dislodge.

For the worse part of fifteen minutes, he'd been alternately chipping and levering at the stone. The fruits of his efforts had amounted to a whisper of motion on the stone, barely perceptible compared to the rest. He was pouring sweat, and had long ago exhausted his limited selection of profanity. But he wasn't even close to throwing in the towel. This was personal now.

He rummaged through the tools he'd fetched from the cart and found a mallet. With heavy, vengeful swings he drove the tip of the spear into the gap like a wedge, then reached up and grabbed the very end of the handle.

"Come on," he rumbled, heaving at the edge. "Come *on*…"

The stone began to produce a quiet grinding sound, and the end of the spear dropped a hair. Energized by the first substantial sign of progress since he started, he redoubled his efforts. More grinding, more motion.

"Yes! Move. Move!" he said, hanging from the spear.

When it finally happened, it happened all at once. The whole block levered free and clattered onto one of its neighbors.

"Ha! Ha-*ha*!" he crowed, hopping to his feet.

He scrambled over to the hole he'd created and held the lantern over it. Sure enough, there was a staircase leading down. He lay on the floor to get the best angle he could, and was rewarded with what he'd been desperately praying for all through the efforts to dislodge the stone. There wasn't a second door at the base of the steps. Once he was through, he was *through*.

Fel placed a hand on the stone beside the one he'd broken free to heave himself back to his feet. It slipped free and tumbled down the steps below.

"Ha! I knew I'd beat you into submission eventually," he said. "I…"

Two more around it tumbled down. The five surrounding those started to slide.

"Uh-oh…"

He turned and tried to get clear of the growing hole, but the stones beneath his feet did not approve of the sudden force of the leap and dislodged. He dropped, flailing arms catching the edge of the hole and only managing to yank a few mores stones free. He dropped painfully onto the steps and quickly shielded his head with his arms. The tumble of stones turned into a clattering cacophony. He held still and took a few dizzying blows from stones the size of a loaf of bread. After a minute, the collapse mercifully stopped.

Fel warily uncovered his head. The lantern had been spared any noticeable damage. Its light revealed a jagged section of collapsed floor above him. Most of the stairwell's ceiling had fallen onto it. There was a patch just beneath the booby-trapped hatch that had held firm, revealing a wooden ladder attached to the wall that would have been a far more comfortable, albeit somewhat slower, way to reach the stairwell. He had two bloody patches. One on his head, the other on his knuckles. At present he wasn't ready or willing to investigate if the blood on his head and his knuckles was from the same injury or different ones. Now that it was clear he wasn't in danger of being buried in a full collapse of the wall or skewered by some secondary booby trap, there was only one thing on his mind. The vault.

He navigated the stone-strewn steps and held up the lantern in the room at their base.

"… Glorious…"

There were nights Fel dreamed of what a vault should look like. Maybe others would have imagined heaps of gold and sparkling gems, but Fel was a Masker, a contraption hunter in his bones. What he dreamed of was something not unlike his father's workshop. Shelf after shelf of devices, only in the vault, they would all be intact. And what he saw before him was as close as he would ever come to that fanciful dream.

It wasn't pristine, but rather than ransacked or decrepit, it was disorderly. This wasn't a vault that was pillaged, it was an archive whose maintainer had to leave in a hurry, without taking the time to clean up. A workbench not unlike his father's—but much better equipped—ran along an entire wall. Smaller workbenches were laid out in a regular grid.

"This looks like a job shop. Or a training shop, maybe," he said.

He glanced at the lantern. The flame was still dancing. Wick wasn't present. Fel pulled a burlap sack from his bag and shook it open. The contraptions in cubbies on the walls and laid out on the tables were far too numerous for him to bring the lot of them home, even *with* the cart. He focused instead on a healthy mix of the smaller items they might be permitted to sell and the larger items his father might learn from. One shelf was brimming with puzzle boxes, hexagonal metal gadgets with tiles that shifted seemingly at random in response to the movement of other tiles. He'd always known them to sell well. A handful of devices that his father liked to convert into alarm boxes would be good for a quick profit, too. In the space of five minutes, even cherry-picking the best of the best, he was left with a sack he could barely carry. Two more sacks like this and the wagon would be fully loaded.

The Bygone Dagger

Fel reached the far wall. He turned to give the place another pass when something with a dull sheen on the wall caught his attention. He raised the lantern. A tool was resting in a rack on the wall. Large, clear runes that he didn't understand labeled it in the manner one might label something that was either very dangerous or very important. It had a leather-wrapped handle, a hilt, and a short sturdy "blade" although it was in no way sharp. Even where it tapered to a chisel tip, it remained fairly broad. This was not a weapon.

He plucked it from the rack and grinned. "The dull dagger, blunt and black," he said. "He could have just called it a Bygone dagger. Probably would have raised the price and he knew it. One out of three, anyway."

Fel slid the dagger into his belt and turned to the first of the row of tables he'd not investigated. His jaw dropped. There, in the very next place he looked, was a heavy canvas pack. Stout straps, worn but still rugged, looped from the back. A flap sagged over the top, and buttoned pockets on either side remained unsecured. A strange, thick bit of metal hung from the bottom through what must have been a slit specially made for it. He tugged the top flap to reveal a heap of gleaming chain tipped with an odd polished-bronze mechanism of some kind. It was roughly oval in shape, and a bit larger than his open hand if he held his fingers tightly together. The bottom of the mechanism had some odd markings, and some component or another must have been missing from the top, because it had a considerable amount of exposed gadgetry. Even with the impeccable build quality of a Bygone Era contraption, pieces that intricate would simply never be exposed to the world.

"Hmm…" he mused. "The guy wanted a heavy pack, full of chain. Technically he didn't say anything about if any parts of it were missing. But for twenty-five thousand duots, I'm not taking chances."

He raised the lantern. The piece closest to the proper shape was a badly mangled piece of similarly aged bronze. He turned it over in his hands. The piece was clearly ornamental, vaguely resembling a smooth sculpture of a serpent's head. Or at least, it *would* have resembled it, if not for the fact that it looked like it had been beaten with a hammer. He held it up and found that it had two primary fasteners and a handful of smaller ones. Each of them would have lined up with a matching mounting point on the incomplete contraption if not for how bent out of shape it was.

Fel looked over the table. There were soft-faced hammers, pryers, pliers, and all sorts of other equipment. They had been working on this contraption, trying to fix it. He was sure of it. And having seen and worked on more than a few of the things he'd recovered for sale, he would say the work was nearly done before whatever happened here chased the workers away.

He glanced at the lantern. Still flickering and dancing. By his count, it would be another ten minutes at least before Wick was back. He would give himself five minutes to see if he could get the piece hammered into shape and reinstalled. It didn't have to *function*. It just had to survive the trip without getting worse. That was a level of repair he was practically an expert at achieving.

He selected a pair of leather-padded tongs and a light tinkering hammer with a rawhide face. Gentle turns and taps slowly eased the half-collapsed piece back into shape. He checked the ornamental cap he was working on against the gadget every few whacks. Soon, with a bit of force, it clicked into place.

"Perfect!" Fel proclaimed.

Metal in tension creaked and then popped, the piece lurching free and skittering across the floor.

"Fine, I'll need fasteners…"

He found the piece. A bit more searching turned up some appropriately sized fasteners in one of the drawers of the workbench. What he failed to find was a tool appropriate for installing said fasteners. He opened every drawer, but none of the many tools had the proper head to fit the broad slot of the "jaw" fasteners.

As tended to be the case when he was looking for something, he mechanically patted at his own pockets at least once every few seconds. In doing so, he grabbed the handle of the blunt dagger. A thought came to mind. He pulled it free and measured it against the fastener. The chisel tip was precisely the right size and shape to fit into the fastener.

"Hah! This is what it was for!" he said.

He clamped the serpent ornament in place, inserted a fastener, and tightened it. A matching one for the other side made the piece nice and secure.

"Good enough for now," he said, sliding the dagger back into his belt. "I'll grab some of these smaller fasteners to finish fixing it later, but Wick'll be back soon and I can't afford to—"

He heard a long, slow jangle of chain. He jumped and slapped his hand onto the pack, fearful it might be falling from the workbench.

It was not.

One of the flaps on the side had popped open, and three articulated steel spikes started to slip free. He caught them and tried to push them back. There was resistance. Then, in a flash of polished metal, a second set emerged from the other side and whipped around. Cold steel claws closed around his wrist.

He yelped in a decidedly undignified manner and scrambled back. The claw remained gripped to his wrist, reeling out more chain as he retreated.

"Off, off, get off!" he shouted, dropping the lantern and tearing at the claw.

Without much effort, he was able to pull it free. Not because he overpowered it but because it loosened of its own accord. He quickly grabbed the lantern and shined it at the pack. The recently repaired contraption was angled toward him. The chain with no clear means of animation nevertheless arched up from the back of the ornament and down again into the pack. What Fel had thought were cleverly placed slotted fasteners in the eye sockets of the snake rotated slightly until they were vertical. He could have sworn these "eyes" focused on him with inscrutable intent. One claw was held up, its gleaming fingers waggling. The other claw reeled back in.

It reached up and tapped its snout. The repaired cover piece rocked up and down. The head tipped down and scanned the workbench. It spotted the open drawer with its many fasteners and plucked up one in each claw. Rotating at the "wrist," the thing deftly spun them in place, then snatched more and installed them until every fastener hole was filled. Thus repaired, it tapped its nose to check for motion again. Rock solid. It retracted its clawed arms back into the pockets and flopped its head down under the flap of the pack. Only its nose remained exposed, though when Fel shifted the lantern, he could see the gleam of its eyes as well.

Fel's heart was rattling, and at some point he'd held his breath. He gasped and shook his head. The thing continued to watch him. He waved his hand. One of the claws snaked out and waved back.

"… twenty-five thousand duots is not enough…"

He looked around and spotted the hammer. He dropped it on the table and slid it forward. The head popped up, the flap perching on the back of its arched chain neck like a cobra's hood. It extended its claws, picked up the hammer and investigated it. It rattled the head, then hammered the handle against the table and tested the head again. Satisfied that it was not loose anymore, it set the hammer down and pushed it back.

"You fix things… you are a contraption that fixes things."

He pulled things from the bag and set them down in front of the odd bundle of chains and claws. Most it picked up, investigated, and set down again. Some it adjusted, tightened, or straightened. Then came the puzzle box. It picked it up and tested the motion of the tiles on each face. They slipped and clicked as they should, so it placed the box down. But a moment later it picked it up again and began sliding the tiles some more. It solved one side, then turned and began toying with the next. When that side was solved, it turned to the first again to discover it had been scrambled. It tipped its head and went to work on it again.

"Heh… I could never figure those things out either," Fel said.

"There is a trick to them," said Wick.

Fel looked to the lantern and slapped his face. He'd lost track of time.

"I see you gained access to the vault," Wick said.

"I sure did."

"Your father provided a code for the door. Did you decode it on your own?"

"No, I bashed a hole in the floor."

"Very effective. You seemed dismayed at my arrival."

"Yeah…" He rubbed his face. "We'll discuss that in a minute. Since you're here, do you have any idea what this thing is?"

"I am not familiar with this mechanism. Does it have any identifying labeling?"

"Uh… yeah." He turned to the contraption, which had now solved three of the six faces. "Can I look at your chin? The bottom of your head?"

Without ceasing its fiddling, it rotated its head upside down. Fel held up the lantern. Now that the time had come to give them consideration, Fel realized that the largest of the marks was actually familiar to him, though he couldn't place it. There was a barbed double hook on the bottom of the shape and a trapezoidal bit above that. Curious.

"The primary mark has no immediate meaning. Potentially a maker's mark. The smaller runes are either a unit or purpose designation. Unclear. They translate roughly to the word 'oiler.' The syntax implies a proper noun."

"A proper noun," Fel said. "Like a name?"

"Correct."

The device finished solving the puzzle and placed it on the table.

"That's everything, Oiler. That's everything I've got."

It clacked its claws together and continued to stare at him.

"Uh… You can play with this?" he said, holding out the blunt dagger.

Oiler reached out, picked it up and promptly jangled to the table, completely limp. Fel gasped and took the dagger away. The mechanism perked back up and returned to the same precise position. After a beat, it looked at its claw and tipped its head again, puzzled that the dagger was gone. Fel held out the dagger a second time. Oiler took it and fell limp again.

"It puts it to sleep. The dagger puts it to sleep. That's why it was over there, it was for putting this thing down so it could be fixed. And that's why the guy wanted…" He trailed off and turned to Wick's lantern. "All right. I guess there's no way around it. Wick, you said if I told you not to tell someone something, you wouldn't, right?"

"That is correct."

"We're not telling Mom or Dad about this."

"Very well."

"Because we're looking to sell it, unappraised, to a buyer, and Mom and Dad won't like that."

"I didn't ask you why."

"And I understand why they don't want us to do that, but it is madness how the assayer's office robs us blind after every expedition like this. They're bleeding us out. If we can get paid the proper price for something just once or twice a year, it would set us on the path to real success instead of scrambling to survive.”

“You seem to feel the need to justify yourself to me.”

“What I’m doing isn’t wrong,” he said.

“I have not accused you of wrongdoing. That is not a service I provide. However, it has been said by sages of the past that anyone who feels compelled to assert one’s moral position unchallenged is himself in doubt of his moral position.”

“… I don’t quite understand what you just said, but don’t say it again. It felt too close to home.”

“I shall keep this observation to myself as well.”

“Just so we’re clear. We don’t tell my parents about Oiler, we don’t tell my parents about this dagger, and we’re looking for a ‘fearsome mask, ready to mount.’ If we find that, we don’t tell my parents about it either. And we don’t tell them that we’re selling anything directly to a buyer.”

“I shall not volunteer any of that information.”

“Excellent. Let’s start loading this stuff, then.”

#

Epiphany, despite being so happy to be back home after her lengthy travels, was beginning to feel the pressure of dealing with her folks. Trying to grapple with the mercenaries and whoever else might be after the contents of the vault would have been trying enough by itself. Persuading her parents to embrace the less legitimate sales venues that served as the secret motivation for this venture made it all the more stressful. And on top of all that, there was the business to look after. She needed a break, and some distance, to gather her thoughts.

She gazed up at the sign for The Fox and Log. “Time to see if Fel’s taste in taverns is any good,” she muttered to herself.

Drinking wasn’t Epiphany’s preferred leisure activity. She might have sherry come the holidays, but she generally preferred to keep a clear head and spend her limited leisure time reading. As it turned out, though, The Fox and Log was *just* near enough for her to get home without too much delay if her parents needed her and *just* far enough away that they wouldn’t come personally to fetch her. It was an almost perfectly calibrated break from her parents without feeling like she was abandoning them. She wrinkled her nose at the wave of smoke inside and let her eyes adjust to the dimmer light.

“Well, Epiphany Masker, in my own tavern. I never thought I’d see the day,” said Allie.

“Hi there. I’d almost forgotten you worked here.”

“Day in, day out. I’m sure the owner would prefer it if I didn’t have to eat or sleep.” She leaned closer and whispered, “The fellow on the other shift skims coffers.”

"And he still works here?"

"He skims less than the last three. This sort of job doesn't attract the straitlaced types like yourself."

"My laces may not be as straight as you think."

"Oooh. Scandalous. What'll be your pleasure, Epiphany?"

"Some sort of a sweet wine. And call me Fanny."

Allie trotted over to the bar and fetched a dusty bottle. "Sit, sit. Let's hear it," she said, cleaning a glass and filling it.

"Let's hear *what*?" Epiphany said, plopping into a seat at the bar.

"Oh, come now. You show your face in here for the first time in memory for some reason other than barking after your drunken brother, and you expect me to believe that you *aren't* grappling with this, that, or the other? Spill your guts! It'll make room for more wine."

"I'd rather not. Some of it is rather personal."

"Oh, rather personal. I see, I see. I killed a man last week because I didn't like the color of his shirt."

"What!?" Epiphany said.

Allie leaned forward. "Not really, but see how nobody turned a head or batted an eye? People in this place are interested in their dice, their tiles, or the bottoms of their bottles. The only one who listens in this place is me. So speak." She shrugged. "Or don't. A girl's entitled to a drink in silence if that's what she wants."

Epiphany swirled her wine and took a sip. It wasn't exactly the finest she'd ever had, but it was a good deal better than she would have expected. "I'm just a bit frustrated with how those mercenaries have been handled."

"Mmm. You mean in the fact that they weren't handled at all?"

"Precisely!"

"Who did you want to do the handling?"

"The watch!" Epiphany said.

"The watch doesn't do that."

"So I've learned. But something needs to be done. Those men could come back. Or they could be working with someone."

"Oh, for sure. They had access to Greater Mystics. That takes money or influence. Seems to me like if you can afford two big, flashy fellas, you can afford a couple others that'll be harder to spot."

"My thoughts exactly. But Captain Boltt wasn't interested in looking into it."

"Eh, he hasn't got half the people he needs to do what he *is* supposed to be doing. They can't keep tabs on everything that's going on."

"I suppose no one can."

"Now I didn't say that," Allie said.

"What do you mean?"

"You're looking in the wrong direction, I think. Think of a city like… well, a city. Everyone thinks, if you want to get to the bottom of something, you have to go to the *top*. If you want to get to the bottom of something, you should be going to the bottom. Everything washes into the gutters. Find the right person in the gutter, and they'll know it all."

"I've typically made it a point to stay out of the gutters. My whole life and personal philosophy have been dedicated to staying out of the gutters."

"A good policy, I'd say."

"… It seems inappropriate to ask, but—"

"I'm not the gutter sort myself, but half of the patrons here are gutter adjacent. Like I said, I'm the only one in this place who listens. Tell you what. I'll keep my ears open and let you know if I hear anything."

"I would really appreciate that. Something tells me you'll make more progress than our illustrious watch captain."

"Eh, it's easier when folks don't run away when they see you coming."

Allie reached behind the bar and pushed a bowl of roasted crickets in front of Epiphany, sprinkling it with a pinch of salt in a positively flamboyant culinary flourish.

"Now you've been up north to Quarr, right? What's *that* like…"

#

Five long hours of tedious, time-consuming work had come and gone, and Fel couldn't have been happier. He'd moved his horse and wagon from the incorrect alcove to the correct one to shorten his trip, then set about picking through every item in the vault. He assessed each for its value and its potential to provide his father greater insight into how these sorts of things functioned, and weighed that against the amount of space it would take up in the cart. Some of the items required no thought at all. Five fully functional puzzle boxes would fetch a tidy sum by themselves. A few of the smaller antique weapons were natural to include as well. What at first seemed like an endless bounty of reference books soon revealed themselves to be the same three texts repeated over and over again—further evidence that this was some sort of training shop. He took two copies of each. When he'd finished making his choices, he had Wick deliver the descriptions to his parents. All the while, he searched for anything that might be the mask they were after. He found no end of spare parts and half-finished or partially repaired gadgets tucked away, but nothing seemed to be the mask they were after.

When Wick returned with his father's priorities, Fel set about carefully packing them so that they would survive the trip. Hauling them up to the main hallway above the vault was no simple task. Even after successfully opening the hatch and thus having access to the ladder, he had to navigate the stone-scattered stairs or take the time to clear them. He'd chosen the former, and had two fresh bruises on his shins to show for it.

But now it was nearly over. He had one more heavy bag of carefully packed contraptions slung over his shoulder. All he had to do was load them up, make sure his horse was watered and fed, and make his way back to Beffshire to deliver the bulk of the goods to his parents and the two key bits to his sister for sale.

He'd made certain that, throughout the entire process, Oiler and the dagger had never been further than arm's reach away. The dagger was tucked securely into one of the side pockets of Oiler's pack, keeping the contraption asleep and making sure the pair was together.

Fel tottered under the weight of his own pack, the final bag of goods, and Oiler's pack. He barely had the strength to keep Wick's lantern aloft to light his way. But despite his exhaustion, he was in higher spirits than he'd been in years.

"Fifty thousand duots," he said dreamily. "Fifty thousand, all at once. They'll have to give us cenots just to keep the payment small enough to deliver. I can't remember the last time I held more than a few of them at once. Fanny's right. Once Mom sees that money, she'll change her tune. And Dad won't stand a chance against all three of us. This is it. This is the beginning of a golden age for the Masker clan. Nothing can stand in our way now."

He reached the door and placed his hand on it. A moment before he could turn the latch, the door rattled under a blow from the other side.

"No…" he muttered.

Fel lowered his packs to the ground and carefully slid the spy hatch aside. There was a hefty man with a scar over his cheek standing directly in front of the door with some sort of rock pick in his hand. He was hammering the door with it, attempting to chip through. Behind him, Fel could see all the carefully packed goods scattered on the ground in the alcove. The worn metal gate, which he'd taken careful effort to transfer the chain and lock to, was torn free and lying out in the sun. His horse was wandering in the field beyond with the now-empty wagon still attached.

"You!" barked the man with the scar on his cheek when he noticed the open hatch. "Fel Masker."

"Who wants to know?" he said.

"Who we are doesn't matter," Temple shouted from behind his partner. "Who you are doesn't even matter. What matters is you've got something we want."

"I don't care if you want it. I found this place fair and square. Salvage rights are mine. You know the rules."

"You didn't find it. You were led to it. With this map," Cheek said, waving the page.

"I *used* the map to *find* it," Fel said. "Before you. Salvage rights."

"You really think your rights matter out here? Who knows who found this place? You and us. And if you don't live to see tomorrow, that just leaves us," Temple said.

"I'm the one who knows how to get in. This is a Bygone Era construction. It's the Greater Lands Wall. Do you really think you'll be able to just bash your way through?"

"There are two ways this happens, Fel. Either you open this door and give us the mask, the dagger, and the pack, or we stay here and watch the door in shifts until you starve to death."

"If I starve, you don't get the goods."

"If you don't give them to us, we don't get the goods either. The bosses want us to bring back these goods, because they've been lost for ages. If they stay lost? We're still paid for our time. The only one who's got anything to lose here is you. So open this door, hand over the goods, and live to see another day. We'll even let you haul back the rest of this junk you seemed to think was worth packing."

"Be reasonable," said Cheek.

"If you were looking for someone reasonable, you are talking to the wrong Masker. I already know what you did in my family shop. You think I'm going to cut a deal with you? You think I'll *trust* you two?"

"You don't have a choice," Temple said.

Cheek started to say something, no doubt yet another attempt to intimidate a man who was in one of the most secure places in the world, but Fel wasn't listening. He was too busy watching something very curious that was happening behind the two mercenaries. Both of their hippogriffs wandered into view. Fel had heard stories all his life about how incredibly well trained such mounts were. Presently they were behaving with the same level of obedience and discipline as his nag of a horse. While the mercenaries took turns assaulting Fel with poorly worded and poorly thought-out rhetoric, the pair of winged steeds trotted off into the field. They converged upon an area of tall grass some distance away and started clawing at it.

"—and if you *don't* give us the packs, we'll make sure your family and your friends pay," Temple barked.

"Uh-huh. Great. Are you going to do that with or without your hippogriffs? Because they seem to have lost interest in you," Fel asked.

The mercs looked, cursed, and dashed for their mounts. Fel grabbed one of the spears he'd determined wasn't worth hauling all the way back home and assembled a plan in his mind. Fel being Fel, the plan amounted to little more than "grab as much as I can, haul it to the horse, and if they try to stop me, stab them with the spear."

He pulled the door open, fully ready to execute the first part of the plan. Something smashed into him at waist level just as soon as the door was open. It knocked him back, thrown off-balance by his heavy bags. He hit the ground, and the door slammed tight.

"What in the world?" he muttered, rubbing his head.

The air in front of him flickered, then a haze of blue seemed to trace out a figure. It dispersed in a wisp of radiance to reveal Tome. He had a cocky smile on his face, which was somewhat incongruous with the amount of dust that had plastered him and the utter disarray of his hair.

"Hello there, Fel," he said hoarsely. "You seem to have come into a small fortune in contraptions and simultaneously acquired some ruffians hoping to separate you from it. How fortuitous that you have made the acquaintance of a paper mage such as I who might lend you a hand."

"Did you send them here?" Fel barked.

"No." Tome paused. "Well… let's not split hairs on the topic, Fel. The more important thing is, I have created the distraction you will need to escape, and more to the point, I can ensure that escape."

"Then why did you knock me back through the door?"

"Because there is the small matter of my fee."

"Your *fee*?"

"I expended a tremendous amount of very valuable ink to craft the spells to travel at a speed sufficient to arrive in time to aid you, as well as to hide myself and to distract the hippogriffs. I don't think it is unreasonable to ask for compensation. Say… fifty percent of what you hope to earn from the sale of these goods?"

"Fifty percent? I can get out of here without your help."

"You were arguing with the men at the door. And you have a spear. What are you hoping to do, fend off two hippogriffs and their riders for a full week?"

"… Seventy-five–twenty-five," Fel said.

"Seventy-five–twenty-five? I'm sorry, but fifty-fifty is generous. I've had to bend the arcane forces to my whims to help you. All you had to do was root around in a dusty hole."

"I'm not convinced you even did anything. Maybe the hippogriffs wandered off on their own. Seventy-five–twenty-five or nothing."

"Not convinced… Do you see how they paw and claw at the land out there? While you were holding their attention, I spied a nice deep hole thereabouts and dropped in a luring spell. Written with my finest ink, it was crafted specifically and exclusively to draw the undivided attention of a winged Greater Mystic. They will not cease their scratching and pawing until they either find and destroy the slip of paper with the spell, or the spell consumes it."

A terrifying pair of screeches split the air. Fel climbed to his feet and slid the spy hatch wide. Tome crammed his head next to Fel's to get a glimpse at what was going on. The mercenaries had grabbed hold of the reins on the hippogriffs and had been trying to pull them away. Something had spooked them enough to ignore the spell and take to the air, dragging the dangling mercenaries until they were able to haul themselves onto the creatures' backs and continue toward the horizon.

"Is this your doing?" Fel said.

"Yes, of course it is. I have layers of plans. Now that they've been entirely chased away—"

The ground shook. A massive sky-blue creature descended on the field. It was large as a building, with wings that could cast half a village in darkness. The stinking breath it heaved made it clear to Fel that this beast and the one that had pursued him on the way here were one and the same. It dug at the ground, precisely where the hippogriffs had been.

"Your spell was a lure for winged Greater Mystics," Fel said slowly. "*That* is a winged Greater Mystic."

"Y-y-yes. You see, a spell as powerful and complex as this requires a level of nuance to craft at all. Limiting its application is, paradoxically, *more* difficult than leaving it vague. But this is a boon! I don't know if you know much about hippogriffs, but I know a thing or two, and they are very wary of larger predators. I guarantee you that it will take them *days* to persuade those hippogriffs to come anywhere near here again, now that they know that there is a dragon."

"But there's still a dragon! You've made things worse!"

"Please, hardly. The dragon will remain until the spell is destroyed or exhausted, and then it will move on."

The beast stuck its head into the hole it dug and belched a blinding blue flame. Something in its fierce eyes changed when the flame had done its work. Presumably it had destroyed the spell, because its expression changed such that it seemed puzzled, and more than a bit angry, to find itself in this new place. It thumped toward the wall and stuck its snout into the alcove. A hot, wet breath of air huffed and snuffled through the spy hole. The beast gave a half-hearted claw at the door. Then it turned.

In the distance, Fel's horse was obeying the same survival instincts that had allowed the hippogriffs to break the influence of the spell and escape. It was dashing for all it was worth, rattling the little two-wheeled wagon behind it. The dragon trotted toward it, covering more ground at a casual stroll than the horse could have managed at full gallop. With unnerving ease, the dragon snatched up the horse like a cat nipping at a mouse. It shook its head until the wagon came tumbling free and took to the air, evidently satisfied with its meal.

"Bluebelle!" Fel shouted. When the shadow had retreated, he turned slowly to Tome.

"Right. Er… Sixty-forty?"

"There isn't going to be anything to split if we don't figure out how to get home. How did you get here?"

"I used a 'motion as the wind' spell. It took me the lion's share of my ink and nearly a full day to write. I don't have enough quality ink left to craft another one of those, let alone two."

"Then we've got a problem, haven't we? You want forty percent of my share? Solve the problem you caused by solving the problem."

"Right… Let us just assess the current status of the problem before I accept your terms."

#

A few anxious minutes in the field beyond the alcove confirmed that neither the mercenaries nor the dragon were nearby. Fel made his way to the remains of his wagon while Tome trailed a few steps behind, watching the sky.

Fel sighed when he saw what had become of the wagon.

"That horse was with the family for six years. And this wagon belonged to my grandfather," he said.

"My apologies for the horse, but what's done is done. What about the wagon?"

"There are bent bolts, torn lashings. The shade is broken off. But the wheels survived. Most of the structure. If I can scrounge together enough rope and find some better tools, I might be able to fix it. And if I do, I'm lashing you in the rig to replace the horse."

"Ah! Ah ha! You fix the cart, and I shall fetch the replacement steed."

"You can do that?"

"Most certainly. I've hidden my gear just beside the alcove. Let me fetch it, and you'll see what even the least of a paper mage's skills can achieve."

Chapter 8

Two mercifully dragon-free hours had permitted Fel to gather the salvageable pieces of the wagon and drag them back to the shelter of the alcove. He sweated his way through the laborious straightening of bent metal struts, lashing of repairs with cords salvaged from within the wall, and whittling replacement pieces from wood. Meanwhile, Tome scratched with his pen.

"Could you be even the least bit useful?"

"Division of labor, Fel. Do you suppose you can attract a creature capable of pulling a cart?"

"No."

"Then leave me to my work while I leave you to yours."

"Well, unless you want this to take until tomorrow, you're at least going to have to hand me tools."

"Very well, but every interruption extends the duration of the crafting of the spell. What do you require?"

"I need something to pry these two tines apart."

Tome sighed and glanced over the scattering of tools around him, some from Fel's toolbox and many more from the shop in the vault.

"Is there a dedicated tool for this purpose or…"

"I just need something sturdy." Fel held up his hands. "About this long, this thick."

Tome paced among the scattered pieces. "You know, something? I envy you. As monumental as my own skills are, it is remarkably difficult to find practical application for them. At least, practical application commiserate with the cost and effort associated."

"You're a magician and you can't find a way to make it pay?"

"Mage or wizard, Fel. We've been through this. If I were a magician, there would be no trouble in earning a living. Dullards love to be dazzled. As a wizard I can find patrons, but it isn't the same. Those who pay for mystic achievements of my caliber don't pay *me* for them. The combined cost of the spells that brought me here and provided the distraction…"

"Still calling that a distraction, are you?"

"Admittedly, it was miscalculated, but you cannot deny it was distracting. At any rate, the cost for the ink was likely in the thousands of duots. Most of the nobles and such I've worked with would simply purchase the supplies for me and think that compensating my time and effort with room and board is sufficient. Unacceptable. It stifles me, prevents me from growing as a practitioner, and limits my freedom to travel and fraternize."

Fel fought with the mangled tines with the claw of a hammer.

"Fraternize? Seems like I only hear people using that word in one specific situation." He looked over his shoulder. "Let me guess. You got kicked out by your last patron after you fraternized with the wrong person."

"I shall not dignify that supposition with either confirmation or denial."

"Seems like people only respond like *that* in a specific situation too," Fel said with a grin. "But if a magician can make the money you want and a mage can't, then why not be a magician? You've clearly got a flare for the dramatic. I'd think some real magic would help a magician 'dazzle the dullards' even better."

"I have my pride, Fel. Being a mage should afford a degree of status, and having done the work to *become* a mage, I shall not squander it on a stage."

"Status I understand," Fel said. "Contraptioneers don't ride high on the social register either."

"Don't they? I'll admit I've never known one."

"Contraptions can be dangerous." He grunted again. "And there's all those people who think the Bygone Era is bygone because they let contraptions get out of control. So working with them tends to put a stink on you. And my family has been working with them longer than almost anyone else. Worse, we don't even get rewarded for it. The things that are actually valuable get taken away. But you know what might get people actually respecting us? What might even get people listening to us and bending the rules to give us some room to work? Being rich."

"Gold does have a way of tipping the scales in one's favor. So the two of us are after the same thing. Wealth enough to forge our own way without being chained to the past or closed-minded benefactors." Tome reached down and selected a tool. "And it is for that reason that I believe the two of us should work together. Pool our resources, so to speak, in pursuit of this common goal."

Fel accepted the tool and wedged it between the tines. A quick twist of the well-wrapped leather handle perfectly spread the tines. He huffed a satisfied breath, happy to be done with the tedious task. His satisfaction lasted precisely the length of time it took to glance down and realize what tool he had been handed.

It was the dull dagger.

"No, no, no!" he yelped, scrambling toward the chain pack that Tome had pulled it from.

It was too late. The flap rose up and Oiler's inquisitive little bronze head poked out.

"What in the world?" Tome cried, jumping back.

Fel tried to slip the dagger back into the pocket that Oiler's left arm was emerging from, but he wasn't swift enough. The odd contraption spotted the broken wagon. Both of its claws waggled gleefully, and an audible sequence of clicks rang out from within its sculptural head. Chain reeled out of the bottom of the pack, hoisting it up onto a curled loop of animated links. It braced its claws on the ground and swung itself forward, hobbling on tail and claws until it reached the largest piece of the wagon awaiting repair.

With a sort of speed and certainty that seemed more like instinct than education, Oiler went to work. The spade-shaped, notched tool dangling at the end of its tail hooked onto the end of a bent strut and levered it back into shape. What would have taken Fel another twenty minutes of cursing was done in no time at all. The tail wove between the spokes of one wheel, both claws grasped the axle, and it shakily raised the wagon to slide the wheel on.

"What is this thing?" Tome said.

Fel sighed and paced up to the wagon to help support the weight while it did its work. "I don't know if it's named Oiler, or it's just *an* Oiler, but it's one of the more valuable contraptions I was able to salvage."

"Contraption?" Tome said incredulously. "That isn't a contraption. Look at the links. There's no way that thing is moving because of a mechanism."

Oiler pivoted its head. A small slot beneath its chin produced a thin, sharp tube that spritzed some oil onto the bushings of the wheel before tapping it fully in place.

"You don't know anything about contraptions, do you?" Fel said.

"What's to know? A spring winds, gears turn gears…"

"That's a mechanism, not a contraption."

Tome glared at him. "And you accuse *me* of being a stickler for terminology."

"A contraption won't work if it doesn't have the right parts… Hand me that nut, will you?"

Tome handed him the stout square-headed nut for the wagon wheel. Fel got it in place and spun it a few turns. Oiler latched its tail to it and spun it tight. Fel and Oiler released the wagon, and it stood on its own wheels again. As Oiler scurried about looking for more flaws to fix, Fel continued.

"As I was saying, a contraption won't work unless it has the right parts in the right places, but it isn't the parts that are doing the work."

"Then what is?"

"Dad calls them 'contraptors.' Some of the older books call them 'the spirits of the machine.' I don't care what you call them. All I know is if you assemble a contraption right, they'll do whatever the contraption calls upon them to do."

"So… this is magic."

"I suppose. Though I always thought magic was a bit more willful," he said, taking a seat on the ground and swigging from his canteen. "We can't really build contraptions. We don't know how. We can only repair and improve existing ones. That's why expeditions like this one are so important."

"Magic, paper magic at least, is willful because people like me have learned the language." Tome snatched up his half-completed spell. "You can't read this, but this is in effect a very polite, formal, and not-yet-complete request to attract tamable land-bound creatures. You contraptioneers are one proper text away from being mages yourselves." He slapped Fel on the back. "We're a better team than I thought! Achieving mystic results via different, complementary methodologies."

"We aren't a team. You are a thorn in my side who is taking forty percent of my share for work you haven't even proved you can do."

Oiler hauled part of the canvas shade up and held the broken bits of wood in place with its claws while its tail coiled tightly around the vertical struts. It retracted its oiling fang and replaced it with a wider one that sprayed a thick goop along the break. It wrapped the chain of one clawed arm around the break and held it in place.

Tome flicked the page and sat on the ground before his wooden case. "May I begin by saying that, with a contraption capable of *that*, I suspect my share will be quite sufficient to satisfy my needs for some time. And may I furthermore point out that I haven't proved my capability to solve the problem at hand because you called me away from the task to help you do your job when you had a perfectly capable automaton that you were neglecting to use for purposes of deception. Observe."

He dipped his quill and traced out a few more runes with a flourish, then held the page up. "Where would we like to see our new steed summoned?"

"Far enough away that if it turns out to be a manticore, we'll have a fighting chance to hide in the wall again."

"It won't be a manticore. Manticores have wings, and I very specifically targeted this spell toward land creatures. More to the point, because I'm now left with nothing but my mundane ink and paper, the very most potent spell I could muster wouldn't be sufficient to command a creature of that level of majesty for more than a word or two of command. I am quite certain we won't get something we can't handle. But if it will make you feel better, I'll walk out a dozen paces."

He held the page before him, ready to tear it, and walked into the open. As he walked, he shouted over his shoulder. "My spell begins with a simple phrase indicating that the words that follow are to be ignored. The spell is activated by destroying that phrase, either with fire or more direct destruction."

"I don't care how it works."

"I instruct you so that, if the time comes that you need to utilize a spell I have prepared for you, you'll be able to do it. The activation must be done from top to bottom. Bottom to top and you'll do nothing but destroy a few minutes of careful work. Here, this should be far enough." He turned to face Fel. "When I activate this spell, the nearest land beast with a weak mystic constitution will approach and remain stationary in this spot for a minute or two. I trust it is within your capabilities to snare a beast that is not moving?"

Fel reached for the remnants of the salvaged rope he'd been using for repairs. "I think I can manage."

"Excellent. Then we shall attract the beast, you shall capture it, and I shall begin work on a taming spell."

"You can tame a beast with a few words on a page?"

"Quite a few words, and only temporarily, but a page of magic for a day of taming should be sufficient to permit me the time to prepare a replacement spell for the next day. We can continue thusly to string together enough spells to get us back to Beffshire. That *is* where we're headed, yes?"

"Yes."

"Then let us begin."

He tore the page, raised a stone on the ground to pin it, and trotted back to Fel's side. Oiler uncoiled its arm from the formerly broken strut and gave it a resounding knock. Whatever the stuff was that he'd sprayed upon it had mended the break. Fel stood and tugged on it.

"It's good as new." He stepped back. "So you have oil *and* glue?"

Oiler pulled its neck, arms, and tail back into the pack and perched itself on the canvas of the repaired shade. That a full pack of chain failed to do much more than bow the shade frame was testament to the strength of its repair. Oiler hung its heavy tail-end over the edge, swinging it contentedly as it watched and waited. Fel scratched his head and looked around. As they were gathering up the parts of the wagon and collecting the equipment to fix it, they'd also collected the assorted contraptions and books he'd been hoping to bring back. He picked up one of the puzzle boxes, scrambled it, and tossed it to Oiler. It gleefully snatched it out of the air and started dutifully solving it again.

"The dagger deactivates it, I assume?" Tome said.

"It seems so," Fel said.

Tome fetched the dull blade and moved it toward Oiler. Fel snatched it away.

"Don't," he said.

"What? It's done its job."

"It's solving the puzzle box."

"So?"

"So let it finish."

Tome nodded slowly. "Oh, I see… You're new to magic of this level."

"What does that have to do with anything?"

"Remember when I conjured that false duplicate of the wagon so we could get away?"

"Of course."

"It had you and me in the seat, guiding your horse. By the nature of the spell, these figures would have acted precisely as we would have, within reason. Naturally they aren't perfect duplicates. They aren't aware of our essential nature. But they would show fear, anger. They might even speak. You'd think they were alive. They weren't. Magic doesn't create life. That isn't a creature. It is what I would call a construct and what you would call a contraption. Maybe these… contraptors or spirits and what we paper mages simply call the Will are one and the same, or maybe they are distinct routes to the same destination. But they can only do what they are told to do. And that's not life."

"Speaking as a person who has spent decades only being able to *afford* to do what I'm told to do, I'll agree that it isn't what I'd call a happy life, but I'm still alive. And even if that thing doesn't think in the same way that you or I do, who are you to say it doesn't deserve a treat for doing its job well? I know I like an ale and a handful of crickets after doing my job."

"Just remember, it's a hammer, not a puppy. And more to the point, we'll be selling it soon."

"I won't get attached," he said.

The grass around the lure started to shift.

"Get your rope ready," Tome said. "Our means of conveyance is likely arriving."

Fel fashioned a quick snare and crouched down. His hopes were not high that Tome had actually managed to bring something that could help, but they weren't spoiled for choice, so whatever had shown up, he would have to make do.

The moment the grass spread and the lured creature trotted out, Fel rolled his eyes. "Of course…"

It was a lesser unicorn. Not merely *a* lesser unicorn, either. It was the very same one that had been drinking from his horse's trough and snacking on the horse feed while Fel had been working inside the wall.

"*That* is what you lured for us?" Fel said.

"Yes! Splendid, right? Quickly, snare it. The lure won't keep it still for long."

"I don't have to snare it. The damn thing has been mooching off me since I showed up," he said, pacing toward the wavering goat-like creature.

"Oh? Well then we're in luck. I may not need to waste so much paper and ink on taming spells after all. Best to put a rope around it just in case."

He dropped the loop of the snare over the wobbly unicorn's neck and tightened it just enough that it wouldn't come off again easily. After a few more moments, it jolted in surprise and scrambled back, but didn't even reach the end of the slack on the rope when it noticed whom it had encountered. Fel fashioned a midrope loop and slipped his wrist through it, then crouched and dumped some of the canteen into his hand. The unicorn tottered up to him and started lapping at the offered water.

"You'll have to waste more on another lure, because this surely isn't going to be able to pull the wagon, fully loaded and with both of us sitting in it."

Tome clucked his tongue. "Oh, Fel. This is precisely why you need a scholar to help you. That is a unicorn. A lesser unicorn, to be certain, but still a mystic. And like all lesser mystics, it maintains some of the features that make its greater counterparts so great. That creature is stronger than it looks."

"Even if that is true, and I'll believe it when I see it, what difference does that make? It is too small for the yoke and too short to lift the shaft."

"You are clearly handy. I'm sure you can fashion *something*."

He narrowed his eyes. "You're helping."

"The division of labor was quite clear, you—"

"Seventy-thirty," he said.

"Fine, fine. I'll help. But I do so under duress."

#

Martin was in his workshop. He'd positioned a magnifying lens on a complex sequence of metal stalks to get it precisely where he needed it while freeing both of his hands for the present task. He'd been able to liberate some valuable parts from the otherwise broken contraptions in Epiphany's recent purchase and was now busy etching a special pattern on one of the parts before installing it in yet another music box. The first family-heirloom Wick lantern was on the bench beside him, at the moment serving its more mundane purpose of providing light. Having worked far more closely with Wick than the rest of the family, Martin was keenly aware of his comings and goings. The flicker had barely started to subside, but already he was setting aside his work and preparing some paper and a pen.

"Mr. Masker, I bring word of your son's expedition."

"Excellent! I trust the code I provided was the proper one for the hatch."

"It was, though Fel's ingenuity earned him entry prior to my arrival."

"He broke through the wall, didn't he?"

"The floor."

"Mmm. I've always said that boy wouldn't let minor obstacles get the better of him. What has he found?"

"The following is an inexhaustive list of the items he has procured. Are you prepared to record them?"

"Extremely."

"Puzzle boxes, five. Six-sided, fully functional. Crossbows, seven. Five fully functional, two requiring light repairs. No bolts…"

For ten full minutes, Wick recounted the findings. Martin marked them all down.

"And, to complete the inexhaustive list, a length of salvaged rope, most of which has been used for repairs to the cart."

"Repairs?" Martin said.

"Correct. There have been some unfortunate incidents, but I will assure you that as of my last departure, Fel was in good health and high spirits."

"That's a relief."

"The mercenaries arrived and were forced to retreat, in part due to the intervention of a paper mage by the name of Tome."

"Oh, yes. You spoke of him previously, when he hitched a ride."

"He has formed a partnership with Fel in exchange for a tentatively negotiated fee."

"Interesting! Anything else I need to know?"

"I regret to inform you that your horse has been eaten by a greater dragon. There is severe damage to the wagon as well."

"No… Not Bluebelle…" he said. "But Fel isn't hurt?"

"He was not directly involved in the dragon incident. When I departed, he was in the process of repairing the wagon. There was some question as to how precisely they would replace the horse."

"I'm sure he'll work it out. He's a clever boy."

"Do you have any message to deliver to him?"

"Things have been quiet around here. Epiphany had a word with the city watch, but there isn't much they can do about mercenaries on winged steeds. She seems convinced she can find out more about them, but I am unconvinced. Just wish him luck."

"Shall I depart?"

"Yes." He glanced at his notes. "No, wait!"

"What service can I provide?"

"You repeatedly referred to this as an inexhaustive list."

"That is correct."

"It seems rather voluminous. I can't imagine there are many other things that could fit in the wagon."

"No. The wagon will be quite full, assuming all listed items are able to be reclaimed and transported."

"So what is missing?"

Wick paused. "Some information is being withheld by request."

"By request from whom?"

"It would not be appropriate to provide that information."

"It can only be Fel, right? You haven't made yourself known to this Tome character, correct?"

"The latter part of your supposition is correct. The former supposition is reasonable."

"You are being evasive, Wick. I've never known you to do that."

"You are typically the only member of the family who deals with me directly. There would be no reason for information to be withheld."

"What information is being withheld, Wick?"

"I can answer that question, but only if you feel you genuinely need to know the answer."

"Is there some reason I might not want to know the answer?"

"Would you like insight on the subject of secrecy?"

Martin furrowed his brow. "I am very curious to hear your insight, Wick."

"I was created to observe, to warehouse information, and to deliver it when requested. There are other services I am capable of fulfilling, and I am happy to fulfill those services. But the primary service is, and has always been, to see things and tell their tale. In my many years, I have seen many things. I remember them all. Some were of crucial importance, and in delivering word of those things, lives were saved and damage was avoided. But there are other things. Things that will do no harm if they remain hidden, but will do harm if they are revealed. Perhaps it is something innocuous, something like a surprise, intended to delight, which if revealed will deprive all involved of what might have been a valued moment. Perhaps it is something else. A mistake, or an act of poor judgment. Something that, if forgotten, will allow lives to continue in serenity, but if revealed, will strain relationships and bring to an end partnerships which have been mutually beneficial. Perhaps it is the story of a terrible injury that has since healed, and to retell it would do nothing more than open an old wound. If something is hidden by someone who is trusted, to seek that knowledge can be seen as a betrayal of that trust, just as surely as the hidden knowledge itself may be seen as a betrayal. Knowledge is important, but wisdom is of greater importance. And there are those who would say that the greatest part of wisdom is to know when it is safe, and preferable, to embrace ignorance. Some secrets should remain secrets."

"I see."

"Would you like me to provide the exhaustive list of Fel's cargo?"

"… No. I suppose I'll just wait and see, shall I?"

"As you wish."

#

Allie paced through the back room, eying up the stocks of various rarely requested spirits. The oddball stuff had a way of running out while no one was looking. About half the time it was because one of the regulars finished a given bottle and no one thought to replace it until the next time he came in. The other half of the time it was because one of the other servers got thirsty and didn't think it would be missed. Given the owner's rather lackadaisical approach to running the place, it usually came down to Allie to spot these sorts of things before they led to a dissatisfied customer. After all, if they were dissatisfied, she was the one who had to hear it. And if they were satisfied, she was the one who got a few extra coins in her pocket. It paid to be thorough.

"Allie!" called the small voice of Davie. He trotted in.

"Hey, Davie. Listen, have you been sampling the wares? I don't remember anyone ordering the Rusty River stuff, but the jug is getting awfully low and it *is* on the bottom shelf."

"I wouldn't wash my boots with that stuff."

"I'm not asking if you've been washing your boots with it. I'm asking if you've been drinking it."

"… Maybe once or twice, to take the chill off."

"Well, just let me know if you finish it. I hate to reach down and grab an empty bottle when I'm expecting a full one. Now what's the matter? Someone trying to help themselves out there?"

"No. But the fellow you said to watch for just walked in."

"Oh! Excellent." She dusted off her hands. "Thanks for watching out, Davie."

She stepped from the back room. A fellow had insinuated himself into one of the booths in the corner of the tavern. He didn't quite count as a regular, at least not by Allie's accounting. If there was a schedule to his comings and goings, it was based upon some sort of arcane calendar the barmaid wasn't privy to. But at least once a month he would show up in a dusty gray overcoat, slide into the booth, and have surreptitious meetings with the patrons. Every neighborhood had a man like him. The man who knew how to get things. In this part of Beffshire, the man was a bearded, grinning little fellow that folks called Honest Hal.

Allie steeled herself for the interaction. Hal was the sort of man it took fortitude to talk to. Not because he was unpleasant or aggressive—at least, not in the way most patrons might be. It was because the man was uncommonly good at finding the *one* thing you'd be willing to pay through the nose for, and wouldn't you know it, he had a supplier. Talking to Hal was a surefire way to find yourself indulging in vices you didn't even know you had.

"Hal! Good to see you," Allie said, marching up with the customary offering of roasted crickets.

"Please, call me Honest," he said automatically.

"I don't think I'll be doing that, Hal."

"Aw, what's the matter? Folks been telling tales about me? I'm a straight talker, a straight shooter, and an all-around good egg. Ask anyone. I fixed you up with that Highland brandy, didn't I? Guaranteed authentic."

"It didn't make anyone go blind, so that's better than it could have been."

"And those lamb's wool socks? They still treating your feet right?"

"Let's not talk about my feet, Hal, I've got some questions."

"Questions? Questions are free. Answers'll cost you."

She slipped into the booth opposite him. "I know the drill."

"So what's the topic?"

"Those hippogriff riders who came through here."

"Oh, sure. Sure. Real notable. Quite a stir. What's to know?"

"I wouldn't mind knowing where they came from."

He stroked his chin. "Interesting. Interesting. You know what *I'd* like? I'd like to fix you up with a drop more of that Highland brandy. Say… two cases?"

"One case."

"My memory might be a bit hazy then."

"I'll attempt to see my way through the fog."

"So, hippogriff riders. You'd think they'd come from down near the Greater Lands, since that's where the greater hippogriffs come from."

"That would stand to reason."

"But you'd be *wrong*. Because the lesser hippogriffs come from the mountains up north. Just north of the capital of Quarr. They practice all the training and such on the lesser ones. Start the riders real young. Practically toddlers. That way they learn on the lessers. It's real fascinating. You should head up there and watch. I know a guy who can get you tickets for a real comfortable—"

"Save your breath on the sales pitches. We're talking about the 'griff riders."

"Just making conversation," he said. "But right, so the 'griff riders come from up north. Top-level training. They all work for the Quarr government, or else get hired out at a high price to private concerns and other governments. So we'd probably be looking at a place with a *lot* of money and a lot of influence to get *legitimate* 'griff riders down here. The Teskal officials have a few."

"Yeah. That's who this crew claimed to be. But I've served drinks to the Teskal folks. These weren't them."

"There are probably a few. You wouldn't necessarily recognize them by their faces and drink orders."

"They attacked the Maskers. Officials don't do that."

"They do if you break the rules."

She glared at him. "I want you to tell me who could get their hands on an *unofficial* 'griff rider, and supply them with credentials and gear to pretend to be an official."

"Getting awfully specific for one case of brandy."

"You've got to get somewhere near an answer to earn *that*."

He stroked his chin. "I've heard tell of people who can get their hands on… I don't know… *amicable* hippogriffs."

"Amicable?"

"Friendly. Obliging. I don't know the details. If I did, I'd be supplying them too, because something like that? It comes at a *high* price. That, and the credentials, are the best clue you'll get. A decent forgery? That's one set of skills. And the kind of person who can bid high enough to get their hands on a rogue hippogriff or two? That's another trait altogether. You draw circles around those two types of people, and you're not going to get much overlap. Understand me?"

"If you're implying you know exactly who funded this, then I understand you."

"Not *exactly* who. But near enough that I can say one name to get you there. Problem is, these are the sorts of people who would put a knife in an enterprising fellow who says that name."

"You're getting an order for a case of brandy."

"My life is worth more than a case of brandy."

"Fine, then what *is* your life worth?"

He stroked his chin again. "Three cases, plus a bundle of those incense sticks."

"I think you have a lofty opinion of your own worth, Hal."

"Two cases and the incense. And you get one name and no more questions."

"You're sure I'll be able to learn what I need to know from that one name?"

"If you're working with the Maskers on this, I guarantee it."

She drummed her fingers on the table. "Deal."

"Bolivan. And if you tell *anyone* you heard that from me, I'll make sure what comes down on me comes down on you too. Forget if they found out I talked about them. I'm not even convinced I want to be around when Donovan Verfessa finds out there are people horning in on his territory."

Allie raised her eyebrows. Verfessa was a name she knew. People in Beffshire used the name in the same context they'd talk about the boogeyman. You did everything in your power to keep your name out of Verfessa's mouth, because if he had business with you, it meant you'd taken a few wrong turns in your life.

"I know how to be discreet," Allie said.

He stood up. "Great. Always nice doing business with you. I'll be through here in two days with the goods. Have the payment ready."

"I always do," she said.

Hal hurried out the door. Allie gave the table a wipe-down and returned to the bar.

"So," Davie said. "You get what you were after?"

"Maybe." Allie considered her words and amended them. "Probably. And I'll tell you this. We might be dealing with some serious trouble, if he's right."

"What makes you think that?"

"He scurried out the door as soon as he answered. Usually he sticks around for more business. I've seen him get threatened with a club and not give up the booth until he'd made his fill of deals. The people involved have got him spooked."

"Should I be carrying my good knife?" Davie said.

"Not just yet. But it might be worth polishing it up."

#

It wasn't his finest work, but Fel managed to complete something of a harness to adapt the yoke of the wagon to the little unicorn. After initial wariness, the creature had pleasantly lingered without testing the leash around its neck, lounging in the shade of the alcove and idly watching the sky.

"I don't think it likes the sun," Fel said.

"I don't blame it. It's punishing this time of year," Tome said, tracing out a few final runes on his page. "I'm pleased we were able to fix the shade on the wagon."

"We…" Fel muttered.

He glanced at the shade, where Oiler was still happily dangling its tail. The contraption held the completed puzzle box. When it noticed Fel was looking, it rattled the box and held it out. Fel trudged over and snatched it down. He paused, puzzle box in hand, and tugged the blunt dagger from his belt. After a few thoughtful moments, he stowed the dagger again, scrambled the box, and handed it back. Oiler merrily set about solving it again.

"I feel like I'm the caretaker at a zoo," Fel said.

"Not much of a zoo if it only has a lesser unicorn."

"I was including Oiler."

"Oiler is more of an item for a museum than a menagerie."

"The point is, I never intended to be taking care of a bunch of critters."

"You're taking care of one critter and a contraption," Tome said.

"Are you going to sit there correcting me or are you going to do something useful?"

"I would think a bit of constructive criticism would be considered useful, but as it happens, I have completed the taming spell. The spell, for its one-day duration, give or take, will allow the unicorn to understand the commands of 'stop,' 'go,' 'left,' and 'right' when spoken."

Fel stretched the shreds of a banner over some quickly knocked-together struts and attached them to the modified yoke to create something of a shade. Tome approached the creature, who backed away warily. Tome tried to follow, but it reached the end of the snare, tugged at it, and ended up pulling free the damaged fence post it was tied to.

"It's certainly strong, you were right about that," Fel said.

"Look, you're the zookeeper, you do this. Tear the top there and press it flat on the creature's head."

"Definitely seventy-thirty," Fel said, snatching the page.

The unicorn tapped a few steps closer when confronted with Fel and bleated happily. He tore the page as instructed and, after two tries, managed to get it flattened just behind the creature's horn. He held his hand over it and was rewarded with a nudge from the little creature that nearly managed to knock him over. A few seconds later the edges of the page darkened and flaked inward until the paper was gone.

"Now what?" Fel asked.

Tome cleared his throat and pointed at the unicorn. "You, go."

It flicked its ears, waggled its tufted tail, and tapped forward.

"Stop," Tome instructed.

It, after a few more steps, stopped.

"Not quite precise," Tome said. "But sufficient. Let's get the creature strapped in and be on our way. I'm beginning to feel as though we're due for a dragon attack again."

Fel walked to the yoke and hefted it from the ground. With a sequence of spoken commands from Tome that left Fel shaking with effort, they finally got the creature maneuvered under the yoke. He lowered it into place. There wasn't a whisper of effort or discomfort on the unicorn's face. Moving slowly so as to avoid startling it, Fel fastened the harness he'd fabricated.

"I'm still not sure about this," he said, loading the last of the goods onto the wagon and climbing aboard.

Tome joined him. "Prepare to be made a believer. Go!"

The unicorn snuffled once or twice, then scrambled its little hooves against the cobbles. After some initial difficulty getting traction, it wedged its hooves between two stones, heaved itself forward, and got the wagon moving. When they rattled onto the dustier, more uneven stones of the decrepit road, it had no trouble at all finding places to dig its hooves in and keep the momentum going.

For a creature that was barely a match in size for a stray dog, it trotted along merrily without a sign of struggle. The hooves made a cute tippy-tap across the stones, and the shade Fel had erected seemed to be well appreciated. There was only one problem.

Fel glanced at the landscape creeping by at barely more than a walking pace, then turned to Tome.

"I know, I know. It isn't a perfect solution. But what would you prefer? Take a bit longer to get home while riding in comfort, or not get home at all?"

"I'd prefer if you hadn't gotten my horse eaten by a dragon."

Oiler clicked and rattled, then reached the completed puzzle box down in front of them. Fel took the box and held the strut to stand on the running board.

"Come down here, you," he said.

After hoisting the chain-filled pack down and plopping it on top of the cargo, he scrambled the box and handed it back. Oiler waggled its fingers in delight and accepted it with the zeal of a dog getting a treat.

"Not putting it to sleep?" Tome said.

"Shut up and write the next taming spell, would you?" Fel grumbled. "I wouldn't put it past you to have it wear off half a day early and leave us chasing down a unicorn with all of our goods."

Tome sighed and pulled his case to his lap. "At least we wouldn't have to chase very quickly."

Chapter 9

A few days had passed. Their travel schedule had been grueling by any standard. The sun was only just rising, and they had already been on the road for an hour. The unicorn seemed quite happy to tow them along, so long as its needs were met. The creature, true to the goat that it most closely resembled, was content while grazing on anything that grew by the roadside. Grass, thistles, flowers, it couldn't care less. However, whenever it had a meal, it would stay put, refusing to obey even mystically enforced spoken commands, until it had been given a drink of water.

"This little guy is always parched," Fel said, emptying his canteen into a dome-shaped spare part they'd brought from the vault.

"He's probably diseased," Tome said offhandedly. "My father always said a wild animal that would approach humans is diseased. Hopefully he'll get us where we're going before he expires."

"He's not diseased," Fel said, patting the unicorn on his back and sending a plume of road dust into the air. "He just works hard. A solid day of work makes a man thirsty." He raised his head and scanned the road in the slowly brightening sunlight. "We haven't even reached the halfway point," he said. "It is going to take close to ten days to get home at this rate."

"What's the hurry?"

"The hurry is, we have a buyer lined up who will be in Beffshire in less than a week, and he won't be staying for long."

"Oh, I see… Well, we're on a decent road now. We could stop at the next city and see if there's a horse for sale. Something with a bit more athletic a stride."

"Do you have money for a horse?"

"I should say not. That little mishap at the grum table cost me the bulk of my nest egg. You?"

"I've burned through what little money I had paying for two people instead of one. This last night we spent at the inn represents the last of my money. Which is a problem, because we're short of food, and soon we'll be on roads without enough plants alongside to feed Parch here."

"Parch? You've named it now?"

"The point is, we need money, because we're close enough to the cities that hunting will be difficult, and we'll probably get nabbed for poaching besides. And I'm not sharing my tent with you after that first night."

"I'm not the only one who snores, you know."

"You've clearly spent more time than I have mooching off people and bilking them. What's your solution?"

"We have no money at all?"

"Not enough for a night for two at an inn."

"Then we have a few duots. That's enough to gamble our way up to a tidy sum of you're comfortable tipping the odds."

"So long as it's your neck getting risked instead of mine, and I'm not the one you're cheating, I don't care what you do."

"Good, good. We may need to get creative, though. I'm running low on paper, and the spells I used when we first made each other's acquaintance required the more potent ink regardless. My abilities, until I can get more paper, are limited."

"I'm really beginning to wonder if you're even worth the thirty percent."

Parch finished his drink and happily trotted forward before he was even ordered to. Fel grabbed the bowl and hopped onto the wagon.

"I wonder why I've never seen any lesser unicorns near Beffshire."

"The horn is a rather valuable commodity. People like to harvest them, so it tends to make them skittish. You really haven't received a proper education, have you?"

"I've gotten this far knowing what I know."

"If you're going to be taking jaunts toward the Greater Lands with any frequency—and the presence of a still *very* well stocked vault suggests you shall—then it would serve you well to learn a thing or two about the Greater and Lesser Mystics."

"You're supposed to be thinking of a way to cheat us into room and board for the night."

"I can pontificate and scheme simultaneously, I assure you. Now, the question you shouldn't be asking is why some Lesser Mystics tend to avoid cities, while others tend to congregate there. The answer to both of those questions is obvious. Mystics are invariably more intelligent than mundane creatures. Sometimes this means they are clever enough to make the best of humanity, and sometimes this means they are clever enough to stay clear. The question you *should* be pondering is why *Greater* Mystics stay in the Greater Lands."

"The wall. Everyone knows that."

"Having clashed with a greater dragon on the safe side of the wall, I should say that is counterindicated by recent events."

"Fine, why do they stay in the Greater Lands?"

"No one knows."

Fel glared at him. "Then why bring it up!?"

"Because I find things that remain uncertain after so many of the wisest of our people have puzzled at them to be fascinating. And more fascinating are the theories."

"You are going to waste my time telling me things that you aren't even certain are correct?"

"Talking helps me think."

"I think talking just makes you feel smart."

"Feeling intelligent is the first step to being intelligent."

"I would think it'd be the last step."

"*The theories regarding the Greater Mystics are many and varied,*" he said, his voice raised. "Some center on the wall. The wall is one of the sturdiest constructions that has survived from antiquity, and thus quite likely the sturdiest structure in the world. That naturally contributes to preventing land-bound mystics from running wild in a world clearly incapable of dealing with them in quantity. But there are many who suppose that it has some inherent magic to it. Not unlike the taming spell that insinuates certain behaviors and desires into the minds of beasts, the wall may compel Greater Mystics to prefer the land on the seaward side of the wall."

"But mystics are supposed to be smarter than regular animals."

"Yes, very good, you've been listening."

"And that would mean that Greater Mystics are smarter than Lesser ones."

"Quite so."

"Then shouldn't the lesser ones be even *more* affected by the spell?"

"Not if it is targeted specifically to Greater Mystics. Though your point remains valid in that hippogriffs and the like are successfully trained to operate beyond the wall. Arguments can be made that some degree of discipline can overcome the effects of the wall's enchantment, but it is hardly the only gap in the theory."

"And all of this hot air is helping you think of a way to earn money rather than just putting the problem off?"

"Quite so. I've already considered and rejected seven different plans. Now don't interrupt. A further theory suggests that there is something within the Greater Lands, possibly *well* within the Greater Lands, that provides something that the Greater Mystics desire or require. It has been shown that all but the best-trained hippogriffs will eventually return to the Greater Lands if not restrained, and the nobles who are capable of maintaining a menagerie with a Greater Mystic within find that great effort must be put forth to restrain them from escaping and returning. Now, as to what it might be that they seek within the Greater Lands, who can say? And then there is the theory that only a limited number of mystics can exist beyond the wall due to some intrinsic aspect of the world. This theory has… sixes.”

Fel turned. “This theory has sixes?”

“If we are going to earn any money through gambling, we’ll either have to earn *some* money in another fashion or depend upon some games of sixes. Unless you are profoundly lucky and have a winning hand dealt to you in a game of grum, there is a minimum amount of money necessary to win a game. You win by wagering for the tiles you need. But sixes typically operates on a set ante per game, and additionally tends to limit that ante to something in the range of twenty duots. Thus, so long as we win our first game, we can work our way up from there.”

“I don’t know anything about sixes. There’s not a running game of that at The Fox and Log.”

“It is quite like grum. The only difference is that it is played with dice, not tiles. And rather than attempting to construct a strong run, you are attempting to work your way toward as many clusters of six as you can manage before the number of dice in the dice pool is expended. And also you lose points for any cluster of six that is composed of the same combination of dice that another player has used. And also… in retrospect, sixes is nothing like grum, beyond the fact it is played for money and relies upon privacy screens.”

“Can you cheat at it?”

“It’s actually quite simple to cheat at sixes. You simply need to know what every other player is doing behind their screens at any given moment, because the final clusters aren’t set until they are revealed, so players can change their minds at any time. I can think of at least four spells that could manage that. I lack the resources to achieve any of them. More thinking is necessary. In the meantime, have you ever heard how—”

“I don’t care if it helps you think, I’m tired of you talking my ear off.”

Oiler clicked and held out the puzzle box. Fel took it and started scrambling again.

“If I wanted someone talking my ear off, I wouldn’t work alone. If it wasn’t you it’d be…” He glanced at Wick’s lantern briefly. The flame was perfectly still. “… All right, if you’re such a scholar, what do you know about sentry lanterns?”

“Mythical,” Tome said with a dismissive gesture. “At least in a modern context. After the burning of the Telestressa archives, they were all destroyed.”

"Do you think you'd know one if you saw one?" Fel said.

"I would imagine if we didn't find one in that vault, we won't find one anywhere."

"Oh, there was one in the vault. But I brought it with me." He pulled Wick's lantern from its hook and set it on the horizontal strut in front of them. "Say hello, Wick."

"Hello! I take that for present company we are making an exception from the policy of only speaking when in the presence of members of the Masker family?"

"Egad!" Tome said with a start. "Is this real?"

"I don't know magic, so everything I show you is real. I can't show lies, like you can. I can only tell them."

"Astounding…" He crossed his arms. "Is it true what they say about sentry lanterns?"

"If what they say is that they can see anything their light falls on and talk to anyone their heat touches, then yes."

"I dare say we have found a means to gain the upper hand in a game of sixes then." He shook his head. "By the high, man, if you had this, how is it that you were losing that game of grum when we first met?"

"Because I'm not a cheater."

Tome patted him on the back. "Well the good news is, I'm cheater enough for both of us."

#

"You enjoy that. And do visit again, my husband is in the shop making another lovely tune as we speak!" Vivian said sweetly as the first customer of the day walked out the door. As the door shut, she opened the dumbwaiter and shouted down. "Martin! Sold another music box! That tune of yours is doing well! Engrave some more."

"So I shall, my love," he called back.

The door chimed. Vivian looked to the newcomer and smiled.

"Allie! My dear, come in, come in," she said.

"Good morning, Mrs. Masker," said the barmaid as she stepped inside.

"Please, to you, it's Viv. And when I get a chance I'll have to fix some sort of a gift of gratitude for you. That little warning you gave us was the difference between an annoyance and a tragedy."

"Your boy is my favorite customer. I've got to do what I can to keep him coming in, haven't I?" she said.

"Sound business sense."

"I take it he's not back yet. I would have seen him if he was."

"No, no. I wouldn't expect him for another two days at least."

"Any idea how he's doing?"

"Any news I'd be getting about Fel would probably be coming *from* Fel. When he heads out, he's seldom spending much time on the beaten paths."

"Well… he might be getting a few more bumps on that unbeaten path," Allie said.

"Oh? Do you know something I don't?"

"That's what I came to tell you. Those two scarred idiots who caused the mess down here?"

"The hippogriff riders."

"I've finally gotten some word. Heard from a guy who heard from a guy, that sort of thing. According to my source, it isn't good."

"Well don't sugarcoat it, dear."

"Does the word Bolivan ring any bells?"

Vivian's expression hardened. "The Bolivan family. If you can call that nest of vipers a family."

"Word has it, they are the people who hired the riders. Or supplied them? I wasn't clear on that point. But my source seemed to think there weren't too many people who could get the riders *and* fake the official badges. Seems like getting together an attack like happened here would take enough money that warding them off once wouldn't be enough. They haven't come back, have they?"

"No."

"If they didn't come back here…"

"They'll be heading for Fel."

"It seems like it," Allie said gravely.

"Mmm… That will be unpleasant for them. Fel doesn't like to be bothered when he's working."

"Ha!" Allie said, the sound a bit more like a release of pressure than a genuine laugh. "He doesn't much like to be bothered when he's playing either."

"Family trait."

"I'd expected you to be… I don't know. More…"

"Worried?"

"Or surprised."

"We've been in this business a long time. There's not much that surprises us anymore. And a mother always worries. It's the default state of *being* a mother. We raised him right. Fel can handle himself. But the Bolivan family… I'd hoped not to have to deal with them again."

"I can't say I'm familiar," Allie said.

Vivian marked down the recent sale in her ledger. "Consider yourself lucky. There are antiquities shops in most major cities and towns. But, on this continent anyway, there are only three groups that do restoration. I don't care if you're a prime minister, a general, or just an enthusiast. If you've got a broken contraption and you ever want to see it work again, you're going to be talking to the Maskers, the Graves, or the Bolivans. All family shops, to one degree or another. You know us. Most people do. The Grave family—"

"Oh, that much I know. Fel has had some choice words to say about them pretty much every time he's been drunk, ever since Euphoria married into them. They're in East Shalia, right?"

"That's right. Shrewd, but mostly on the up and up, like us. And then there's the Bolivans, spread out across the northern edge of Quarr and Shalia. They're more of a crime family than a clan. The Graves are cutthroat in the figurative sense. The Bolivans are cutthroat in the literal sense. They're like terriers. They latch their little jaws on and shake and shake. There's no adequate defense against those people. No way to break free once they've got their teeth into something. The last time we ended up after the same thing was when Martin was still doing the expeditions personally."

"How did it go?"

Vivian looked up from the ledger. "Poorly for all involved. We lost half the contents of a vault we rightfully unsealed, and they lost some of their best men."

Allie glanced about and leaned close. "Mr. Masker *killed* someone?"

"We like to say that the Bolivan mercenaries precipitated a sequence of events that took their lives. Martin may have had a hand in setting up that sequence, but it's the one who lights the fuse that blows the bomb, eh?"

"I guess so. Gosh, I wouldn't expect Martin Masker to have that in him."

"I wouldn't marry a man who didn't," Vivian said. "And neither should you."

"Ha. I'll keep it in mind." She pushed the door open. "I pulled the early shift today, so I'd better get moving. Good talking to you, Mrs. Masker."

"Viv."

"Quit being such an intimidating lady, and maybe I'll start calling you Viv."

"In that case, Mrs. Masker is fine."

Allie laughed and stepped out the door. A few seconds later, the door from below opened and Epiphany climbed up.

"You heard all that, I assume?" Vivian said.

"I did. By the high, the Bolivan family…"

"I know. This had better be the end of something. Because if it's the beginning of something, I'm not looking forward to what comes next."

#

That evening, after much planning and a fair bit more traveling, Fel and Tome found themselves at a roadside place of entertainment and refreshment. This was one of the endless sequence of small towns that existed simply because the road was long enough for the average traveler to need a place to stop. It had the usual staples of a roadside town, including a tavern, an inn, a general store, a smith's shop, a stable, and a smattering of homes. It also had the curious addition of a three-story wooden wall surrounding it. Like most strange features of the landscape, Fel had written it off as a relic of the Bygone Era and dared not muse about it aloud for fear of Tome expounding upon his own theories for the next hour.

Presently, the wizard puffed at a pipe and settled into the final free chair at the inn table where a handful of rather distinguished gentlemen were playing sixes. He hadn't bothered with the naive-foreigner routine. For reasons likely associated with the specific proportions of luck, skill, and intuition involved in sixes, it tended to attract people who fancied themselves more clever than the average person. A grum table was always looking for a fool with heavy pockets to fleece. The same act would keep you from earning a place at a sixes table, as though one required a certain level of education to even deserve to play a game that was just a few steps more nuanced than flipping a coin to see who wins each game.

Tome tried to keep Fel in his peripheral vision as Fel finished subtly dipping a lit taper into each of the lanterns and candles that cast light around the room. When he was through, Fel threw down the single duot he'd held back for himself and had a tankard of ale.

"The game is sixes," said a man named Chepson, apparently the local who had taken it upon himself to run the table. "Does anyone need a refresher on the rules?"

The table rumbled with shrewd laugher. Tome joined in.

"Very well. Twenty-duot ante," Chepson said.

Tome tossed in his coins and took a long puff on his pipe. As the smoke curled into his mouth, he heard a voice peep up in his head.

"Fel has mingled flame from my lantern with every light around the table. With the flames so near to each other, I can see and hear from them all simultaneously, including Fel's lantern," Wick stated. "I am capable of selecting which heat source can hear me when I speak. You should be the only one hearing me at this moment, as you have just puffed from the pipe. Can you acknowledge me to confirm this?"

"Yes, yes, yes," Tome said. "It's been ages since I had a proper game of sixes. I apologize, gents, if I smell too strongly of the road. It's been forever and a day since I had a proper place to stay, and I fear tonight will not be the night."

"Excellent," Wick said. "After each dice throw, I will give the current status of the dice tallies for each player, beginning at your left and continuing around the table."

Tome grinned. It was a marvelous scheme, really. His success in providing himself with an advantage in the other games he'd played had largely centered on the simple fact that most people cheated via mundane means. Hiding tiles up sleeves or under tables. Conspiring with other players. Setting up polished surfaces to peek behind the screens of other players. And to cheat in that manner was perilous, because if another player can conceive of a way to cheat, that player can plan for it, or accuse someone of it. But cheating via means that any normal man would suppose was impossible was much, much safer. It wasn't reasonable or sane to suppose that one tile might be masquerading as another, so rare was the person who would check for it. And sentry lanterns were considered to be a myth even by people as well educated as himself. No one at this table would suppose that the very light that was allowing them to see their slates was collaborating with one of the other players.

As a matter of fact, there was only one potential flaw in this plan, and it was sitting at the bar, glaring angrily at him.

"I say! Driver boy!" Tome said, craning his neck and shouting to Fel. "When you finish your refreshment, go see to the steed and the wagon."

Fel's eyes narrowed. He took a slow sip from his mug.

"Good help is so hard to find these days," Tome said to the other players. "Good for carrying luggage and guiding a horse, but sharp as a bag of wet leather."

He picked up a piece of chalk. The head of the table rolled first, all five dice. Two fives, a three, a four, and a one. He marked down a five and a one and took a puff.

"From your left. Five, one. Five, one. Five, one. Five, one. Five, one. And five, one," Wick said.

"Not much interesting from that roll, eh?" Tome said.

"Only one six to be found, but the game is young," Chepson said.

Five more dice were rolled.

"Five, three fours, and a one."

Wick worked his way around. Some added a second five and one. Others erased the first and replaced it with a four and two ones. Tome picked the combination that would tie him for first and waited. Even with the edge on his competition, there was still a great deal of calculation to earn a win, or a tie. And then there was the artistry of undershooting perfection by just enough to not be accused of cheating, while still avoiding a loss.

Fel finished his ale and walked out the door. Tome settled in for the long haul. Top score took five antes, split evenly if there was a tie. Second best score got the ante back. It would take at least a dozen wins to make the money they needed to finish out their trip without resorting to camping or hunting. A bit more never hurt.

#

It had been hard for Allie to keep her mind on the job during her shift.

119

To her credit, she was a better barmaid distracted than most of the rest of the employees were when they were at their best. But as she topped off drinks and sleepwalked her way through endless conversations with drunks trying to woo her, her thoughts circled around what she'd learned about the Masker family's likely troubles.

The Maskers, like Allie's own family, were Beffshire old blood. It didn't carry the same weight as the nobles on the north side of town, but it still meant something to her. Beffshire was a city of merchants and traders. Most of the money in town came from folks passing through and making a deal along the way. If you were interested in business and wanted to make a go of it, you came to Beffshire, opened a shop, and generally closed it a year later and left with empty pockets and a sour attitude. It was a town fairly light on locals. But she and the Maskers grew up together. There was a kinship to the rare folks who called this place their home.

Allie had been chewing on the riddle of these Bolivan fellows. Were there others already in town? Almost certainly. How many were there? How could she identify them? How could they be chased from the town, and kept from returning once they were gone? There didn't seem to be any good solutions. But Allie had been tending bar and tackling the unique challenges of her job for quite a while. Being a woman in charge of keeping a room full of potentially hostile drunks from boiling over had taught her that if there weren't any good solutions to a problem, you had to consider whether it was preferable to endure the problem or pick one of the bad solutions. After a few hours, she came to the conclusion that she was willing to give the bad solution a try.

And this one? It might be one of the worst.

"So, boys!" she said, setting down some bowls of salted crickets at a table where a spirited game of grum was just finishing up. "How's the luck?"

The losers rumbled unpleasantly. The winner just smiled and raised his ale.

"Glad to hear it," she said. "Listen, would you mind if I borrowed Billy Boots for a minute?"

"You can keep him," said the winner. "He's tapped out."

"Oh, sorry to hear it, Billy. Come on to the bar, have a drink on the house."

He gave her a look like a stray puppy who'd received his first ever pat on the head. "Much obliged, ma'am. Much obliged."

He trudged over to the bar and took a seat. She filled a mug and set it before him.

"Billy, forgive the observation, but it seems to me you're hard up for money pretty often."

"Can't ever seem to get lucky with the grum tiles," he said.

"Mmm. And yet you're back in here pretty often."

"Gotta get even," he said, nursing his beer.

"You polish boots. That's your trade, yes?"

"I'll polish them up so bright you can use them like a mirror," he said. "You need a polish?"

"No, no. It's just that, the money you throw down on that grum table? Seems like more than you'd make in a day of polishing."

"I come by a little extra from time to time. Odd jobs."

Allie rubbed her face and lowered her voice. "Look, Boots, we can do the dance if you want, but we both know where this is heading. You're doing work for Donovan Verfessa."

He paused with the cup to his lips.

"You don't need to confirm it. But I've got a few questions about how the man does business."

"Mr. Verfessa's not the sort who likes a fellow talking about his business, ma'am."

"If I ask a question you'll get in hot water for answering, just skip it. I'm mostly interested in how he runs things."

Billy clutched his mug with both hands and tried to huddle down into his jacket.

"First," Allie said. "How do you think he'd feel about someone in a similar business trying to run something here in Beffshire?"

"He wouldn't much like that. No, sir. He would be very cross."

"And do you think he'd be aware of it if something like that was happening?"

"Before just about anyone else, I figure. Someone like that wouldn't last long in Beffshire."

"And if he didn't know about them? If they were very clever? Very skilled? What then?"

"They'd have to be *very* clever to keep Verfessa in the dark. I don't think there'd be anyone who could do it."

"We had those 'griff riders in through here. They got past him."

"Well, sure, but who knows what their deal was? And they were in and out."

"But let's say the same people who could get a 'griff rider had the notion to put someone new in town? If you can get a greater hippogriff or two, you can probably put in the work to pull the wool over the eyes of someone like Verfessa."

"Maybe…"

"Do you think he'd be amenable to taking direct action if someone spotted a person stepping on his toes before he did?"

"That uh… depends on what 'amenable' means."

"Do you think he'd agree to take care of someone who slipped past him if he was asked."

"Verfessa knows what Verfessa knows. And he knows what he doesn't know. I think you'd have a hard time convincing him he missed something. And I wouldn't like to be the person to suggest it."

"So proof would be the first order of business."

"Good proof. And it'd have to come to him by way of someone he trusts."

Allie drummed her fingers. "I'm not so big on middlemen these days, Boots. They get expensive."

"Are we talking about maybes or are we talking about for-sures?" Billy asked.

"Let's just say it's a maybe, but I'd like to know how things will go if it turns out to be a for-sure. How does one earn the rank of 'someone he trusts'? How would I talk to him directly?"

Billy shrugged. "Work with him longer than I have… That is, if I'd been working with him, that is."

"Right, right."

"Or… I mean… rumor has it…"

Allie prompted him with her hand. "Yes, Billy, spit it out."

"Get in good with his wife. You get on his wife's good side, you'll be sitting by his fireplace with him that afternoon. But Mrs. Verfessa is *real* picky. Guess that's why it works so good."

She nodded. "Good. Good, Billy. Enjoy your drink."

She wiped her hands with a rag and ran the new information through her head. The good news was, Verfessa would be hunting for these people, so there was every chance they either never made it here or had already been caught. But if they *had* known what they were doing and found a way to work in Beffshire unnoticed, she needed proof. Nothing could happen before she had faces and names for the potential interlopers. And after that, she'd need a way to win over Mrs. Verfessa.

Two steps, and she didn't have a clue how to achieve either of them or even if she would have to. Still, it was a list. Once she had a list, she was very good at checking things off.

#

Fel leaned against the side of the wagon and stared through the slats in the window, eyes focused on the form he knew to be Tome.

"How's he doing in there, Wick?" he asked.

"He has increased our total nest egg from twenty-one duots to one hundred and eighty. I believe his target is two-hundred fifty," Wick said.

"It's been hours. What's taking so long?"

"It is a low-risk, low-reward game. One moment, he requires an update."

"Low-risk, low-reward. Sounds like a coward's game," he grumbled.

The Bygone Dagger

With the dagger tucked away in Oiler's bag to keep it from causing a problem or making a scene now that there were other people near enough to notice, and with Wick busy helping Tome, there wasn't much for him to do. If he had his druthers, he'd be sitting inside drinking, but his pockets were empty and Tome clearly felt as though his presence inside was a liability. Parch had his head buried in a feed trough, which technically belonged to one of the other people in the stable, but what his fellow traveler didn't know couldn't hurt him. It was late at night, the street was utterly dead. Fel poked at one of the puzzle boxes he'd been using to keep Oiler content during the ride, for lack of a better distraction.

"How does it solve these..." he mumbled.

Technically, Fel had solved a Bygone puzzle box before, but it involved disassembling it and reassembling it in the right order. Actually playing by the rules was another matter entirely. That something with a head full of gears could put one in the proper order in just a few minutes while he'd been working on this one for hours didn't improve his mood at all. He knew that there were contraptors involved, and according to his father there was very little contraptors couldn't do, but that didn't change the fact that a bag of enchanted chains and linkages was outsmarting him.

He succeeded in solving one side and was debating with himself if that was enough for him when something drew his attention to the hazy, moonlit sky. A pair of dark forms far too large to be normal birds flitted across the moon. He squinted at them. They turned toward the city with purpose. Fel retreated into the darkness of the stable and peered out through the open gate of the city's wall.

After a few seconds, the two mercenaries' hippogriff steeds touched down. They landed just outside the town gate and released the 'griffs to trot off into the neighboring countryside, probably to hunt down their own meals. Fel snatched the Wick lantern and stowed it as best he could to keep the light from catching their attention. He crouched beside it and watched as the mercenaries stalked through the gate.

"The 'griff riders are here. We need to get out of here."

"I shall inform Tome," Wick said.

The mercenaries reached the edge of town. He could see them having an exchange. Judging from the looks on their faces, they were deriding the quality of the town in between making a plan of how to search it. As they continued forward, Wick spoke up.

"Tome attempted to excuse himself from the table. He was chided, as they have fifteen more dice to roll before the game is ended."

"We're going to be in more trouble with the mercenaries than a couple of upset gamblers!" Fel hissed.

"He has made an idle comment that I suspect is more intended for you than them. Specifically, he said, 'Oh well, it isn't as though I'll be able to leave very quickly anyway. With any luck, the people I have an appointment with will be distracted in some way until I'm through.'"

Fel remained hidden and watched. "All right. There's still a chance. They could have stopped here just to spend the night. Or they could check the rest of the town first, and we'll be gone before they check the tavern."

The pair stepped into the general store, which was already a rare stroke of luck. He coaxed Parch back and strapped him into the yoke. Perhaps he could bring the whole wagon to the outskirts of town and hide. Then it would simply be up to Tome get himself out safely.

"Go," he whispered to Parch.

The unicorn flicked an ear and swished its tail.

"Go!" he said more harshly.

Still no reaction. Fel shut his eyes and did some quick time-of-day calculations. It struck him that the little creature was due for its taming spell to be refreshed. He cursed under his breath.

The door to the general store opened. Both of the mercs stepped out and set their eyes on the tavern.

"No, no, no," he growled.

His mind entered a swift internal debate. A rather loud voice was demanding that he find some way to abandon Tome here, as the man represented a thirty-percent financial liability and a less-than-pleasant companion. Another, more reasonable, voice reminded him that he would be condemning the wizard to a beating and interrogation at best, murder at worst, and there was still the question of how he would get away without Parch. Indeed, there was some question how they would get away even *with* Parch, as it wasn't as though the slow and steady plodding of the unicorn would outpace the hippogriffs or give them some sort of magical means to escape from their eagle eyes once on the road.

To his great dismay, logic and morals teamed up on him and demanded he find a way to keep the mercenaries from finding Tome. Alas, the same logic didn't present anything useful for him to do. His limited capacity for scheming, when confronted with short notice and an intractable problem, presented a solution that, in retrospect, wasn't an ideal one.

"Hey! Over here!" he shouted.

Temple paused, his hand on the handle of the tavern door. He and Cheek turned toward the stable.

Fel snatched Oiler and slipped the pack on his back. He took his cudgel in hand and stepped out into the moonlight. "Congratulations on surviving the dragon attack," he said.

He retreated as he taunted, trying to lead them away from both stable and tavern. They took the bait, stalking toward him.

"Uh-uh-uh," Fel said. "We sicced a dragon on you once. We can do it again."

"Don't make me laugh," Temple said.

"We know what happened," Cheek said.

"That friend of yours is a paper mage. He worked up some sort of lure," Temple said.

"Even if he could do it again, there's no way he'll get anything big enough to scare off the 'griffs again."

"That's what you think," Fel bluffed, he hoped, convincingly.

"That the chain pack you've got there?" Temple asked, pulling a crossbow from his belt.

"And that the blunt dagger tucked into it?"

"What difference does it make? You're not getting your hands on it," Fel said, giving his cudgel a threatening swivel in his hand.

"Tell you what. We'll let you dig through your stuff and find the mask to give us too, rather than tossing it," Temple said. "We're reasonable men."

"No sense getting yourself killed. Still plenty of stuff to sell in that junk shop your family runs," Cheek said.

"Masker's Antiquities is the finest antique and jewelry shop on the continent," Fel snapped.

"You won't get another offer like this," Temple said.

"Good. I don't want to talk myself hoarse turning you two down. The goods are mine. All of them," Fel said.

"Mmm. If that's how you want to play it," Temple said.

He raised the crossbow. Fel dove aside. The bolt glanced off the gravel street.

If not for the heavy pack, Fel likely would have rolled to his feet and perhaps even charged in fast enough to deliver a blow to one of them. Instead, he hit the ground like a sack of wet sand and flailed his legs. The two mercenaries closed in on him and hauled him to his feet. Cheek held Fel's arms. Temple loaded a fresh bolt.

"Now, before I make a mess of this nice clean street, are you going to save me the trouble of digging out that mask?"

"We didn't even find the mask!" Fel barked.

"Mmm. You'll excuse me if I don't take you at your word," Temple said. He leaned forward and claimed the blunt dagger. "Get the pack off so we don't stain it," he instructed Cheek.

Before his partner could attempt to comply, the pack jingled and rattled with Oiler's awakening. His head snaked out and pivoted, scanning the surroundings and taking them in. At the sight of the crossbows, the head jerked up and produced a startled clicking sound.

"What in the world!?" yelped Temple, raising his weapon.

Oiler's claws reeled out of their pockets. One of them closed around Temple's crossbow and wrenched it out of his hand. The other plucked the bolt out and deftly unhooked the string from the limbs, rendering it safe.

"Get it! The thing's alive!" Temple shouted.

"On it," Cheek shouted.

Oiler flipped its head upside down, spotted Cheek about to fire, and snapped its tool of a tail up to clamp down on the string, keeping it in place. Again it pulled the weapon away and rendered it inert.

"Hah!" Fel said, backing away. "So quickly the tide turns!" He raised the cudgel. "Hand over the dagger and—"

Before he could even finish the threat, Oiler grabbed the cudgel, twisted it out of his grip, and tossed it away.

"Oiler!" Fel snapped. "You traitor!"

The mercenaries were already reaching for other weapons. Fel dashed forward, bowling Temple over and retrieving the dagger. He tucked it into his belt and dashed into an alley. Behind him, he could hear the mercs fighting with their crossbows, attempting to restring them.

"So let me guess," he huffed as he circled around into the back alleys. "You don't just fix things, you disarm things."

From the tone of the shouting behind him, they weren't having any luck rearming their crossbows.

Oiler's head reeled out and pivoted to look him in the face as he ran.

"Don't look at me like that. It's all well and good that you don't want those crossbows to fire, but one way or another those two are going to find a way to kill me. They are *bad*. I am good. Or at least not bad. And the rules are simple. A person who is *not* bad is allowed to defend himself against someone who *is* bad! Understand?"

Oiler showed no sign of understanding. Not that it would have been apparent on its nearly immobile face.

"Great. Just great," Fel said.

He reached the city wall. It was far too tall for him to have any hope of scaling it. He dashed toward the nearest gate. Cheek appeared ahead, blocking the way. He turned. Temple showed up behind him. There was nowhere to go but the wall behind and the two-story building ahead. The mercenaries began to a stalk closer.

"Oiler, you've been better than you have any right to be at doing everything you've tried to do. You better be just as good at disarming these two every time they pull out a weapon, because if you aren't, they are going to kill me, and the last thought I'm going to have in my head is that it was your fault."

"You put that thing to sleep and hand it over," Temple called with the sort of tone intended to intimidate Fel but not alert many townsfolk. "So far it doesn't seem anyone's seen what's happened. This will be a lot easier if that thing stays secret. Just put it to sleep and hand it over. We'll let you live."

"I may not be smart, but I'm not so dumb as to think you're going to spare my life. You can try to take it from me, but I'll die before I make anything easy for you."

"I accept your terms," Temple said, hefting a throwing dagger in his hand.

"This is it, Oiler. These men are trained killers," he whispered. "Unless you can snatch two blades out of the air at once, in a few seconds something's going to be buried hilt-deep in my neck."

Fel tried to keep an eye on both of them as they advanced. Oiler did likewise. Cheek raised his blade and threw it. Fel lurched forward to avoid it. Oiler tried and failed to snatch it out of the air. The failure, it seemed, was the motivation Oiler needed to take more decisive action. It reeled out both clawed hands, extending them far further than Fel expected them to be capable of. He could feel the pack emptying as the claws launched to the edge of the inn's roof. The "thumb" of Oiler's three-fingered hands inverted, joining the others in a sort of garden rake configuration and holding tight. It reeled its arms back in, pulling the straps taut and dragging him up and forward. Fel panicked and kicked his feet up, slamming boot-first into the wall. He walked up the wall as Oiler reeled up, and before he knew it he was tumbling onto the roof, breathless and bewildered.

Below, he could hear the mercenaries cursing and scrambling for what to do next. One of them dashed for the edge of town, whistling for his steed. The other marched toward the stable.

Fel looked over his shoulder. "That was… good thinking."

The gears in Oiler's head clicked merrily, and it waggled its fingers.

"Can you do that again, whenever you want?"

Oiler nodded.

"So you *can* understand me. You could have done a better job of making that clear… But I've got an idea. Listen close and be ready."

#

Inside the tavern, Tome had tied another game.

"Really, gentlemen," he said, adjusting his chair. "Much as I've enjoyed our game, I have a long night ahead of me. There are servants to pay, supplies to purchase."

"One more game," Chepson said, a touch of threat in his tone. "You've had quite a run tonight, and as you'll inevitably be walking away with a great deal of my money in your pocket, I think you owe me the courtesy of a final game to help even the distribution just a bit."

Outside, the first hints of shouting could be heard from the altercation Fel had been involved in across town. Tome took a nervous puff from his pipe.

"I cannot see what has happened to Fel. He has positioned my lantern to hide it from view, thus depriving me of an external view of the tavern," Wick said.

"What's going on out there?" said one of the other men at the table.

Tome drummed his fingers on the table. This was a dilemma. On one hand, if he allowed the others to become distracted by whatever Fel was doing outside, he could probably bring the game to an end, which he desperately needed to do. On the other hand, it was just as likely to bring the game to a halt, rather than an end, and it was clear that someone sweeping up his earnings when the other players weren't ready for him to depart tended to raise a fair bit of ire. That these men were ostensibly better educated than the typical grum player didn't rule out violence if they felt as though their chance to balance the ledger was being taken away.

Whether he should embrace the distraction or counter it was a choice, it turned out, that would not be his to make.

"I'll tell you what," Chepson said. "You've been cramped in that seat for hours now. What do you say the whole group simply rotate, eh? Stretch our legs and pick a new location. Then one more game and I'll be satisfied."

Tome smirked. This was the first clear evidence that Chepson thought he might be cheating. He thought Tome had some means to spy on the others, and he was quite correct, but swapping seats wouldn't make a difference. This meant two things. First, there was no possibility of escaping this situation without at least one more game. Second, Chepson and the other players would be watching him very carefully throughout. Whether he liked it or not, he was in this for another round.

"If you insist," Tome said, gathering his things.

All shifted around until Tome was left with a clear view of the window. While the others were gathering the dice and clearing their slates, he repacked his pipe and relit it from the nearest candle. A puff conjured Wick's voice.

"There is a mercenary digging through the back of the wagon," Wick said. "He is attempting to be subtle and quiet."

Tome breathed out the smoke and tried to remain calm. He glanced out the window. For a brief moment, he thought he could see someone stalking over the roof across the way. Surely an excellent sign.

"Let's get to rolling, gentlemen," he said quickly. "I really am rather eager to be moving on."

#

Fel stalked along the rooftops, trying to stay low and out of sight from those on the ground. He was lucky that the buildings were mostly of similar heights and huddled quite close together. It meant he could navigate the rooftops of everything on this side of the road. Most importantly, that included the stable.

He hopped, quietly as possible, to the hay loft over where the horses were kept. For the second time, one of the mercenaries was rummaging through his carefully packed wagon.

"All right," he whispered to Oiler. "I see some rope down in the loft. I am going to slip down and grab it. I want you to lower me down, and I'll tie him up. Nice and peaceful. No weapons."

Oiler clicked and rattled far more energetically than Fel had ever heard before. He glanced back to see what it was up to. The contraption had huddled into its pack, barely peeking around the edge of the flap. Before Fel could turn to see what it was looking at, something slammed down upon him. It felt like he'd been hit with a falling tree branch. Something slashed him, slicing easily through his coat and shirt and gashing his side. The pack on his back was pulled taut, and he was hauled into the air.

The roof of the stable dropped away beneath him. He held tight to the straps of the pack to keep from being thrown free as the flap of mighty wings shook him. A hippogriff had hauled him skyward.

"You've got to admire the quality of that pack, eh?" shouted Temple astride the monster's back. "How many shakes before the 'griff tears you loose? I don't think you'll make it past five."

The great eagle claws gave him a shake. There were few things more capable of clearing a man's mind than seeing the ground retreat away. Fel felt a few things click into place in his mind. First, he realized that fifty thousand duots, while it was more money than he'd ever earned at once, was not worth losing his life for. A shake threatened to force his arms from the straps. Another diamond-clear thought seized his mind. If he was going to die, he most certainly wasn't going to die alone.

Another shake dislodged one of his arms from its strap. Oiler struggled, but the eagle claw was clutched tight around it, preventing anything but the tail from escaping. Fel flailed from the remaining strap, but his eyes were set on the belly of the hippogriff. At the point where the feathers transitioned to the short pelt of a horse, a belt was drawn tight to hold the saddle in place. Another shake nearly dislodged him, but when he swung, he reached out and grabbed the belt.

He released the pack and dangled entirely from the belt. He didn't know how long his grip would last. If he was going to get the proper revenge on this person, he was going to have to act fast. He hauled at the stiff leather, inching a bit of it out of the buckle. A sharp shake dislodged the tab of the belt, and it started to slide free. Evidently even a whisper of motion was enough to capture the attention of a rider. The instant the saddle started to slide, the mercenary barked orders in a blind panic.

"Beast, down! Beast, down! Go down, you idiot!" the man raved.

The 'griff tucked its wings and went into a dive.

Fel continued to hold tight to the belt, now gripping either side of it as the strap continued to slide. Strong equine legs and fierce avian talons flailed at the air, as if trying to propel it faster in its dive. With a much more pressing task to fulfill, it lost interest in Oiler's pack. Oiler swiftly grabbed tightly to Fel and pulled itself to him.

The saddle started to pivot. The mercenary scrambled to keep from falling from the hippogriff's back. The ground loomed closer. Wings stretched to catch the air and level off. The swift aerial maneuver finally pushed beyond what Fel's hand strength could manage. He lost grip of one side of the saddle's belt. The saddle slipped free, dumping the mercenary a dozen feet into a tumbling but likely nonlethal landing. Fel followed, but Oiler coiled its tail around his midsection and tangled both claws with those of the 'griff.

Once again Fel was left hanging beneath the flying beast, now with a heavy saddle in one hand. He should have been preoccupied with survival, but he of all people understood that there came a time when such things were no longer in his control. If he was going to survive, it would be a combination of Oiler's strength, the flying steed's whims, and a healthy dose of luck. He was, essentially, unwanted cargo at this point. And thus he had enough of his mangled wits available to him to observe that some telltale brass-work and inlay in the underside of the saddle looked like the sort of thing his father would work on.

"The saddle is a contraption?" he murmured.

There was little doubt what sort of purpose the contraption served. Now that it was no longer strapped to the 'griff, the creature's flight had become far wilder and more erratic. The saddle had some role in controlling the beast, taming it in the same way that the spell had given him some control over Parch.

The epiphany was cut short by the pluck of a tense bit of chain. Oiler had either lost its grip or been otherwise dislodged by the hippogriff, and now the pair was arcing through the air.

He only had a moment or two to assess this change of circumstance when it changed yet again. He was suddenly tumbling and rolling across something far less kind and forgiving than the overgrown field outside the city walls. It felt like the wooden shingles of a roof. This theory was proved correct when his painful tumble flew past the edge of the roof. Another twang of chain and he came to a jarring stop. Oiler had caught him and the edge of the roof. Gravity asserted itself, and Fel swung down to slam into what turned out to be the back side of the stable.

Fel's head spun and his vision swam. Oiler lowered him to the ground and then reeled back into its pack like a turtle taking cover.

Just like that, Fel was safe on the ground again. At some point during his flight and tumble, he'd lost grip of the saddle. He checked for the blunt dagger and found it tucked into his belt where he'd left it, nestled right in the center of a dagger-shaped sore spot thanks to landing on the tool at least twice.

He managed to haul himself up onto his hands and knees before his body decided that it no longer had any use for his lunch and quickly relieved him of it.

"… Never mind that. I've got the saddle. We've got to catch my mount and get it saddled up again. They'll kill us if we don't return these things to them," barked Temple.

"But Masker! And the pack."

"Forget them for now. We know where they're headed. We'll catch them in no time."

He heard the flap of wings and the screech of an eagle, then the mercenaries were gone. Fel leaned on the back of the stable. He pulled himself painfully to his feet and pulled Oiler to his back. Once the world stopped spinning, he hobbled around to the front of the stable.

A handful of people were in the street now, evidently attracted to the commotion. Fel slipped into the stable without being noticed. Half his goods had been dumped on the ground again, and he sat heavily in the wagon, gave Parch a pat, and kicked around at the dislodged gear until he found the puzzle box he was working on. He held it out. Oiler eagerly snatched it and went to work.

"Fel, I am pleased you were not hurt," Wick said.

"I'm bleeding and bruised, Wick."

"Then I am pleased you were not hurt killed."

"Right. Wick, we're not telling Mom and Dad about this part either."

"Understood and cheerfully agreed to."

A few minutes later, Tome approached. "Ah! Excellent. There seemed to be some disturbance out here, but I'm pleased to see you have it handled."

Fel looked him wearily in the eye. "Do you have the money?"

"Three hundred and twenty duots. I managed to get some side wagers in on the final game."

"Good. First, you're giving me twenty duots for me to spend on some liquor. Then you're writing one of those healing spells for my side here. Then you're loading all of this back up. After that, we'll talk about what to do."

"A word of gratitude for parlaying our pittance into enough to finish the journey on would not be out of place."

"Tome, in the last few minutes I have been shot at, I've had knives thrown at me, I've been pulled onto rooftops and pulled off them, the eagle half of a hippogriff slashed my side, the horse half almost kicked me, and I dangled in the sky under one until it went feral. My mouth is full of sick, my side is bleeding, and I'm going to have to hope that hippogriff claws aren't poisonous. Give me my twenty and get to writing."

"Right, perhaps you've had the more trying evening," Tome said, counting out the requested share of the winnings. "I'll just do some shopping so that we can be on our way, shall I? I assume the shop is still open."

"If you've got money, the shops never close. And buy a bit extra. Maybe see if you can trade the family wagon for something less distinctive. Those mercenaries aren't done with us, and we're too close to home to get caught again."

"I'll endeavor to do so."

Fel took his coins and muttered under his breath as he hobbled to the tavern.

Chapter 10

The traveling bazaar had arrived in Beffshire. As a trading hub, people were always coming and going through Epiphany's hometown, but this bazaar in particular was an event. Ever since she could remember, she'd looked forward to it. Most trade caravans that made their way through Beffshire had a fairly tight circuit, tracing a constant line back and forth between two towns on either side of her home. The traveling bazaar traced a wide loop, zigzagging through the three major regional kingdoms in a six-month cycle before reversing and making the trip again along a different course. It meant that any product from anywhere on the continent—and a fair selection of products from beyond it—could be found in one or more of the well-stocked wagons for the right price.

Epiphany paced through the city square, where rowdy traveling merchants were still setting up their booths. Orders were barked from bosses to underlings. Plans for how to spend their earnings were openly discussed, and the first deals of the four-day bazaar were being made. That's why she was here. In one of these wagons was the man she'd purchased the map from. And to locate him, she need only use her nose.

She took a whiff near each cluster of wagons she came upon until one of them made her nose wrinkle.

"Badgerweed," she murmured, trotting toward the smelliest of the wagons.

Epiphany knocked on the wooden support of the thick canvas cover for the wagon. The cover was flamboyant, the better to catch the eye of would-be customers. In this case it was bright purple with white stripes. In addition to the stench of the northern blend of tobacco that she dearly hoped wouldn't become popular in Beffshire, she caught whiffs of all manner of herbs and spices. It seemed an odd way for an artifact collector to travel, but then it was clear this was a man with things to hide, and what better way to hide them than by booking travel with an unrelated merchant.

"A bit busy," shouted someone within in response to a second knock. "We'll be open for business in an hour."

"I'd hoped to discuss a thing or two before the start of business.

Regarding… navigation."

She tried not to make it terribly obvious that she was placing emphasis on the final word. She was new to subterfuge, and it seemed like an area where subtlety was called for.

"Mmm… One moment," the man said.

A tall, gaunt fellow with a sallow expression and a thin pipe stepped out. He was dressed impeccably well, crisp, creased trousers and a matching coat, and a well-kept overcoat. He wore a felt cap on his head, and smiled with yellowed teeth.

"Ah, yes. Miss Masker. Proactive. That is admirable. You're interested in a discussion?"

"Yes. I believe you know the topic, but there may be some other issues worth mentioning," she said.

"There is a rather quaint tavern in this town. Now what was the name…"

"If you're using the word 'quaint,' it's The Fox and Log," Epiphany said.

"Let us have our discussion there. I fancy a pint."

#

A short walk across town led the pair to a reasonably secluded booth in The Fox and Log. Allie, as always seemed to be the case, was working. She set them up with two tankards of their better ale.

"Now. The fact that we're having a discussion rather than an exchange implies the items are not presently in your possession?"

"They are still en route with my brother."

"Do we know if he's been able to acquire all three?"

"Only the pack and the dagger."

"Unfortunate, but any of the items are better than none. You do know that I'm only in town for four days. Do you suspect he shall arrive in time?"

"He should, but if he doesn't, I'm sure we can find a way to deliver the items to your next stop."

He puffed his pipe. "Acceptable, but not ideal. I was hoping to acquire them here. A large town with something approaching a capable watch and, more to the point, a decent wall. It puts a man at ease when he needs to do significant business. I may have to charge a bit of a penalty if you violate the terms of the agreement."

"And if there are extreme circumstances?"

"That would depend upon the circumstances."

"We have had some run-ins with a pair of mercenaries riding hippogriffs. They were posing as officials from Teskal."

"I see."

"They were aware of the map, and the specific items you were after."

"Not wholly unexpected."

Epiphany's fist tightened a bit about the handle of the tankard. She took a sip. "Not wholly unexpected…" she said. "You knew the mercenaries would be on the way?"

"Not specifically hippogriff riders. But I'd anticipated interest from the North Quarr contingent."

"That's a very soft way to refer to something as vicious as the Bolivan family."

"You're a rather well-informed young woman."

"When two men come into my family's store and threaten our lives and livelihoods, I make it a point to familiarize myself with their history. And I'm fortunate to have some very good friends with very large pools of knowledge."

"I trust no one was hurt?"

"Nothing tragic has happened, but not for lack of trying. If not for some fast acting by an awful lot of people, things could have gone far worse. And the mercenaries have complicated things. More importantly, if you suspected something like this would be part of the process, what possible excuse could you have for not warning us?"

"I suppose you haven't been operating at my level of commerce for very long. With the sums of money at play here, there will *always* be other interested parties."

"And how precisely did they find their way here?"

"I'll give you the benefit of the doubt and dismiss the accusation in your tone. Though you may have modest standing within the social strata of the city, the Maskers are known the world over for their work in antiquities. There aren't more than three people on the continent with a chance at making sense of that map to the degree that was necessary to access the items in question. Your father is foremost among them. Couple that with the fact that you were doing business in those parts not so long ago, and it doesn't take a wise man to assemble the pieces."

"They're after the items. If all goes according to plan, you'll have them within a few days. Then they'll be after you."

"I am aware, and quite well prepared. Though it is now doubly important to me that the exchange be made here in Beffshire, where a violent clash is less likely to be successful."

"Tell me this. Once the goods are transferred, is that going to be the end of it?"

"I'm not a prognosticator, Miss Masker. But to my employers, and I must assume to the Bolivan family as well, the items of greatest interest are those I listed for you. While the mask is unaccounted for, I suspect your family, as the only people with easy access to the vault, will continue to be a target. All the more reason to devote all you can to the discovery and delivery of the mask."

"My brother was prepared to risk his life and limb in the acquisition of the items, but that was with the understanding that the vault itself and the creatures of the Greater Lands were the threat. Given the hazards involved, and the friction they have introduced, I'm going to have to request a higher fee for our service."

"The price we'd agreed upon was calculated with the understanding of the threat involved."

"Maybe on your side, but not on mine."

"The original fee is already significant. What makes you think I have enough to cover any more than we've already agreed to?"

"We're bringing you two items, not three. I should hope you'd at least have the money to cover the entire agreement."

He sipped his ale. "Remember, you only have leverage if you have another buyer."

"I don't need another buyer. There are two vicious killers looking to claim those items in exchange for our lives. You're looking to outbid that."

He took another sip. "Thirty thousand for each item."

"Fifty thousand."

"Thirty-five thousand."

"Forty-five thousand."

He swirled his tankard. "Forty thousand would be acceptable. 'Griff riders can be dogged foes. But the enhanced price comes *only* if you provide the goods before I depart Beffshire. And lest you feel compelled to seek still higher fees from other interested parties, I offer this advice. You do not want the Bolivans to get their hands on those items. I am not at liberty to share specifics, but suffice to say, you would make an enemy of my employers at the least, and you would bear some responsibility for the consequences of the Bolivans' eventual deeds."

"You seem to be awfully well informed."

"Mmm. Though I am well-funded, information is the most valuable thing I have in ready supply."

"And you don't care to share?"

"Even if you were to turn in all three items, I don't think you could afford the price of the least of the secrets in this head of mine." He stood. "This has been a productive meeting, but I believe I should be on my way."

"One last thing," Epiphany said. "Provided we *are* able to deliver the two items in a timely manner, what are the chances we'll be able to continue doing business? Ideally for somewhat more mundane items in somewhat greater quantity."

"Until the mask is found and delivered, further business between us is quite certain. After that? It is all a matter of supply and demand, Miss Masker.

If there is something you are able to supply that meets our demands, there will be business to conduct. And given the skills present in your family, I very much doubt this is the last time we'll be on either side of the bargaining table." He dropped his payment on the table. "Good day, madam."

He marched out the door. When he was gone, Allie appeared as if summoned by magic.

"You, of all people, bring a man stinking of badgerweed into *my* tavern?" Allie said. "The trollops from the west end of town don't bring in boys who stink half as bad."

"Don't judge a man by his smell, Allie."

"You can say that, but it's been an impressively effective predictor of who's likely to cause trouble."

"Oh, I didn't say I didn't think he was going to cause trouble. He's caused a fair bit already. But I'm thinking it might still be worth it, if Fel can get here soon."

Allie collected the man's tankard. "Fanny, tell me you didn't get Fel in over his head."

"My brother can handle himself and you know it."

"I know he can handle himself when he's digging his own holes. He can just *barely* handle himself, but he can do it. But I've known the Masker family long enough to know that it's the Masker women who find the real trouble. I've heard stories about your mother. And we won't discuss your sister."

"No, we won't."

"So what I'm asking is, if you'd known what this was all about before it started, would you have sent Fel out wherever you sent him on his own?"

"If we'd known what this was all about before it started, Fel would have insisted."

"I've seen Fel gamble. I don't think his insistence in something necessarily makes it a good idea."

"We've been through worse, Allie."

"Maybe so, but that doesn't mean you should make it a contest."

Epiphany dropped payment for her own drink on the table. "I'll tell Fel you send your regards when he gets here," she said.

"Better yet, tell him to head down and dish about what happened on the trip. First drink's on me."

Epiphany nodded and took a few more steps toward the door.

"Epiphany! Just a moment," Allie said, her tone of voice a bit less sharp and a bit more serious.

Epiphany looked back, her patience and politeness taxed.

"As long as we're talking about making trouble…" She gestured with her head toward the booth again.

Epiphany paced back and took a seat. Allie slid in across from her.

"I've been asking around a fair bit about the Bolivan family and if they might have anyone else here," Allie said quietly.

"Anything?"

"Nothing to confirm they're here, but nothing to confirm they aren't. Not that it's so simple to prove someone *isn't* here. But I've still got my suspicions…"

"As do I. But suspicions don't help anyone, do they? Why call me back if that's all you've got?"

"Because if I'm going to dig any deeper, I'm going to have to have a better idea of what I'm looking for. And it seems to me the Maskers are the only people in town who know anything about the Bolivan family. And your father never leaves the shop, your mother's pretty tight lipped on the subject, and Fel's off gallivanting. That leaves you. What can you tell me?"

"Not terribly much. They're a very tight-knit organization. A firm division between people who work *for* them and people who work *with* them. As I understand it, members of the Bolivan family are all from the same city, more or less. Baalhaven."

"I know the place. Up in the mountains. And those mercenaries didn't strike me as being from there," Allie said.

"I agree. Which would place them on the 'work for' list rather than the 'work with.' They were probably hired. But if there is anyone else in town—"

"Then we'd be looking at the 'work with' list. Inner-circle types."

"Or at least people they'd trust more. I'm guessing, of course."

"I'll take an educated guess over just wondering. Anything else I should know?"

"They're contraptioneers. They have access to things no one else does. Even things *we* don't."

"Oh?"

"They're the one family who is willing to work outside the oversight of the assayers and officials regularly. They have things that even *I* agree should be wrapped up in chains and stowed in locked rooms."

"Such as?"

"Potentially anything. Unique weapons. Gadgets to help them defeat defenses… If they have had half the success Fel has had in their local vaults, or my father has had repairing old contraptions, there is no end to the sort of gear that would be available to them."

"Do you think they'd be equipped with that sort of thing?"

"It would be very brazen to try."

"As brazen as sending 'griff riders, do you think?"

"Good point."

"Is there any way I'd know if they had something like that?"

"Hmm… Yes and no. There's a type of contraption that we used to send Fel out with when he was going to old sites and hoping to find things to sell. We called it a 'contraption compass.' It points in the direction of the nearest contraption or collection of contraptions. We don't use it anymore."

"That sounds marvelously useful," she said. "Why doesn't he use it anymore?"

"Because it takes a fairly substantial collection of contraptions to activate it. Within the town, it will always point back to the shop, unless there's a *particularly* potent contraption much closer. There just aren't collections of contraptions like that out there to be stumbled upon anymore. And as for the individual things that might trigger it, nothing complex enough to do so is simple enough to be permissible to sell. So all it was good for was identifying things that would get snapped up by the assayers. But this far from the shop, it *might* have a reaction near something of extreme complexity or potency."

"If you're comfortable loaning one out, I could keep it behind the bar."

"I'll run one over."

"No, no. You head back and I'll send Davie for it. You're a busy woman."

Epiphany stood and headed for the door. She paused. "You know something, Allie? I think I'm beginning to understand what keeps Fel coming back to this place."

"Good fresh brew, excellent service, the best grum games in town, and all the crickets you can eat. What's not to like?" Allie said.

#

Fel hated to admit it, but Tome was easily the quickest wheeler and dealer he'd ever met besides his mother and sisters. Despite the fact that it had been nearing midnight in a town that wasn't precisely the most bustling place he'd ever visited, the wizard was able to find a buyer for the family wagon, a supplier for the assorted equipment they needed, and even a new wagon and fresh horse. Somehow he still had a handful of coins left afterward to show for it. Fel very much doubted all the transactions were on the up and up, but after the night he'd had, he was more interested in escape than square business deals. At the moment what bothered him most was that Tome had persuaded him to send Parch off to fend for himself rather than bringing him along. It was the right decision, but it seemed horrid to have taken him so far from home only to cut him free. A kinder thing would have been to keep him until he could be taken home again.

The replacement vehicle they'd acquired was a rickety but serviceable hay wagon with a tattered roof. It had more than enough storage for their cargo, plus enough assorted rags and such to hide under with room to spare. The sun was rising, and they were moving at a fairly brisk clip thanks to finally

139

having a horse properly sized for the vehicle again.

The fine work he'd done had earned Tome a bit of a respite from Fel's ire, and he'd seen fit to squander all that goodwill with a nearly unbroken string of complaints.

"It's just that I'd budgeted the gambling earnings to include nights in inns. I'd expected a *bed*. And now I'm left with nothing but straw and a rumbling cart to sleep on."

"Yes, well. This would be a terrible time to be a sitting duck, now wouldn't it?"

"For all we know, they've seen fit to abandon whatever bounty was placed on the items we're transporting once you set the hippogriff free."

"I don't think so. I think, even if the money was off the table, those two would still come after me at this point. I've made a fool of them. You can't lose face like that and remain a mercenary. If word spreads, you'll never get work again. Just keep an eye out for them. There aren't a lot of other wagons on the road. It wouldn't take them long to figure out which is us."

"It does very little good for me to keep watch," Tome said, eyes turned to the road behind them. "If you'd at least let me sleep, I'd be able to take over at the reins while *you* sleep and we wouldn't have to stop at all."

Fel looked over his shoulder. "You've been hitching rides for too long, Tome. The horse needs to rest. We're lucky this new one you picked up was rested enough to pull us all through the night."

Tome muttered something under his breath.

"What's that?"

"Just the sounds of generalized irritation. This doesn't look like the main road to Beffshire any longer. I don't remember trees on the main road while we were headed south."

"We aren't on the main road. We're taking the rural route and coming in from the northwest."

"I was under the impression time was of the essence."

"It is. At this rate it'll take us three days to get home, and we've only got three days left. But survival is important too. And our enemies have wings. So we need some cover."

Oiler's claw emerged from the pile of hay it'd been hidden beneath. It was clutching a solved puzzle box.

"Scramble that for it, will you?" Fel said.

"I don't know why you don't just tuck the dagger in so that we don't have to keep it entertained," Tome said, obliging.

"It saved my life. I'm not putting it to sleep if I don't have to. It deserves to have some freedom while it can."

"You keep thinking like that, and I just know we're going to end up keeping it rather than selling it."

"And if *you* keep talking like that, there's not going to be a 'we' when the time comes to sell it."

"Oh, fuff," Tome said, handing back the puzzle box and setting his eyes on the sky once more. "We make an excellent team. And if you owe gratitude to that bag of chain, you certainly owe me similar consideration."

"You're getting thirty percent. That's your consideration."

"If you keep that attitude, I may not be inclined to continue our partnership in the future."

"Partnership!?"

"As I said, we make an excellent team. Surely you agree, even if you stubbornly indicate the contrary. Your strengths—which are chiefly physical and mechanical in nature—are my weaknesses. And my strengths—chiefly scholarly, metaphysical, and social—are your weaknesses. Without the rather significant obstacle of the 'griff riders, this would have been a very smooth and successful enterprise. Between the remaining contents of the vault and your contacts in the world of antiquities, there is a small fortune to be made in our continued allegiance to one another."

"A large fortune. And we aren't a team. We're a guy with prospects and a guy who clings to him like a barnacle."

"You really ought to hold yourself in higher regard than that."

"You're the barnacle."

"Ah. Well, now you're just being daft. I'll have you know that I have been upwardly mobile in this world since I completed my mage training, and it is one of the greatest travesties of this world that you've got me watching the sky instead of resting my valuable mind. First, because you have a mystic artifact specifically for keeping watch."

"It is a service I fulfill happily," Wick said.

"And second, because it is a task so thoroughly beneath my capacity that you may as well be extinguishing a campfire with fine wine. You may as well feed the chickens with truffles. You may as well—"

His moping was suddenly cut off by a strangled yelp as a gray form leaped up from the tall grass beside the road and toppled him backward. After startled cries, the clip-clopping of hooves, and some playful bleating, Fel turned to find that Parch was standing on Tome's chest.

"It's your blasted unicorn!" Tome said.

"Parch! I thought I told you you were free," Fel said.

"The stupid creature doesn't understand freedom. It understands that you're the soft touch that has been hand-feeding it water like a *pet*, and it's gotten comfortable with that." Tome shoved it off. "What bothers me is that the thing followed us for a whole night and kept pace. Makes me think maybe it wasn't giving its all when it was pulling the old wagon."

Parch tapped over to the open bag of feed and munched contentedly at it.

"Tell me the truth. Does this always happen? Do you head out on expeditions and collect strays?"

"You and Parch would be the first," he said.

It wasn't strictly true, but Tome didn't need to know that. They'd made their way deep enough into the forest road that Fel was confident they were well hidden from above.

"The horse needs rest, we need rest. We're stopping here," he said.

He led the horse off the road near a brook and freed it from the yoke. Parch hopped down and pranced out onto the slippery stones in the river to slake its endless thirst.

"That thing is diseased, I'm sure of it," Tome said. "Nothing needs to drink that much."

"Let's just break out the supplies, have a meal, and get some rest," Fel said.

Tome tugged a crate from the back of the wagon and sat down. Fel waded into the brush around the river to gather kindling. He was remarkably efficient and able to fashion a proper base for a fire nearly as quickly as Tome was able to unfasten the twine that secured their meal for the day.

"Meat pie," Tome said, holding out a congealed, greasy bit of pastry. "I'd honestly prefer a bit more specificity with regard to the content of my meals, but when it comes to something that'll keep you alive on one meal a day, this is the best in ready availability."

"Give me a moment," Fel said.

He grabbed a hand shovel from his tool pack and wiped it clean with a rag. He took both pies from Tome, arranged them on the blade of the shovel, and propped them on some river stones beside the fire.

"Ooh… clever," Tome said.

"Faster and easier than the pan, half the time. Provided you haven't done any digging recently."

He opened the front of Wick's lantern, stuck a bit of tinder inside to catch it on fire, and tossed it into the bed of the campfire. A bit of blowing and puffing was enough to get the blaze started properly.

"A few minutes and we'll have a hot meal," he said.

"You're quick with a campfire."

"I'm impatient. When you're impatient you either learn the best way to do something so you only have to try once, or else you learn the quickest way to do something and hope you don't need to keep trying. This is one of the ones I learned right. Why, how do you make fires?"

"I don't. I am a city man at heart. Having the sky as my roof doesn't appeal."

"If you're a city man, why don't you settle in a city?"

"I'm intending to. I just have to find one large enough for me to keep from wearing out my welcome before I find a way to make my fortune."

"You could just work for a living."

"Perish the thought. One does not devote his youth to a proper education because he wishes to be a laborer."

"There are other jobs than laborer."

"Nor am I interested in the tedium of a life behind a desk. I assure you, I'm well aware of the width and breadth of jobs available to a man who knows his numbers and how to handle a quill. That's no life for someone who has learned to harness the forces of nature through the power of words."

The fire started to crackle. Fel pulled his pack from the wagon and plopped it down to recline against while he stretched out on the ground.

"No being a wizard because you get no freedom or wealth. No labor because you're above it. No desk work because it's too tedious. If you put half the thought into making a normal life for yourself as you put into coming up with excuses for not making a normal life for yourself, you'd be in a mansion by now."

"You ran headlong into the Greater Lands looking for precious artifacts. You don't get to lecture me about leading a normal life. At least the only people *I* ever had chasing after me rode horses instead of hippogriffs. The hottest water I've ever been in was this pot you've got me simmering in."

"I'm not interested in making a habit of it. Items like this dagger and Oiler back there are precious *because* they're in short supply. You don't make a living hunting them down. I'm not going to pass up a payday like this one, but the end goal isn't finding huge treasures, it's finding a buyer for the more mundane and available things that we've been getting robbed of for generations. And to persuade my parents to risk finding a buyer like that."

"Generations… Feels odd to hear a young man talking about generations."

The pies started to sizzle. Fel gave the shovel a shake.

"Beffshire is an old town. Most jobs have been handed down from parent to child. Well, that's not true. Most jobs are around for six months and then vanish when the money runs out. But most of the *established* jobs are handed down. I'd think it would be the same way for you. Paper mage seems like the kind of job that runs in the family."

"Not in my family. Father was not terribly pleased with my decision to take up the study of the word."

"What does he do?"

"He is a priest. On the west coast, near Graytide."

"A priest, near Graytide… isn't that where the old monastery is? Door of the Old Man or whatever it's called?"

"Gate of the Ancients. Yes. That's where he studied. That's where I was raised. That's where I learned to write. And that's where I learned about the power of words. The donations don't come like they used to. The monastery makes most of its money hiring out its sages to hand-copy books. The problem was, I started reading what I was writing."

"How are you supposed to copy a book if you aren't reading what you're writing?"

"Word for word, letter for letter. Not even that, usually. Shape for shape is the way. A proper scribe can copy books when he doesn't know the language. But we were given a stack of texts about paper mages. Imagine, if you will, spending your every waking hour from childhood perfecting the art of quickly and accurately putting words to the page, only to learn that there are those with precisely the same skills who are able to sculpt the very firmament with their words. I've tread the path of the paper mage for a few years now. I've had my fill of the west coast. Thus, I've come east."

"Now let me get this straight," Fel said. "You just write words on paper and magic happens?"

"Very specific words, but yes."

"I don't understand why everyone doesn't just learn to use magic, then."

"Because it is an art. Everyone doesn't learn magic for the same reason everyone doesn't learn to sing or paint."

"If singing or painting could make magic happen, I'd make the effort to learn."

Tome stroked his head. "How to simplify a staggeringly complex subject for easy digestion… Imagine if you will, the spell is a request. 'Please start a fire.' If I just dropped that request on a table in a tavern, do you suppose I would get the fire anytime soon?"

"No. Why would anyone start a fire just because you asked?"

"Precisely. And where should the fire be started? And how large of a fire? And to what purpose? And what's in it for them? Crafting a magic spell has to answer all these questions, and many more. Because one of the key aspects of a spell is who composes it. Think of it as a signature at the bottom of the page. Although in this case it is usually nearer to the start, but that's not relevant to the discussion. The point is, for spell writing, just a signature isn't enough. The name you ascribe to the spell must be uniquely yours. Not just what you are called, but your legitimate identity. Working out your own true name, which changes subtly depending on the spell that needs to be cast, takes years. There are also minor differences in the spell based upon the location the spell is being written. The time of day. The time of year. Once again, as I believe I've covered this, but one of the reasons a spell loses potency with time is that it moves farther from the point in time that it was crafted." He raised his hand. "Now before you ask, yes, you *can* preserve some of that potency by writing the spell with the time and date of its activation farther into the future, but there are limits. It is all about nuance, and balance. And learning how to handle that nuance and balance takes a lifetime to master. I am but a novice. But you've seen what a novice can do. Imagine if you'd seen these possibilities and known that they could be within your grasp."

Fel flipped the pies. "That does seem tempting."

"'Temptation' is precisely how Father put it. And ascetics aren't fond of anything that comes from temptation. He saw magic and mechanism as wicked. Said it had brought the world to ruin and would do it again. He denied my request to be permitted to go. Told me he would disown me if I did." Tome shrugged. "And so I am disowned. Suits me. I'd grown weary of being owned anyway. Don't tell me you don't dream of getting loose of the shackles of your family."

"That's not what I dream of. I dream of my family getting loose of the shackles of antiquities."

"You want them to get out of the business?"

"I want them to see that the business shouldn't be the way it is. You, you're a wizard. You talk about having patrons. You may not like serving them, but do they respect what you do? Do they respect you for doing it?"

"Generally the mage for a wealthy family is treated with a degree of reverence."

"Contraptioneers, when we're actually being dealt with *as* contraptioneers rather than silver polishers or jewelry merchants, are treated like we're working with sewage. All anyone focuses on is the danger of the most potent contraptions. Because there are some contraptions that could cause damage, we're watched like hawks and picked apart by the assayers. People act like we're chomping at the bit to concoct or resurrect some sort of world-threatening this or that."

"Sounds like the locals and my father would be in agreement on that."

"I won't say there isn't danger. The mechanisms in those hatch doors in the wall would be terrifying if they fell into the wrong hands. But… something like Oiler. How could the world be made anything but better if we were to learn how to restore or re-create things like that? The fizzle rod kept a dragon off my tail when I was headed for the wall. But if we'd had a halfway adequate assayer the day we presented it, they'd have dropped their twenty-five duots on the table and tucked it away in the vault up in Teskal. It isn't even the vault that bothers me. Fine. Hoard the contraptions. We're getting along without them. But my father spends hours, days, sometimes weeks repairing a contraption, and they give him a handful of coins. I just want us to get what we're worth. And if that means going around the people who don't want that, I'm willing. My sister is willing. But my parents…"

They both took their warmed pies.

"I suppose it's simpler just to keep doing things the way they've always been done," Tome said.

"But things *can't* have always been done this way, can they? Someone must have made the decision to start swindling contraptioneers."

"Yes," Wick said.

Tome jumped at the unexpected voice. "You'd think I'd become accustomed to the fire talking to me after last night," he said.

"What do you mean 'yes,' Wick?" Fel said.

"I apologize, I was under the impression you were asking if it had always been this way, or if decisions were made to institute the current policies. Yes was the answer to the latter question, though this is an inference from the former question, as it most assuredly was not always this way."

"Well, naturally it wasn't *always* this way," Tome said. "What I mean is it may as well have been."

"Wait, wait… how much do you know about how things were?" Fel asked.

"My direct knowledge from the Bygone Era is very limited. I have discussed my direct knowledge with your father at length. However, as a sentry lantern I was tasked with observation, and I did observe both a large number of contraptions, of complexity and functionality vastly exceeding what has been deemed acceptable by the assayers, in common use. I also observed that those who could craft them were considered skilled tradespeople and no different from masons, carpenters, or the like."

"What about magic?" Tome asked.

"I observed little magic, but that may be a result of my placement rather than actual scarcity."

"So why did it change?" Fel said.

"I do not know. It must have happened during the period of time that my flames were extinguished."

Fel thought for a moment. "Wick, we're close to Beffshire now. That means you can deliver a message faster, right?" he said.

"That's right. Only a few minutes to reach Beffshire from here."

"How up to date are they?"

"I last communicated with them shortly after your survival of the 'griff-rider attack."

"Tell them we're stopping for the morning, but we'll be on our way soon."

"Right away."

Tome finished his meal and wiped his hands on a rag. "Fel," he said. "You shovel a fine pie. Now why don't you get some rest?"

"We both need to get rest."

"Maybe so. But you've just sent Wick off to deliver a message, so we are at the moment without a lookout. I shall take that task, at least until his return. It will give me some time to work up some fresh spells. I was able to purchase some mundane but passable ink among our other supplies, and some paper as well. I will feel much more comfortable if I have a reasonable collection of spells at my disposal."

"I'd argue with you, because I don't know if you can keep watch and write spells at the same time. But I won't be able to keep my eyes open much longer, so just try not to get us killed while I'm resting."

"Keeping myself alive is my primary skill, and lining my pockets is a close second. As you need to be alive in order for me to reap the rewards of all the effort I've put in in the last few weeks, I can assure you, you'll be safe as a kitten."

Fel climbed into the cart. He didn't fully trust Tome's assessment, but his head was heavy and his belly was full. He settled down onto the heap of hay. Oiler's head popped out and, upon spotting Fel, produced the puzzle box for a refresh. He wearily stirred its faces and handed it back. Before the clicking of its slowly solving faces could continue, he was fast asleep.

148

Chapter 11

Allie leaned on the bar and gazed over the clientele. For most of her career, she'd trained herself to be mindful of the locals and regulars. A newcomer was all well and good, but so many people passed through Beffshire that the chances were good any given person sitting down in the tavern for the first time was also sitting down there for the last time. For many, the town was simply a brief stop for refreshments on their way to a place like Teskal or Oldover. She always gave good service, but going the extra mile for them didn't usually pay off in the same way that remembering the drink orders that regulars favored did.

Ever since she'd set her mind to the issue of the Bolivan family, she'd been a lot more mindful of just how many new faces the tavern saw each day. Any one of these people could be the provocateurs threatening the lives of her friends. Lately her conversations had been short and subtle, teasing information out of people. This woman was in town to help restore a painting. Those men were carpenters brought in to add another floor to one of the noble's houses. There were new volunteers for the watch, a few clusters of the typical traveling-merchant type, and the cluster of newcomers who were in town to buy or sell at the traveling bazaar.

Never had she been more aware of just how much of her life was shaped by strangers and how much trust or ignorance it took to push the possibility of treachery from her mind.

She leaned behind the bar and glanced at the needle of the device Epiphany had given her. It was still pointed squarely at the antiquity shop. The device hadn't budged from that orientation since it had been given to her. Allie now understood why the Maskers had given up on using them. For all intents and purposes, it may as well have been a standard navigational compass with a needle that curiously chose to point southwest instead of north.

Still, something was off about this bunch. The place was packed because of the bazaar. Instincts that seldom failed her insisted that something was amiss. Someone in here wasn't who they claimed to be. She finished delivering assorted orders to tables and updating the running tabs. For the moment, there was a lull. She shut her eyes and listened. Even she didn't know precisely what she was listening for. The bar was filled with the usual drone of conversation. As the day progressed and more alcohol flowed, the volume of the din tended to get louder and less coherent. A few other languages mixed in periodically—when conversations got heated, people liked to slip back into their native tongue to make a point or to provide some profane color.

Slowly, something tickled her mind. It wasn't something she heard, but something she didn't. She opened her eyes and looked to one of the tables. It was the pair of watchmen. They'd been doing a fair bit of drinking, but the volume of conversation had remained at the same even, controlled level. There was something odd about how they were sitting, too. They'd managed to arrange themselves at a circular table such that even in the standing-room-only bar no one had bothered to try to wedge into either of the two remaining seats. That in and of itself wasn't *so* strange. A bizarrely large number of people came to a bar to be with other people and then tried to find a place within the bar to be alone. But their specific orientation made it more difficult to have whatever conversation they were having. Just about the only thing that made sense about their positions and the angles of their chairs was that it provided an excellent view of both the main entrance and the door to the back room.

These men were quiet, reserved, and mindful of who was coming and going. For watchmen, all desirable skills. But Beffshire rarely attracted watchmen who were in any way desirable.

One of them had just finished his drink. She wove gracefully through the bar and stopped at their table.

"Enjoying yourself, boys?" she said, taking the empty cup. "Thirsty work, defending the city."

They murmured something in reply. She glanced at the bowl of crickets on the table. It was untouched.

"What are you drinking? I'll top you both off, on the house. As a special thanks for keeping us safe."

"Just the ale is fine," said the first man.

"House ale, that will do," agreed the other.

He tipped back his cup to drain it and handed it to her. She placed the mug on her tray and worked her way back to the bar. As she dodged the shifting bodies of a dozen patrons, she ran the limited exchange through her mind again and again. They sounded like locals. *Just* like locals. Which was odd, because they were newcomers. Probably recruited or conscripted from Toyl's Crossing, which attracted people from all over the region. It'd be awfully odd for someone to leave the town to go to the fort, only to come back as a watchman, *and* for that person to be a complete stranger to Allie.

She set down the mugs and jangled some glass bottles behind the bar.

Over and over she repeated their words in her head. There was a precision to how they spoke. Like they were correcting for something. Overcorrecting, maybe. Covering for another accent?

Allie shook her head. She was grasping for straws. But the clock was ticking, and this notion was the best evidence she had. She selected a small glass bottle of Mountain Salt Bitters. It was a mixer for some of the fancier cocktails she prepared whenever the son or daughter of a noble decided to irritate their parents by slumming. It had a dense, pungent flavor, but a drop or two in a tankard of ale had a way of giving it the same strange twist at the back of the tongue that the mountain springs up near Baalhaven had.

She dosed both cups and filled them to the brim with ale. Before placing them on her tray, she subtly palmed the compass in her bar rag.

"Here you are, boys," she said, delivering the drinks to the table. "Fresh from a new keg."

They wordlessly accepted the free drinks with the same lack of gratitude she'd come to expect from the less mannerly of the watchmen. But the gratitude wasn't the part she cared about. She watched their faces. One by one, they finished their first sip, and the aftertaste settled on their tongues. And sure enough, one by one she saw a faint grin and a spark of recognition flicker across their faces.

"If you're feeling particularly thankful, let's have any other refills you might be sending our way come out of that same keg, hmm?" said the first of the watchmen.

His partner raised his mug in agreement.

"Anything for our boys on the wall," she said.

Allie edged past them, ostensibly to tend to the table behind them. But as she rubbed at the table with a rag, she glanced down at the face of the contraption folded into it. When she slid it closer to the table of watchmen, the needle made the most imperceptible of flickers in their direction. A bit closer, a bit more of a nudge. These men were carrying contraptions, they were taking care in the way they spoke, they were watching the doors, and they were fans of the mountain water. Weak evidence, every last piece of it. But an *awful lot* of weak evidence was as good as one solid piece.

"Oovay! I'm taking my break!" she shouted.

"Break? We are having busy time!" came the thickly accented reply from the back room.

"Yes, we're 'having busy time' and you've been in the back room for an hour while I've been handling it by myself. Fair's fair. I'm taking my break."

Oovay grumbled and emerged from the back room, his one eyebrow twisted in a surly grimace as he tied his apron. Allie hung up her own and pulled on her coat. She waved Oovay over.

"Tables one through three are starting to push it on their tabs, the bruiser in the back with the matted hair has had one too many. Water it down or else we'll have a fistfight before the night is over. If the watchmen there want refills, they're on the house and each mug gets a dash of Mountain Salt Bitters, but don't let them know you're doing it."

Oovay nodded, knowing better than to question any of his instructions.

Satisfied that the bar would hold together without her for a while, Allie stepped out into the street. She had proof enough for herself. Whether or not it would be proof enough for Verfessa was questionable, but there was only one way to find out. The next step was getting in to meet him. Except that *wasn't* the next step. The next step was letting Epiphany know what she'd learned.

#

Epiphany leaned on the counter, staring out through the windows at the row of four lesser harpies on the roof across the street. All four of the crow-like creatures were staring back at her, heads cocked one way or the other, a single bead-black eye glaring at her.

"They're going to start causing trouble soon, I know it," she muttered to herself. "I can see them plotting. This is all Fel's fault. He's been feeding them, and now they expect it."

"Rat bird?" croaked one of them, muffled through the windows.

"Rat bird is right!" she shouted back at them.

"Don't antagonize the harpies, dear," called her mother from below.

"They're staring at me," she called back.

"That's what the box of washers is for."

She crossed her arms. "I'm not rewarding them for stalking our doorway. That's what got them started stalking our doorway to begin with."

"When Fel is here, they're very well behaved."

"That's because he stuffs them with pastry!"

"Small price to pay to keep them mannerly."

"Not if he keeps getting them from Divinity's."

"Rat bird!" croaked one.

"Go on!" squawked another one.

"Get! Get!" added a third.

"Just give them some washers," Vivian called. "Those don't cost us anything. They're worn out bits that have been replaced."

Epiphany grabbed the box and counted out four shiny disks. "I can't believe I have to do this," she griped. She pushed the door open. The jangle of their bell got the birds hopping excitedly on the roof. "You get one each! Just one! And then you go, got it?" she said.

"Go on, filthy rat bird!"

"I'll have your guts for garters!"

"Wait'll I get my hands on you."

"Those are my suspenders!"

She flipped a washer into the air. Two of the harpies fought over it. She flipped the other washers up, one after another. The birds wrestled until they each had one, then fluttered off a few houses down to investigate their prizes.

"You'll have them doing tricks soon," said Allie, trotting up along the street.

"The only trick I want them to learn is how to stay clear of the doorway during business hours. This is all Fel's fault, you realize. It's been this way ever since he was seven years old and Mom and Dad wouldn't let him have that caged lesser dragon that came through during the bazaar. Every few months he just gets it in his head to adopt whatever empty-headed creature he can find. We're lucky it's just the harpies right now. Do you remember? Two years ago?"

"He found that… dog thing that started following him everywhere."

"It was a dire rat! He found himself a rodent the size of a house cat."

"Animals know a good heart when they see one," Allie said.

"Animals know a soft touch when they see one," Epiphany grumbled. "But enough about that. What brings you to the shop?"

"I wanted to return this," Allie said, handing her the cloth-wrapped compass.

"Mmm. No luck?" she said quietly.

"Depends on how you define luck," she said. "I think I know who our mysterious friends are."

"Oh?"

"There's two of them… well, there's at *least* two of them. And bad news. They're in the watch. I've got names and faces."

"Lovely… Can you prove it?"

"Not to the degree that'd convince Boltt to oust some of his already-struggling team."

Epiphany stuffed the compass into her pocket. "I suppose it's nice to have our suspicions confirmed, but it hardly improves our situation. Where do we go from here?"

"Nowhere good," Allie said.

"Nowhere at *all*. No one with the authority to do something is going to do anything about this."

"Sure. But there's different kinds of authority."

Epiphany eyed Allie suspiciously. "If you've got something, you'd best come out and say it. All this cagey, ominous talk isn't doing anyone any good."

"The issue is, I don't know how dirty you want your hands to get in the pursuit of a solution for this problem."

"If we don't do something, I'll have blood on my hands. I'll trade any amount of dirt to keep that from happening. What have you got?"

"Are you familiar with someone named Verfessa?"

"Donovan Verfessa or Eveline Verfessa?"

"Who's Eveline Verfessa?"

"Donovan's wife."

"You know them both?"

Epiphany shrugged. "I know Donovan by name. Eveline I know a little better. We polish her silver."

"Would you say that she trusts you?"

"She trusts us with her silver. Why? What's all this about?"

"Let's just say Donovan is the kind of person who would be very cross about the Bolivan family being in Beffshire, but getting his ear is a bit difficult."

"Ah… I had it in my head he was an investor. The sort of person who earns enough money to have… well, silver and a budget for polishing it, but doesn't need to do much physical labor. I hadn't put much thought into what precisely the nature of his investments might be. We *are* talking about the seedy underbelly of the city, aren't we?"

"I certainly hope so, because the bright and shiny pelt of the city isn't going to do us any good."

"I'd wager that 'allowing us to polish her silver' falls well short of whatever level of trust would gain us entrance into… the sort of business that may or may not solve our Bolivan problem."

"What can you tell me about Eveline? From what I've heard, she's the key to all of this."

"I don't know if I should…" She huffed a breath. "Allie, you're talking to *me* about whether or not I want to get my hands dirty. At least this is my family. It seems like you're getting yourself deeply into something, and you don't have a drop of blood in the game."

"I'll be honest, if I'd known just how long a road this was and precisely where it was headed, I probably wouldn't have started the journey. But I'm halfway there, seems like a shame not to take the last few steps if it'll get us where we need to be. I can take care of myself. Now what can you tell me about Eveline?"

"She's got a sweet tooth."

"Oh?"

"I've never seen silver so caked with sticky gunk. Little bits of orange rind and honey. Weird flecks of some spice or another."

"What sort of food has honey *and* orange rind?" Allie said.

"Something expensive, if they're serving it on silver."

Allie gazed up at the harpies as they admired their prizes. "Expensive, ridiculous sweets. I may not know what it is she likes so much, but I'll bet I know where she's been getting it. I've got time enough left on my break before Oovay starts yelling at the patrons. May as well pay Divinity's Oven a visit." She turned to hurry away.

"Allie?" Epiphany called after her.

"Mmm?"

"We're going to owe you for this."

"Oh, trust me. I know how to run a tab."

#

Allie stepped through the door of Divinity's. After working for so many years in a place that smelled of spilled drinks and bad tobacco, she'd trained herself to ignore the generally unpleasant messages her nose was sending her. Thus, the sweet, spicy scent of the bakery struck her to an almost dizzying degree.

Mariss smiled at her from behind the cake that she was presently sprinkling with slivered almonds. "Hello and welcome! How may I help you today?" she said.

"I'm in a bit of a hurry, but I'd hoped I could ask you a few questions. I need help identifying the favorite treat of a friend, and I really don't have much to go on."

"Oh! Well, most of our customers come here with a very specific order in mind, but I'd be happy to help you if I can."

"My friend—and forgive me if I'm vague, but she probably wouldn't want anyone knowing I'm asking this about her…"

"Mum's the word," Mariss said brightly.

"Right, but my friend is rather well off. She just adores something that has orange rinds, honey, and some kind of spice."

Mariss tapped her chin. "Let me see. There really aren't many items we make that feature all those ingredients. Orange rind is the odd one. We have the honey rum baba. Was there any cream?"

"Not that I'm aware."

"We have marmalade puffs. Any powdered sugar?"

"Again, not that I'm aware."

"Mmm. Neither is heavily spiced, either…" She snapped her fingers. "Oh! Of course. The honey butter spice cake! We do a special version once a month with orange-blossom honey and orange zest."

"That could be it."

"If it is, your friend has discerning and *expensive* tastes. Orange-blossom honey is quite pricey."

"Then that is certainly it."

"Wonderful! Well, if you'd like to have one, you can place an order now. We'll be making a fresh batch at the beginning of next month."

"I see… And, may I ask, how much would such a cake cost?"

"Eighty duots."

"… For a cake."

"The orange-blossom honey is *very* expensive."

Allie looked down and considered what she'd learned. Not until this moment had she considered just how far this ridiculous trail had led her from her goal. It was supposed to be about helping ferret out the people who might threaten Fel and his family. Now she was contemplating finding a way to buy a single cake that cost more than a good bottle of wine in order to potentially earn the trust of a woman who *might* allow her to talk to her husband, who *might* have a relevant concern with the dangerous men.

"It seems to me this might be about more than a cake, ma'am," Mariss said.

Allie winced. "Please don't call me 'ma'am.' I'm Allie. Call me that. I work in The Fox and Log, and people who call me 'ma'am' are usually either begging not to get thrown out or trying to blow smoke up my butt."

"Oh! Such colorful language!" she said, mildly scandalized.

"Sorry. Again, Fox and Log. We don't worry about being genteel."

"Not a problem. Just not what I'm accustomed to. So, Allie, what precisely is this about, beyond the cake?"

Allie sighed. "Look, there's a fellow who comes in here, once a month. Do you know him?"

"We get a fair amount of business."

"He's about this tall? Very broad. Looks like he shouldn't be able to afford whatever it is he's buying?"

"Oh! Oh yes… I forget his name… Something Masker, yes?"

"That's the guy. Fel Masker."

"Fel is his name? I don't think he ever told me that."

"… He's been coming here once a month for ages, and he never told you his first name?"

"Such a sweet man. A little awkward and quiet, but just lovely. Always returns the baskets. That's very rare, you know."

"Awkward and quiet, huh," Allie said. "You've never seen him when he had a few drinks in him."

"I suppose not. Wait a moment… The Fox and Log. He's talked about you! You're the clever barmaid who 'busts his chops' all the time, aren't you?"

"That's me." She paused. "He's spoken about *me*, but he hasn't mentioned his first name?"

"Like I said. Awkward. He seems nervous all the time. Go on, though."

"I can't get into the details. It'd be more trouble than it's worth for both of us. But I'm hoping to get my hands on this cake as soon as possible in order to curry some favor with a Mrs. Verfessa so that, in a roundabout way, I can get a favor done on Fel's behalf."

"If he'd let me know he needed the cake a few weeks ago, I would have had it ready for him."

"He didn't know he needed it. He still doesn't. And he probably couldn't afford it regardless."

"He shops here all the time! I'm sure he can afford it."

Allie rubbed her forehead. The runaround and the stakes of this little scavenger hunt were beginning to get to her. Otherwise, she might not have said what she said next.

"Do you know why he shops here so often?" she said.

"We have the best pastries in town!" Mariss said proudly.

"Sure, but that's not why. He's shopping here because *you're* the one selling them. If you sold shoes, he'd be getting a new pair after every scuff. Every duot he earns either gets spent here, gets gambled away at the grum table in the hopes of getting enough to be the kind of man who shops here more often, or gets spent drowning his sorrows when he doesn't get what he wants out of the tiles or his monthly shopping trip."

"We always give him what he orders. But you mean… golly…" Mariss felt the pockets of her apron, then pulled open a few drawers in the counter behind her. Finally she found what she was looking for. It was a heavy, shiny bit of copper. She unclasped it and revealed the stationary pin of the compass and the flattering drawing of his face. "It *did* seem strange he'd given me a gift with his picture in it," she said. "I get gifts all the time."

"Gifts like *that*?"

"Again, not with a picture in it, but sure. Little baubles. Bits of jewelry. You don't?"

"I mostly get a couple of duots and business propositions that are well outside my line of work."

"Business propositions from… oh, I see. That sounds terrible."

"It just takes a bit of know-how to navigate it. But I'm not here about that. I'm here because he needs help."

"Right, right. What sort of help?"

"Did you hear about those 'griff riders who caused a stir a few weeks back?"

"Certainly. Was that about him?"

"About his family. And I'm hoping to make sure that sort of thing doesn't happen again."

"And you're *sure* a cake will make the difference?"

"I'm not sure of anything, but I'm hoping it will."

"Hmm… Give me a moment." She knelt and shuffled around in

something hidden behind the counter. After a few moments, she unearthed two jars. They each had a bit of honey left in them. "I might have enough to make one small cake. I'll make it personally. I can have one for you in a few hours. Free of charge."

"Really?"

"He's been a perfect gentleman, a fine customer, and he needs help. One little cake using some scraps is a small price to make sure he comes back next month for his sweet buns and yeast roll."

"That is damn decent of you."

"It's nothing, really. I should get started, though. Before you go, if you don't mind me asking, he didn't ask you to do this, did he?"

"No. I imagine he'll want to have a word with me when he finds out I did."

"Did his family ask you to? I know his sister just came home from a long trip."

"Not in as many words, though his sister has been a part of it."

"Then why go through such trouble?"

"He's my best customer too."

"Well, sure, but I'm just creaming and whipping some honey and zesting some citrus. You're running all about town, earning favors. I'd think his *sister* would be in here before you." She tilted her head. "Unless you're his sister, too? I half remember something about him having two sisters."

"No. No. Just the barmaid and a concerned associate."

"Well you're a fine friend to him, and I'll make sure to let him know it next time he comes through. Two hours and you can pick up the cake. I'd recommend you deliver it straight to Mrs. Verfessa. It's best when it's still gooey and warm."

"Two hours… I should be able to swing another break by then, if I get back and take over as soon as possible."

"Excellent. See you then!"

#

Fel gazed up through the trees as they rolled forward. If they'd taken the direct route, and certainly if they hadn't had to rely upon Parch for so long, they would have reached Beffshire by now. But the wisdom of taking the route that provided overhead cover was reinforced almost hourly. He squinted.

"There. The hippogriffs again. Good. They're still following us," he said.

Tome dragged himself to the front of the wagon and spotted them. "I am not certain I'd use the word 'good' to describe that discovery, Fel."

"Yeah, well, it's not *your* family that they're going to go after once they give up on us."

"Mmm… I hadn't considered that."

"You'd better start considering, because we need a plan for when it happens."

158

"What plan could we possibly have? They could do it at any moment. And what good will a plan do us if we're still hours away when it happens?"

"No. If they've stuck with us this long, they won't do it until we're practically in the city."

"How do you know that?"

"Because they wouldn't be circling us like this if they didn't have a contraption compass."

"Which is?"

"A device that points to potent contraptions. They're tracking us with one. I know it."

"Then why haven't they *found* us?"

"Because either the person who handed them the compass didn't know how to use it, or they didn't know how the mercenaries were controlling their hippogriffs. Those compasses point to the most complex contraption around, or largest concentration of contraptions. If you're flying around holding the compass and you're literally sitting on a contraption powerful enough to control a Greater Mystic—"

"It will constantly point at the saddles."

"Right. Unless they get close enough to us. Oiler and the rest of the goods we grabbed, combined, are probably enough to make the needle wiggle a bit when they get close enough, but you'd have to be a better compass reader than me to be able to tease out our exact location. But once we get close enough, I'm willing to bet the antiquities shop will be enough to grab their attention and hold it. So what is our plan when that happens?"

"Beffshire has a watch, doesn't it? Surely we should call them."

"They didn't do much good last time. I can't imagine they'll do any good this time. We'll call them, but we can't depend upon them."

"What other option is there?"

He squeezed the reins tight and considered the question. "Allie," he said.

"Who or what is Allie?"

"She works in my favorite tavern. She'll rally the troops like no one else. You'll take the goods and go get her. Just tell her what's happening. She'll know what to do."

"Just to be clear, you said *I* will take the goods."

"We both know they'll assume I'm the one with the stuff. They'll come for me more readily than they'll come for you, so it's safer with you. Go get Allie, I'll go see to my parents."

Tome looked to Oiler, who was simply sitting and gazing out from under the flap of the pack. It wasn't even fiddling with a puzzle box.

"If I am going to have to carry this thing, I suppose I should see if I *can*." He grabbed the pack and hauled it aside. With some effort, he managed to get it onto his back. "It's heavy, but not quite as heavy as it looks. I wouldn't want to haul it a few miles, but I think I can… no, what are you doing?"

The claws on either side of the pack reeled out, as did the tail. Oiler propped itself up on its tail, somewhat awkwardly slid the straps from Tome's arms, and dragged itself to Fel's side. The unicorn was already on the other side, leaned against him as he guided the horse along the road.

"You see, now that is likely to be a problem," Tome said. "The blasted thing has imprinted on you. This is precisely why you don't pick up baby birds you find in the forest."

"It's a contraption. You said it yourself," Fel said, tugging out a crease in the flap and giving Oiler a pat.

"It's a contraption built to mimic life for some reason, and you've gone and got it attached to you."

Fel pulled the blunt dagger from his belt and handed it to Tome. "When the time comes, you tuck this in. Problem solved."

"It's not solved, because you're not going to sell it. You're going to look the salesman in the eye, and you're going to let your heart overrule your pockets."

"I think you underestimate how badly I want to earn enough money to climb the social ladder."

"I think you overestimate it. I've seen the mad lengths you go to achieve your goals. If it was *really* all that important to you, you'd be there already."

"It isn't that easy," Fel said.

"No, it's tremendously difficult, but I've known you for a few days, and you've pierced centuries-old defenses and overcome trained assassins. If those sorts of odds aren't enough to stop you, it seems to me the only person standing between you and greatness is you."

"Why would I stand in my own way?"

"You find the key to *that* lock, and the world will be yours, Fel."

Fel stewed the words in his mind for a few seconds. "You think too much, Tome."

"Either that or everyone else thinks too little. I'm inclined to suspect the rest of the world is wrong and I'm right."

Fel snapped the reins. "Why does that not surprise me?"

#

It took a bit of haggling with Oovay and Davie, but Allie was able to cut her shift short with *just* enough time to dash across town, grab the cake, and walk it to the Verfessa household. Fortunately, Mariss had the address. Unfortunately, upon locating it, Allie had her doubts about gaining entry, cake or no.

The estate was uniquely Beffshire in its design. The bit of the building visible from the street was squat and low. It was made from gray stone, slabbed and mortared into rather artless walls that looked like they could turn away a

160

battering ram. Here and there, attempts had been made over the generations to dress it up a bit. They came mostly in the form of dangling willow trees, gruesome gargoyles, and a fountain that was almost fully swallowed by moss. The building had the worrisome look of a mausoleum scaled up to house a few families. But despite the unassuming exterior and only slightly larger ring of greenery around the place, Allie knew this home belonged to someone with old money, and that it was the tip of an iceberg of luxury.

A black iron gate was open, flanked by two small shacks, each bearing a guard with a sunken expression and a very large truncheon. They watched her silently as she stepped along the twisting path toward the front door, but they made no move to stop her. She stepped up to the heavy, ancient oak door and was confronted by a door knocker that had been polished to a ruthless shine. It was shaped like a ram's head, with a smaller ram's head pivoted above it to butt between the horns with each knock. Allie steeled herself, raised the ram, and thumped it down a few times.

She still had the knocker in her grip when the door opened. A woman in a crisp gray maid's outfit opened the door. Her sunken gaze was such a close match for the guards beside the entrance that Allie wondered if it was somehow part of the uniform.

"Can I help you?" she asked.

"I have a cake here. Made specially for Mrs. Verfessa. I wondered if I could deliver it personally. Perhaps I could have a word with her while she enjoyed it?"

The maid gave Allie a measuring look. She took the basket and tugged up the checkered cloth keeping the confection warm. Her brows rose. "Stay here," she said.

The door shut. Three minutes ticked by with painful slowness. When the door opened, she was greeted not by maid, but by a tall, thin woman with a weary and dour expression. She was impeccably dressed in stiff, thick gray fabric. The creases in the skirt and sleeves were knife sharp. Allie didn't know how someone could achieve and maintain such immaculate creases without pressing the garment while it was being worn. This could only be Eveline Verfessa.

"Audience granted," she said. "Follow me."

She marched Allie through the uncomfortably warm entryway and down a curving staircase that led to a lower level nearly double the size of the one above. Here it was cooler, and warm yellow light was cast from smokeless candles. Comfortable antique chairs stood on either side of a tea table upon which a pot of fresh tea and the cut cake were waiting.

"Sit," Eveline instructed.

Allie did as she was told. The older woman sat opposite her and held a finger over the cake.

"This. Orange-blossom honey butter spice cake. Warm from the oven. A full nine days into the month. This is a very difficult item to acquire."

"So I learned," Allie said.

"And you have provided it to me without invitation and without appointment."

"The timing was a bit tight. I apologize if I overstepped my bounds."

"You went vaulting over your bounds," she said. "But you made a clean landing." Eveline divided a wedge of cake from the rest of the delectable, oozing pile and deftly deposited it on a plate. She set it before Allie. "Please," her host said, presenting her with a fork before preparing a slice for herself.

Allie took the utensil. "This is a gold-plated fork," she said, hand shaking as she held it.

"Heavens no. Solid gold. A bit extravagant for a tea cake, but it does avoid that nasty flavor forks can sometimes inflict upon a meal. Please, eat."

She took a bite. The cake was sweet, buttery, and complex. Eveline watched her sample it and waited until she'd swallowed before she took a bite of her own. The older woman paused to reverently allow the confection to melt upon her tongue.

"Divine," Eveline said. "Your thoughts?"

"It's good," she said. "Given my preference, I'd probably go for brown bread with butter and jam. But I suppose I don't have the palate for this sort of thing."

Eveline laughed. "There's value in knowing your tastes so well." She took another bite and enjoyed every moment of it before setting the plate down. "The statements that follow would have, in the past, been presented as questions. There is value in giving someone the opportunity to lie to you and seeing if they choose to. It reveals character. But as you've said, you are working on an abbreviated timeline toward an as-yet unspoken goal, so I will do you the kindness of being direct. You did not want to speak to me, you wanted to speak to my husband. You hoped, through me, to gain an audience with him and you hoped, through this gift, to curry my favor to that end. Incidentally, the traditional gift for that purpose is jewelry. Furthermore, the traditional gift is unsuccessful."

"No sense clinging to tradition, then," Allie said with a nervous laugh.

"Mmm…" She had another bite of cake. "Your name is Allie, short for Allizon with a Z, a name that you detest in full but adore in short. You come from the family Waverly, and you are born and raised here in Beffshire. You are a criminally underpaid barmaid at The Fox and Log, and you've waded hip deep into matters best left alone on behalf of a friend and customer named Fel Masker, whose family has recently become the target of agents likely to be under the employ of the Bolivan family."

"… Yes."

"As you might imagine, some of our employees frequent your establishment. Now, we have not been able to determine to our satisfaction if there are indeed additional Bolivan agents encroaching on our territory. I take from the efforts you've taken to gain this audience that you *have* satisfied yourself with the available proof."

"I have."

"The question that remains is whether your judgment is sound. That you aren't enchanted by this exquisite cake is a vote against, by the way. But the fact that you brought it as an offering is a vote in favor. So on balance you are doing well."

"That's a relief." Allie sipped her tea and grimaced. While it was a good counterpoint to the cake, it had an odd, bitter, sour flavor. "Um… If you don't mind me asking… who does the… business around here? You seem to be very well connected. Should I be discussing this with you and leaving Mr. Verfessa out of it?"

"Oh, there is a strict division of labor. I see to the house and the comings and goings, he sees to the business. I keep him informed, because that falls within my aptitudes, but I lack the constitution and inclination to engage in some of the activities that afford us this luxurious lifestyle. Now tell me, what did you do to seek out these individuals you believe to be Bolivan agents, and through what means did you come to be convinced that they were reliably identifiable as such? Leave out no detail."

Allie took another sip of the tea. Despite the taste, it did have an odd allure to it. "It started a few days ago…" she began.

#

"And that brings me here," Allie said.

As Allie had recounted her investigation, growing less confident in her findings with each detail, Eveline consumed cake and information in equal measure. She'd nearly finished the sweet bit of bribery and had called for her tea to be freshened.

"And that is that. Well summarized."

"Is it enough?" Allie asked. "Because if it isn't, I wouldn't mind heading back out. I was able to get the evening off from the job, and there are chores that I could be doing."

"The chores, I'm afraid, will have to wait, as I believe Mr. Verfessa will want to speak with you after all. He tends to linger on the next floor. See yourself there. And don't touch anything."

"You're not… you're not going to introduce me or send me with an escort or something?"

"If I felt as though you required an escort, I would send one. Thank you for a pleasant conversation, and I hope my husband will be able to render some manner of aid. I'll see you when you're through."

"Right… Yes, all right," Allie said.

She stood and shakily set down her cup and fork. Instantly her mind started to paint pictures of just what sort of a man Verfessa might be. As she paced along the plush carpet toward the stairs, she conjured someone downright vampiric in presence and coldness. If his wife, who was intimidating enough to cow the worst troublemakers of The Fox and Log and *then* some, didn't dare get into the business he ran, what sort of man might he be? Even more severe? Even more calculating?

Allie crept down the stairs.

"Oh! I hear someone comin'!" shouted an excited and avuncular voice.

As she turned the curve of the stairs, she saw a round, aging man with worn canvas work clothes and hands rough and callused as a miner's. He waved her down.

"Come on down, come on down. If you got past the missus, I know you're worth my time," he said.

"Mr. Verfessa?"

"Don! And you're Allie, from The Fox and Log. I have the boys bring me a keg now and again from that place. You've got it in good with some really worthwhile breweries. What's your poison, by the way? I hate to have a discussion without a drink in my hand."

"I just had some tea upstairs, I—"

"Did Eve pour that stuff down your throat? Terrible, isn't it? She pays an arm and a leg for it, and the stuff tastes like bark. I'd rather chew on a boot, personally. You'll want something to wash the taste out, right? What'll you have? Brandy? Sherry? Whiskey?"

"Water is fine."

He slapped her on the back. "Good thinking. Good thinking. You're two floors down in a house most people would be scared to visit, best to keep your wits about you. Tell you what, I'll have a water too. Keep things civil, right?"

He had a fast, almost dizzying way of talking. It made Allie feel as though he'd started the conversation a half hour ago and was trying to catch her up.

He opened a cabinet and pulled out a pitcher and two glasses. "Mostly I keep this here for mixing. I'm not a man who takes his whiskey neat. I gulp the stuff, and if I don't water it down, I'll be passed out before the good part of the night." He poured two tumblers to the brim. "Good clean stuff. Cool, too. We've got a deep well."

He sipped his water, she sipped hers.

"Now! Word has it you've been doing some sleuthing, eh? Looking after those Bolivan boys. I assume they're boys. The Bolivans never seem to send any ladies too far from home. Mistake, if you ask me. There's places ladies can go and things ladies can do that folks would chase off a fellow for trying, but you know that, I'm sure. So, give me the quick version. Who are they and how do you know it?"

She swallowed her water hard. "Two new members of the watch. I've got the names they gave and descriptions if you need them."

"Write them down. I've got some paper right here. And what makes you think that's them?"

"They were carrying contraptions, according to a gadget the Maskers loaned me."

"Doesn't necessarily mean much. The watch recruits from the fort, and the fort brings in boys from all over. One of them could have been carrying one of those… what do they call them? Handheld something or other. Shoots those little bolts. Crossbow but smaller? Doesn't matter. Point is, contraptions are awfully Bolivan, but not *just* Bolivan."

"They also seemed to really enjoy the taste of ale with some Mountain Salt Bitters," Allie said, trying to keep up with him as she jotted down the information.

"I don't see what a man's drink order has to do with if he's working for a rival."

"Have you ever had Mountain Salt Bitters?"

"Can't say I have."

"They're hideous. They make drinks taste like you licked the bottom of a rock that's been left out in the rain for two weeks. The only time I've ever heard of them being used in a palatable way was when you mix them with an overly sweet drink to tone it down. I snuck a couple of drops into their drinks, and those boys grinned like they'd had a taste of their mother's cookies."

"Could just be from the north."

"They talked like they were locals. They talked like they were *trying* to sound like locals, at least, and doing a good job of it."

"Lots of little pieces then." He sipped his water. "Do you have a hobby, Allie?"

"Mostly when I'm not working I sleep."

He whistled. "I remember those days. I've got guys now. Guys I trust. Gives me a chance to while away an hour or two. Let me show you."

He marched her over to a table covered in little clay fragments. The wall behind it was hung with similar arrangements of fragments in frames. Some frames displayed plates or other bits of pottery perfectly reassembled with contrasting glue or clay highlighting the cracks. Others were different, complex clay patterns made from irregular fragments.

"I do a lot of digging in my line of work. Normally it's more about what we put in the hole, but plenty still comes out of the hole while we're working. Sometimes, you end up with *loads* of pottery from the Bygone Era. I like putting things back together. You can come close to madness looking for *just the right piece*. Especially because sometimes the right piece isn't there. Or sometimes it's two pieces. And when you've been at it for a while, you can convince yourself that this little piece, or that little one, or maybe these three put together? They might be close enough to the right shape. But you've got to be careful. Because if the pieces are small enough, and you already have a picture in your head of how you want them to look, you can end up with not a restoration, like this plate here, but a mosaic, like that one there. Still pretty, but one's fact and one's fiction."

He glanced at her. "The missus calls this a metaphor. You picking up what I'm laying down?"

"You think I'm imagining things when I say these men are Bolivan."

"I'm saying you might be taking little pieces and making them look like the big piece you were looking for."

"I can appreciate that you feel that way, but I'm convinced."

"Convinced enough that if something needs to be done about these boys, you won't worry you got it wrong?"

She paused.

"See, that's the kind of thing you've got to think about when you work at the level I work at." He gave her another slap on the back. "Lucky for you, you already came up with better than I got, so regardless of if I talked you out of it just now, you talked me into it. I'm impressed you got there in only a few days."

"I work long hours. I've got to get things done fast or not at all."

"Ha! You and me both."

"It helps that this was all focused around some friends of mine, so I knew where to start looking."

"You looked in the right spots. Boy, oh boy. Bolivans. You know, on paper, you'd think I'd be able to get along. They deal in contraptions. I deal in… *not* contraptions. But I just don't like them coming down this far and not doing me the courtesy of an introduction. And they're *all* about stepping on toes these days. Getting their dirty little fingers into everything they can. Can't let them get their roots down in my garden, or I'll be pulling weeds forever. But, and this is the bit that rubs me raw, they picked *just* the right spot to plop their boys in. I can't just start pulling blades across the necks of the watch. For one, we need *someone* on the walls in case someone comes a-knocking that shouldn't. For another, the nobles pay for them, and the officials make sure we have them, and the more I fiddle with stuff the nobles and the officials do, the more likely I'm going to have to start pushing through a lot more nonsense to get my job done."

"Don't tell me there's nothing you can do."

"Oh, there's always something I can do. I just don't get to choose *when* it happens. The nice thing about the watch—and I'm stretching that word pretty far to fit—is that they have a job that'll get a fellow killed even if he's doing things right. I don't like seeing a man die who doesn't deserve it, mind you, but when a man's gotta die, it sure helps when his job can get the blame. But if they were smart enough to put their boys on the watch, and to GET their boys on the watch, they won't make it easy. Regardless, I'll put some boys on them. Maybe I won't be so subtle about it, let them know I know. That should give them some cold feet if they're thinking of pushing their boundaries. And when they slip up, that'll be it. How's that suit you?"

"So long as my friends stay safe."

"Mmm-hmm… Let me make something clear. I don't think you need to be told this, you seem pretty sharp, but it's not the kind of thing I like to leave dangling. Probably, what I'm planning to do? It'll keep your friends safe. Safer than if I didn't do it. But I'm not doing it to keep your friends safe. I'm doing it to keep some rats out of my garden before they chew up the roses. And if it so happens that there's two ways to do this, one that's hard and keeps your friends safe and one that's easy and doesn't? I'm doing the easy one. Not out of spite. But that's how business is done. I appreciate the information—information isn't without value—and I know the missus appreciates the cake, but even if you put those two things together, you don't come close to covering what it'd cost to hire me. This isn't even a favor. This is you finding a thing that just so happens to be on both our lists. And trust me, that works out for you, because I'm not a man you want to owe a favor."

"… Right."

"But, to show you I'm not a bad guy, let me make some more things clear to you. The way you handle someone on the watch? You lean on a situation that might go sour for them to *make sure* it goes sour for them. No one's surprised when it happens, and all the guesswork gets taken out. But these boys? They'll be expecting someone like me to try something like that. So they'll try to avoid a situation like that, or they'll try to make sure we can't lean on it. The difference between pulling it off and not pulling it off? Speed. Something comes along that'll put those two in danger? I gotta know. And I've got eyes in a lot of places, you know that. But I don't have them everywhere and even if I did, sometimes someone blinks. So for the purposes of this little job, I'd recommend you volunteering your eyes. You see something happening that'll give me a chance to do my thing? You let me know. Personally. You run up, you give a nod to one of my boys out front, and the wheels'll start turning. And the quicker you do it, the quicker they're out of our hair. Understand?"

"I understand."

"Great!" He slapped her back again. "I do love doing business with someone who works for a living. Nice and clean and easy. Finish your drink, see yourself out. I've got to get some boys in here and tell them what the need to do. It's been a pleasure, Allie. Maybe I'll see you around."

"I'll say this as kindly as I can, sir, but I don't think you will. Once this is settled, I'll go back to pretending I don't even know you exist."

He laughed. "You say that now, but I can count on one hand the people who made it down here once and didn't show back up eventually. The missus can pick 'em. She sends them down, it's usually the beginning of a long, profitable relationship. But for now, you're not on the payroll, so I won't keep you."

Allie drained her water, set down her glass, and hurried toward the door as quickly as she could without seeming rude. She made it as far as the front door before a voice called from behind.

"I trust things went well?" said Eveline.

Allie turned.

"Oh, yes. Yes, thank you so much for your help and your time."

"You earned your audience. No thanks necessary. But before you go, I'd like to applaud you. Finding your way here, unannounced, and ending up with an audience with my husband? A rare achievement. I'll be keeping my eye on you. I suspect you'll be a useful woman to know."

Allie didn't know how to respond. She respectfully nodded and slipped out of the manor. Her back tingled and twitched as she left their home behind her. There was something about that place. It wasn't sinister, precisely. But it felt... heavy. Like the longer she lingered, the more likely she was to be stained by whatever hung in the air. There was the terrible feeling that by having touched that knocker, she'd be leaving fingerprints on everything else she touched that would lead right back to that place.

"This had better be worth it..." she muttered.

Chapter 12

Epiphany hurried toward the bazaar. Most of the stalls were still set up, though the bulk of their more exotic goods had been purchased or traded for local goods. Only a handful of wagons were loaded and ready to roll. One of them was a purple one, stinking of badgerweed.

"Stop! Wait!" Epiphany said, dashing toward it.

At the sound of her voice, her still-nameless prospective buyer poked his head out of the flap.

"Ah, Miss Masker." He hopped out and stepped close, his breath almost unbearable as he whispered, "I trust you have the goods?"

"Not yet. My brother should be arriving any minute. If you leave now, you'll pass him on the road."

"Miss Masker, yours is not the only deal I've been tasked with closing. I have my deadlines, and I face consequences for missing them just as you do. The offer of purchase still stands, less the forfeit of failing to meet the agreed-upon timing. Perhaps next time you'll learn to be a bit more punctual."

"We aren't talking about a day. We're talking about an hour, perhaps two. You can make that up on the road."

"It is not my obligation to push my crew harder to make up for your shortcomings."

"My brother has had *multiple* run-ins with bloodthirsty mercenaries in order to bring you your goods. I'm not letting you weasel out of an agreed-upon price because of obstacles you could have warned us about to begin with."

"You're upset. I'll forgive your indelicate wording, but I'm afraid if I don't have those items before I leave the city, the price drops. That's the cost of doing business."

"You haven't seen me upset, sir. But you and I both know that if you could get what you want from anyone else, you would have. You have the money, I have the goods. Money is money. I can get it elsewhere, if I search hard enough. But those goods are unique. I am the one with the leverage here."

He grinned. "That would absolutely be so… if you had the goods. But you don't. Not here. Not yet. And frankly I'm curious how you know of the travails of your brother. If he's heading here as quickly as he can, word of his troubles and tribulations surely wouldn't precede him."

"Well then I suppose you don't know everything about how we do business. Why don't you…" She trailed off as she noticed his focus shift to the sky.

"It seems you may be right about your brother's proximity. And I suppose there is at least one way that word of his clashes could precede him."

Epiphany turned. Two sleek forms were slicing their way through the air. Hippogriffs, and they could only be headed for her parents' shop.

"You've earned yourself a few minutes reprieve, provided this doesn't go south for you." He climbed back into the wagon, his head lingering in the opening just long enough to add, "Good luck."

#

Tome huffed and puffed. Despite his time on the road, he was unaccustomed to this level of physical activity. He'd been heading for Beffshire partially because he knew it to be a rather large city, but at this precise moment he found himself wishing it was a bit smaller. Fel had dropped him at the gate, and it felt like he'd been running for ages with the heavy pack on his back and his traveling case in his hand. Finally he seemed to have reached what he'd been sent toward. He stumbled through the door of a tavern and dropped the pack on the ground with a clank.

"This is," he panted, "The Fox and Log, yes?"

"That it is," said the barmaid. "Can't say our reputation has brought many people running, but pick a seat and what'll you have?"

He waved off the offer and caught his breath a bit. "No, no. Not here for a drink. At least, not yet. Fel sent me."

"Oh, is he back in town?" Allie said hopefully.

"He is, and he needs help. He sent me here. Said it was better than the watchhouse."

Allie's expression hardened. "Is Fel in trouble?"

"Unless he's able to talk himself out of it."

"He's more of the talking-himself-*into*-trouble type than the talking-out-of-it type."

"So I've observed."

"Where is he?" Allie asked.

"At his family's shop. The hippogriff riders are—"

Allie didn't need to hear any more. "Davie!" she shouted.

The little runner appeared from behind the counter. "What do you need, Allie?"

"Nothing happens to this guy, you got that? This guy stays safe. And keep people away from the bar. No moochers."

Davie saluted and pulled a heavy, leather-wrapped stick from behind the bar.

170

Allie threw her rag on the counter. "Boys! Fel's in trouble. Let's get moving!"

Half of the clientele of the tavern stood, some a bit more shakily than others. Allie rushed out the door. They followed.

"Does Fel have that many friends?" Tome asked.

Davie shrugged. "About half of them are friends. The others are just folks who'll do what Allie asks, hoping for free booze."

Tome glanced out the door. "Even so… I don't imagine there's a place in this world that would empty out like that if someone mentioned my name. It's enough to make me rethink my transient lifestyle." He tugged open his coat and splayed his remaining spells on the table. He sifted through them. "Healing… Defensive… Defensive… Why in blazes did I do nothing but write down things to keep myself safe and no one else?"

"Well, you sure can't depend upon that knife of yours. Looks dull as a spoon," Davie said.

"What are you talking about?" he said.

Davie pointed. The dull dagger was at his feet. Oiler, notably, was not.

"The dagger must have slipped out when I dropped it." He cradled his forehead. "Oh… this won't end well…"

#

In Masker's Antiquities, Vivian was showing off a silver teapot.

"As you can see, this maker's mark here indicates the Loyah smiths. That means this is no less than two hundred years old. There are six such teapots left in the world, and I personally sold one to Lord Stiller just last month. This is an heirloom in the making."

"I don't know. Four hundred duots…" said the customer.

"That's just two duots a year since its creation. And don't think of it as an extravagance. Think of it as an investment."

Wick's voice came from the lantern in the corner, heard only by Vivian. "The time has come. The 'griff riders are nearly here."

She shut her eyes for a moment. "I'm sorry, ma'am, but we'll have to continue this tomorrow."

"Now, now, I didn't say I *wasn't* going to buy it," the woman said.

Vivian pulled a club from behind the counter. The customer's eyes opened wide.

"Fine, four hundred duots!" she yelped.

"Leave, quickly."

She nodded and rushed out the door. Vivian turned and shouted down the open dumbwaiter.

"Martin! Wick's given us the heads up, and not a moment too soon. The blasted harpies finally went quiet and I just saw a shadow. It's time."

"I'll be ready," he shouted back.

She rushed to the door and dropped a brace across it. One by one she shuttered and locked the shelves built into the walls. As she turned the final key in its lock, the ground shook. She didn't bother squinting through the shutters she'd just secured. She rushed to the dumbwaiter, set the keys inside, and sent it down.

"Vivian and Martin Masker!" barked Temple through the glass. "You are in violation of Thayn Antiquities Ordinance. You will open your doors and allow a thorough inspection, or we will use force!"

"The Bolivan family has no say in how I do my business, and you're wasting breath pretending to be working for anyone but them."

"How'd they find us out?" Cheek mumbled.

Temple thumped him on his head. "Your fool mouth, most likely. But fine, if this is how they want it." He turned to the hippogriffs. "Beasts, defend!"

The creatures turned their backs to the storefront, flicked their tails, and adopted a hostile stance, eying up their surroundings for threats.

Cheek put his boot to the door and started bashing. It rattled and creaked, but one didn't run a place full of jewelry and one-of-a-kind contraptions without investing in a proper door and brace.

"Forget the door, you idiot. Go for the glass," Temple ordered.

Vivian winced. In part, it was because a glass window so large was terribly expensive and she wasn't looking forward to replacing it. Mostly, it was because she knew what came next.

Cheek finished smashing his way through the window and put his foot through. A glimmer of faint blue raced along the edge of the window and vanished into the ceiling.

One of the nice things about the assayers was they only appraised contraptions in their intended form. Many a time, Martin had assembled and restored a contraption that had an innocuous function, like releasing curtains at the merest tug of a thread, and been given permission to sell them. But replacing some mundane linkages and adding some specialty equipment could make contraptions of that sort a good deal less innocuous.

Thin wooden planks shattered under the force of a horizontal iron bar dropping down through the ceiling. It dragged a net of crisscrossed chain behind it. Cheek tried to pull his leg free, but didn't quite get it clear before the bar struck and trapped his foot under a hunk of metal that weighed more than he did. He screamed in pain and yanked his foot free.

"She broke my toes! She broke my blasted toes!"

"You broke my window. Fair trade," Vivian called.

Temple picked a broken slat from the ground and tentatively tested one of the chains now barring his entry. "Full of tricks, aren't you?"

"Keep trying to get in, and you'll find out how many tricks I've got," Vivian said.

Despite the early morning, the streets were starting to fill with curious and concerned townsfolk. As well-meaning as they might be, the snapping beaks and fierce gazes of the hippogriffs had a way of sapping the bravery from the average city-goer. Calls for the watch rang out, but Vivian wasn't going to count on them having much more interest in facing off against the Greater Mystics.

"Fortunately, I don't need tricks," Temple said.

He paced to his steed and pulled a set of hooks and ropes from the saddlebag. He looped them through the beast's harness and drove them into the door. A few shouted orders had the door straining at its hinges. The brace splintered and the door gave way. Temple, rather than risking the cleared doorway himself, shoved the limping Cheek through. No further defenses activated. He paced after him. They both drew blades from their belts.

"I'll make this very simple. The chain pack, the blunt dagger, and the mask. You give them to us and we leave. You get cheeky and we will tear your shop apart, we will tear your home apart, and we won't stop digging until we've found them."

"You've done an awful lot of damage for nothing then. We have nothing of the sort."

"Your boy has them. And your boy is headed here."

"My boy does *not* have them."

He stalked closer. "We've tangled with the boy. And though we don't know how, we know for *certain* that you've been in contact with him. Either he's been here already, or he'll be here shortly."

"I'm telling you, you've made a terrible mistake. Nothing like that is on its way here," Vivian said.

Temple tipped his head. "You really believe that, don't you?" He grinned. "Then your boy's been hiding something from you. And you'd better hope he's headed this way rather than straight into the arms of whoever he's looking to sell it to, or he'll miss his chance to save his mother."

Vivian took a step back and inched toward the corner of the room, where the stairs to the next floor were hidden.

"Don't try to escape." He stepped forward onto the rug in the middle of the floor. "Unlike you with your assault on my associate, I'm not interested in spilling any blood today. This doesn't have to get any messier than it already has."

"It'll have to get a little messier, I'm afraid," Vivian said.

"If that's how you want it." He brandished his weapon.

Vivian stomped her foot twice. An instant later, a hefty click rang out, and the rug sank down into the floor. The already-hobbled Cheek dropped through a trapdoor that the rug had been hiding. His shouted complaints were brought to a sudden end by a dull thump below. Temple managed to roll clear of the trap. Vivian charged forward and dove atop him, hammering him with her club.

"This one's out!" Martin shouted from below.

Temple, bloodied and furious, heaved Vivian off and put a meaty mitt around her throat. "This one *isn't*," he shouted back. "I've got my hand around your wife's throat. Either we start behaving ourselves, or the family is going to get a good deal smaller."

"Mom!" shouted Epiphany.

Temple turned to the street. Epiphany burst from the crowd and slid to a stop just before the hippogriff could get a piece of her.

"You're this wench's girl," Temple shouted. "Do you have the goods?"

"I don't!" Epiphany said. "Call off your beasts and come out of there now. There's no way this goes your way, mercenary."

"You are in no position to make demands."

"No, but I am," Fel shouted. He emerged from the crowd as well.

"You…" Temple growled. "Send the goods through."

"Oh no. I don't have them with me. I'm not giving you the chance to just sic these monsters on me and claim them. They're with my associate for safekeeping. If you want them, you and I are going to parlay. When I'm satisfied my family is unhurt and you agree to never show your face in this town again, then we'll do the exchange."

Temple smoldered with anger for a moment. Finally he shouted to the hippogriffs. "Heel! For that one and that one only…"

#

Allie skidded to a stop in an intersection.

"You boys head that way, down to the Masker's place. I'll join you just as soon as I take care of something."

The collection of tavern patrons hurried down the street. Allie sprinted to the upscale part of town.

"This is what it was all about," she huffed. "This is what you did this for."

Her chest was burning as she rounded the corner and spotted the Verfessa estate. All she had to do was make eye contact with the men guarding the gate, and she was treated to a synchronized knowing nod. One of them headed for the door of the estate. The other pulled what looked like a halberd from a rack just inside his booth.

Allie didn't wait around to see what would happen. She was still needed at the antiquities shop. But hopefully that cake was about to pay off.

#

In Masker's Antiquities, Fel had made little progress. Temple's hand was off his mother's throat, but only to replace it with a knife held against her

174

skin, ready to bring a swift end to negotiations if things didn't go as he wanted.

"All three artifacts. In my hands. I don't take one step out of this place until I have them."

"I didn't find the mask."

"For your mother's sake, you'd better be lying and you'd better come clean about it, because it's all or nothing."

"Listen," Fel said, his voice low, "we've got a buyer for these goods. We'll split the money with you."

Temple laughed. "You don't get it, do you? I've got a contract. I don't care if you offer me ten times what the contract is for. I break that contract, I never work again. The mask, the dagger, and the pack. Hand them over. All of them. You can't hide them from us."

"I'm telling you, we didn't find the mask. There may not *be* a mask."

"Well then, if it means more searching, then there's no reason to keep you around, is there?"

Temple's grip tightened. A voice rang out from the corner.

"Not so fast!" Wick shouted, his voice heard by all.

Temple turned, expecting to see someone trying to get the drop on him. Fel took full advantage and heaved himself forward. Temple prepared to defend himself, but Fel wasn't aiming for him. He tackled his mother to the ground, separating her from the mercenary. Temple swiped his knife at him, but the blade failed to slash completely through his heavy jacket. Fel rolled and delivered a heel-thrust between Temple's legs. The blow missed its mark, but struck his thigh and threw him off-balance. It bought Fel enough time to scramble to his feet and charge Temple. The better-trained warrior sidestepped, but it turned out that fighting against Fel was very much like gambling against Fel. It's true that Fel was no expert, but his complete lack of knowledge on which moves were the most intelligent meant a more skilled opponent tended to be confounded by his boneheaded plays. In this instance, it might have been wise to try to knock down or disarm Temple. Fel had something else in mind.

Temple's sidestep brought him to the edge of the open trapdoor. Fel threw a shoulder at him, and they both went tumbling through.

A more calculated maneuver would have placed Temple on the bottom at the point of collision. Instead, they twisted in air and both struck the floor hard. The merc got his feet first, but he soon found himself on the receiving end of a chair to the back from Martin. Fel tried to climb to his feet, but the surprise attacks weren't enough to offset the accumulation of injuries and the lack of formal training. Before he could stand, he took a boot to the neck and slumped back down. Martin didn't fare much better. He was sent sprawling into the dining room table, under which the other mercenary was shackled. Temple hauled Martin up and used him to replace Vivian as his hostage.

The door from above flew open, and Vivian appeared on the stairs, armed and ready to fight. But she stopped in her tracks when she saw the blade to her husband's throat.

"All right…" Temple breathed. "All right… You put up your fight. But it's over. Here is what's going to happen. You are going to hand over the goods. You are going to unlock the shackles from my partner. And *maybe* I'll let some of you live. If you don't do as I say *immediately*, then I'll paint this house with your blood and start tearing this city apart to find what I'm after. No more tricks. No more bargaining. Bring me the goods *now*."

"I don't have them. They're being kept safe by——" Fel began.

Temple slid his knife against Martin's throat, nicking it slightly. "I don't want excuses. You figured out this whole ambush, you can figure out how to get the goods now, or your father's blood is on your hands."

Fel's mind swam as he staggered to his feet. Even if he wanted to give in, he wasn't sure how he could do it fast enough to save his father. "I… I just need…" Fel stammered.

Above him, a rattling, jangling sound rang out, like metal being dragged across the floor above. Then a blur of glittering metal dropped down through the trapdoor and landed heavily between them. It was Oiler. He looked up, assessed the situation, and extended a claw to snatch the weapon.

"Mom! Get Dad downstairs and barricade the door."

Vivian didn't waste the breath to argue or question what would become of Fel or where this mysterious mechanism came from. She charged in, gave the mercenary a boot to the side, and hauled Martin away. The door and hatch to the next floor slammed shut, and a pair of heavy braces could be heard sliding in place behind them.

Temple tried to pull yet another of his seemingly endless sequence of weapons. Oiler disarmed him again. He glared at the contraption with disdain.

"Fine…" he rumbled. "You want me to beat your keeper to death with my bare hands? I can oblige."

Temple moved in. Fel raised his arms in defense and immediately received a thrust-kick to the stomach. Oiler just watched, expressionless face darting between the two of them. The contraption evidently only wished to disarm, not actually prevent combat. Fel wheezed and stumbled back. A vicious backhand staggered him. A few more blows like that, and it would be over for him. He just didn't have the skill Temple had. He blinked his eyes and tried to focus his doubled vision on the mercenary.

"First you," Temple murmured. "Then your family. Then your friends. I'll cut a bloody swath through everyone who has ever met you until I find what I need. You toyed with the wrong people…"

He raised a fist. Fel shut his eyes, turned his head aside, and raised his arms in defense. A chaotic clatter of chains filled the air, and he felt something tight and heavy curl about him. Chains wound around his arms and midriff. Temple delivered a punishing blow to his midsection, but it did little more than knock Fel back. The blow was mostly absorbed by the chains wrapped around him.

Fel opened his eyes to find that Oiler had wrapped its chain arms around Fel's own and similarly wrapped his midsection in tail. The contraption closed its claws over his fists, forming something of an improvised set of brass knuckles.

Fel smiled. He launched toward the mercenary. Still, the greater skill was an obstacle, but knowing precisely how to mount a defense didn't matter much when the attack was from someone nearly double one's size and wrapped in steel. The battle raged on between them, and slowly the tide started to turn.

#

Tome dashed down the street. Davie was with him. Despite his smaller size, the little runner was more than capable of keeping pace.

"This way. Just around this turn and you'll see the antiquities shop!" Davie said.

"Right…" Tome huffed. "Great… Why is Beffshire so *large*?"

He had three spells gripped tightly in his right hand. With the limited time and limited resources, he'd been able to dream up a grand total of three possible ways he might be helpful if Fel needed him. As they rounded the corner, there was no need for further instruction. Between the small crowd of concerned or curious onlookers and the veritable army that Allie had gathered, he knew precisely where Fel was located.

As he got closer, he could see that the crowd was being ably held at bay by the pair of hippogriffs. In theory, the crowd could overwhelm the beasts, but persuading any individual person to be the first to face a beak that could crack a skull like a walnut was a bit much to ask someone.

Tome shouldered his way through the crowd until he reached the front. Allie was there, flanked by a pair of particularly hefty bar patrons, both looking as though they were having second thoughts about their role in this.

"They're just a couple of birds!" she shouted, waving her bat. "We can take them!"

"Listen," Tome gasped when his lungs would allow him. "If we can just get the saddles off, these things will fly off. They're being tamed."

"Yeah? Well you first," said one of the burly helpers.

He fumbled with one of the spells. "This is a taming spell too. It'll work for a day on something small and weak. For a hippogriff, it might work for a few seconds."

"'It might work' isn't good enough for me," the brute said.

"I'm quite certain… I'm *moderately* certain…" Tome stumbled for a bit. "… Fine, I'll do it myself…"

He pocketed the remaining spells and readied the relevant one. As his mind helpfully provided all sorts of potential concerns with the plan, from the interaction with the other taming enchantment to the age of the spell and the fact that it was written quite a distance away, he waited for his opening. When the nearest hippogriff decided that someone on the other side had gotten a little too close and snapped at them, Tome struck.

He tore the edge of the spell, sprinted forward, and slapped it against the 'griff.

"Stop! Stop, *stop*, STOP!" he cried with escalating concern as it turned toward him.

It opened its beak, then gradually became still. He didn't waste a moment. With a panicked dive, he dropped to the ground and fought with the saddle strap until it came free. The heavy bit of contraption fell away, and instantly the hippogriff's eyes widened and it scrambled at the ground, hoofs fracturing cobbles and nearly trampling Tome. He rolled back into the crowd, and the thing took to the sky. The remaining hippogriff retreated toward the doorway and widened its stance.

Allie helped him to his feet. "Good job, stranger. Do that again and we can go in and help Fel."

"Thank you," Tome said, one hand on his chest in hopes of preventing his heart from rattling out of his body. "But that was my last of that spell."

"What's left?"

"I've got one that makes a lot of flashing lights as a distraction, and one that… I think it makes a four look like a five on a rolled die. I'm not sure why I thought it would be helpful. My mind hasn't been as sharp as it could be."

"Well snap out of it. I don't like the sounds I'm hearing from in there. As soon as we get an opening, I want everyone ready to take advantage. That includes you," Allie said.

#

Fel had gotten the hang of the heavier motions now that his arms had been wrapped in living chain, and was scoring more hits than he was missing. Temple, for all his superior training, simply couldn't overcome the raw strength and impenetrable defense of the combined Oiler and Fel assault.

"Enough!" he spat, backing toward the steps. "I'll be back. With reinforcements."

He dashed for the steps. Fel followed, but as soon as he was no longer in mortal danger, Oiler dropped from him and industriously set about repairing the broken furniture. Fel rushed up the steps in pursuit. Dealing with these two was almost more than he and his family could handle. If this person got away and managed to bring down more of this onto his family, it would be the end of them.

Temple sprinted across the shop floor. Fel bounded after him. The mercenary scrambled onto the back of the remaining hippogriff. Fel stumbled into the street and grabbed hold of his leg.

"You're not going anywhere!" he barked.

"Do you honestly think there's anyone here who can stop me?" Temple said, trying to kick him free. He pointed his hand and raised his voice, ready to issue a command that would see Fel and anyone foolish enough to help him shredded by griffin claws. "Beast…" he shouted.

"DIRTY RAT BIRD!" croaked a chorus of voices from above.

The four lesser harpies, bright enough to know they were at risk of losing their meal ticket, descended upon Temple. He shouted and swatted at them as wings buffeted and claws scraped. Fel dragged the merc off the saddle and raised his fists to pummel him into submission.

"Beast! *Kill!*" Temple shouted.

Fel threw himself aside and barely avoided being slashed to ribbons by a sweeping claw. The crowd scattered as Fel dashed for the cover of the nearest alley, as he very much doubted his family's ransacked shop would offer much protection. A terrified dive sent him sprawling onto the scummy ground of the narrow alley. The 'griff scratched and tore at the heavy stone walls of the neighboring buildings. The good news was, there wasn't room enough for the thing to get to him. The bad news was the alley was a dead end.

He heard voices shout as the bravest among them tried to work out how to take down the maddened beast without being trampled by its powerful hind legs. Behind it all, he could hear the increasingly anguished screams of the mercenary as the harpies continued their harrying assault. Then came new shouting, a bit of confusion, and the clip-clop of tiny hooves. As Fel backed farther into the alley, he saw the spirited gray form of Parch come trotting into view between the monster's legs. It spotted Fel, then took a few steps back. It pawed the ground, lowered its horn, and charged.

With all of the force the little thing could put behind its horn, it assaulted the unsuspecting 'griff with a leaping headbutt. From the stricken cry the monster released, the blow landed somewhere very sensitive. The 'griff took a faltering step back and turned to see where the attack had come from. Fel rushed out, slid beneath the distracted beast, and unfastened its saddle.

The combination of pain and suddenly restored freedom inspired the creature to leap skyward the very moment it was no longer tamed. It spiraled into the sky. Fel, a bit bewildered and badly battered, surveyed what had become of the street around him.

The hippogriffs had churned the street and the neighboring buildings up a bit, but nothing that a few hours' attention from a mason couldn't cure. The crowd and the watch together had subdued Temple once the harpies retreated.

Others had hauled Cheek out to join him. His parents hurried out to the street, spotted first Allie and Epiphany, then Fel. All four of them rushed to Fel.

"Are you all right? Are you hurt?" his mother asked.

"I've been better… but I could have been worse," he said.

"What in the world have you been up to?" Allie said. "I'm a little hurt that I had to hear you were back in town from a wizard instead of from you."

"You'll be hearing all about it as soon as I can scrape together the money for a couple of pints. Do me a favor, take Tome with you back to The Fox and Log and get him started on a tab."

"Will do," Allie said. "But you better get over there soon. Seems like this story will take a while."

"Wait." Tome handed him the blunt dagger. "You'll need that."

Tome was flanked by the contingent of bar patrons, who all agreed he was owed a few drinks for his display of fortitude and mysticism. Fel's mother dusted him off a bit.

"If you're not hurt, you're helping to prop up that door," she said.

"And answering some questions," Martin said.

"Mom, Dad, there are plenty of questions to answer, but first, there are things to discuss, and fast," Epiphany said.

"Fine. Inside." Vivian turned to the crowd. "And off with the rest of you! The show's over."

#

A few minutes later, Fel was inside. He had a wet rag over one eye and was becoming increasingly aware of just how many aches and pains he'd accumulated. Oiler was inert in the middle of the room, dagger tucked into the pack to keep him asleep. Martin was glaring at it and tugging at the bandage on his neck. Epiphany had taken it upon herself to fill them in.

"… the man is, hopefully, still in town. But if we're going to take advantage, then we'll need to act quickly."

Their parents sat in sullen silence for a few moments.

"You took the map with the full intention of making a sale to someone willing to bypass the assayer's office…" Vivian said.

"… I did," she agreed.

"You brought this upon the family."

"I didn't know the mercenaries would come. And by then it was too late," Epiphany said. "No one else knows about the goods. We can still make the sale."

"Oiler had to have come into the shop somehow," Fel said.

"There were *two* hippogriffs," Epiphany said. "I don't know how Oiler got past them, but I can guarantee you the rest of the crowd was so distracted by them that the moon could have fallen from the sky and they wouldn't have noticed."

"But it had to have run through town," Fel said.

"I think your many interactions with them has skewed your understanding of just how much of a sensation two hippogriffs invading a town can be, Fel," Epiphany said.

"Don't change the subject. How *dare* you two do this? You knew what you were risking," Vivian said.

"Mom, we both know we just don't have the business necessary to keep the shop going for more than a few more years unless we change something."

"So we adapt. We take on more work. It's what we've always done."

"This is us adapting, Mother!" Epiphany said.

"Don't you raise your voice to me, young lady. And just how much were you willing to risk the lives of your family and the legacy of the business for?"

"I negotiated the price *before* I knew—"

"How much, Fanny?"

"… Originally, twenty-five thousand duots per item."

Vivian's eyebrows raised. Epiphany continued.

"And once the mercenaries showed up, I negotiated it up to forty thousand."

"For each item," Vivian said.

"Each, for three specific items. Fel found two. The dagger and the pack of chains."

"Oiler," Fel said. "And we're not selling it."

"It's a contraption," Epiphany said.

"It saved my life, and probably Mom's and Dad's too."

"Many of the contraptions Dad sent you with saved your life."

"But this one *chose* to save my life. We can't sell it. It wouldn't be right."

"So forty thousand duots," Vivian said.

"*If* we hurry," Epiphany said.

Vivian turned to Martin, who was tapping the chair Oiler had glued back together with his finger.

"What do you think?" she said.

"Sell the dagger," he said quickly.

"Are you sure?" Vivian said. "If the assayer finds out—"

"We're always at the mercy of the assayer. This changes nothing. They can decide music boxes are too dangerous and we're through. But this contraption… Oiler… it stays. I need to know more. I need to know what it can do."

"Without the dagger, we won't be able to put Oiler to sleep," Fel said.

"That's a risk I'm willing to take if you are," Martin said.

"It's bad enough we didn't find three, if we go through all of this without making a single duot from this man, it will be a travesty," Epiphany said.

Fel looked to his father. "Get a puzzle box. One of the big ones. We'll need it."

Martin quickly fetched a box easily twice the size and complexity of the ones Fel had found. When it was properly scrambled, Fel slid the dagger from the pack. Oiler perked up, looked around, and spotted the puzzle box. It held its claws out and waggled the fingers pleadingly. Martin handed it down, and it eagerly went to work. Fel gave the dagger to Epiphany.

"Go. Hurry."

#

Mere minutes later, Epiphany reached the town square. The purple cart was on the move. She charged out and stood in front of the horse to stop it. A puff of badgerweed smoke coiled from within the wagon.

"Miss Masker. Cutting it close, aren't we?" the man breathed.

He held open the flap. There was little room inside. Most of the goods he'd brought must have been sold. Two other men, heavy-lifting types, were reclined against this piece of their remaining cargo or that.

"Privacy," he said, vaguely motioning at the door. They silently left. He puffed at his pipe. "I don't see a pack," he said.

"There was a problem. A miscommunication. He wasn't able to find the pack either."

"That is disappointing," he said.

She presented the dagger, wrapped in a rag. He took it and carefully unwrapped it. While it rested on the rag in his hand, he reached over and brushed the flap of the wagon aside to let some more light in. Then his fingers disappeared into his jacket pocket and returned with a jeweler's loupe. He looked over the details of the artifact.

"It is genuine. Or at least it matches the description I was given in every detail. I would vouch for its authenticity." He looked up and removed the lens from his eye. "I would have preferred all three items. I was willing to accept two. I am loathe to bring only a single item back to my employers."

"Would you prefer to bring nothing?" she said.

"You are absolutely certain you won't be selling me the pack."

"Absolutely."

He puffed his pipe. "A deal is a deal. Even in this diminished form, you've still done what no one else could. And I understand the mercenaries are now in custody. A net improvement for the world, that."

He handed her a small wooden case and opened a larger one beneath it. The large case had row upon row of coins, all lined up neatly. The last few rows were empty.

"Hold this, will you?" he said.

She held the smaller case. He opened it and, as she watched in agony, pulled stacks of coins out to return to the larger case.

"There," he said, turning the case in her hands to face her. "Forty thousand duots in the form of four hundred cenots. Do double-check my accounting, would you?"

"Fifty in a stack. Four stacks in a row. Two rows. That's four hundred cenots," she confirmed.

"Excellent. Your work leaves something to be desired with regard to comprehensiveness, but I can say with confidence you still provide a singular service."

"Tell me, sir. Would you consider making future purchases from us? Similarly unburdened by official appraisal?"

He grinned. "I believe so. Particularly if you come up with the mask and/or the pack. You'll be receiving a correspondence from me in a week or two. I would recommend you read it thoroughly. I look forward to future business, Miss Masker."

Epilogue

The Masker family sat around the dining room table. In a vanishingly uncommon event, Vivian had conceded that the store would need to close for the day. Fel and Martin had boarded up the broken window and repaired the door sufficiently to keep their goods safe. Now they were staring silently at the contents of the table. It held one of Wick's lanterns, the case filled with the payments from Mr. Badgerweed, and Oiler. The contraption was fiddling with a music box that had been stubborn enough in its malfunction that Martin had set it aside.

"It *thinks*. Look at it," Martin said. "It isn't pulling from some… previously installed information. Not entirely. It is working things out."

"Is it dangerous?" Vivian asked.

"It's the opposite of dangerous," Fel said. "It fixes things and it disarms people if it sees that they have weapons."

"Were there other things like this in the vault?" Martin asked.

"No. And believe me, I searched that place from top to bottom."

Oiler managed to carefully lever the top of the box open to reveal its innards. Using the very tips of its claws, it tested the motion of individual components.

"Does it sleep?" Epiphany asked.

"Only when it is in contact with the dagger. As far as I can tell. But if it has nothing to fix, it sits there quietly. And it likes puzzle boxes. They're like treats."

"This thing is worth more than forty thousand duots," Epiphany said.

"We're not selling it," Fel said. "It saved my life at least twice."

"No, no, no. I'm not suggesting we sell it," she said. "I'm just pointing out that it is worth more than the negotiated price. And that's *after* I renegotiated to include the pain and hardship. The biggest deal of my life, and it turns out I'm the one who got swindled."

"You didn't know, dear. But now you do," Vivian said. "Forty thousand is a more than respectable sum. More than I've made over that counter in my best weeks combined. But when we do business with that man again, we are going to play a bit harder."

"So we *are* doing business with him again?" Epiphany said.

Vivian motioned toward Oiler. "The deed is done. Every moment we are in possession of this thing, we are in violation of Thayn's laws governing unsafe contraptions. And we've made the sale. The damage is done. If they find out, we are ruined. Either we make sure they never find out, or we become rich enough to be the sort of people they bend the rules for. I don't much like either option, but of the two, wealth has its appeal."

Oiler's screw-slot eyes twitched and shifted. It waggled its fingers and clutched the box. A needle-thin fang emerged from its mouth, and it used it to press the music box's axle from its housing. It gently removed the axle and the free-spinning gears on it. With motions more delicate than one would have imagined would be possible with metal fingers, it removed and sorted the gears into an orderly row on the table. It hovered its head over the row, then pushed one of the gears forward. Martin snatched it up and fished a magnifying lens out of his pocket.

"The teeth are rounded over." He gingerly bit the gear. "This is entirely the wrong sort of metal, it must have been an old repair that wore out. I can grind up a replacement in no time. Brilliant diagnostic work, Oiler."

He patted the mechanism on the head, producing an oddly musical bell-type sound. It laced its claws and retracted into its pack.

"Even *without* any questionable trade, this mechanism is going to vastly increase our stock of functional contraptions. Though I imagine it would be best to keep it out of the workshop. That many broken contraptions at once might drive it a little mad."

Epiphany turned to Fel. "I know this trip was trying, but—"

"Oh, I'll be going back to that wall. I'll need to equip myself a bit better. Also, Dad, I might need a few hundred duots and a quick trip south if you want me to buy back Grandpa's wagon."

"It isn't without sentimental value, but a thing is a thing," Martin said, gathering up the parts to the music box. "But there are two points I'd like to make regarding any further trips to the wall."

"I'll take any advice I can get."

"First, isn't it going to be significantly more dangerous, now that the Bolivan family knows it contains a vault that we know the combination to?" he said.

"There's a dragon there, Dad. It was never going to be safe. I can handle it."

"Good. Because the second point I wanted to make was this." He reached under the table, where the sack with the items Fel had deemed "educational" were stowed. "These books. You said there were multiple copies of each?"

"I think so. I can't read them, but they all looked pretty similar."

"Even this one?" he said, sliding forward a thin black book with a gold-leafed title.

"I think? Look, Dad, I still have a headache and I haven't dulled it with any booze, so if this is a riddle, let's skip to the answer."

"The other two books are contraption references. They'll be enormously helpful. But this one? This one I think is the reason the workshop was so thoroughly locked and guarded."

He opened the book and flipped to a random page containing a familiar diagram of circles, dots, and crosses.

"That's a door combination," Fel said.

"They're *all* door combinations. I think you found the code book to the entire Greater Lands Wall, Fel."

"One trip to one vault that you could only gather a few bags of loot from was enough to change our whole family's fortunes," Vivian said, practically salivating. "And you're telling me we have the keys to a city-sized structure?"

"That is my belief," Martin said.

Vivian and Epiphany both looked to Fel.

"I guess it's good that we have the bigger wagon now," Fel said. "Because once I heal up and settle some debts, I'll be heading down south again."

"You've got debts to settle?" Epiphany said.

"That paper mage's help didn't come free. I'll need my share, and I'll need to get down to The Fox and Log before he tries getting into a game of grum and gets his teeth knocked out."

#

"Kings and a milkmaid," Tome said, flipping down his screen.

"And we're sure he's not using magic," said Tem.

"I've been watching him, boys," Allie said, setting down drinks and crickets for the table. "Unless he's pulling the wool over my eyes too, he's on the up and up."

"Grum is so much more of a rewarding game than sixes," Tome said, collecting his winnings.

"Yeah, well, have fun while you can. These boys don't like to lose. Things'll start getting real tense if you pick up another pot in a row. And that's your last free drink, by the way. Heroism gets you tipsy, not drunk," Allie said.

The door swung open and Fel walked in. The tavern erupted in excitement and approval.

"There's our boy! Ol' 'Griff-slayer Fel," Lou said.

"I didn't slay any hippogriffs. I just chased it away."

"Same difference. Get in here and tell us what you've been up to. Your boy here has been cleaning up at grum."

"Yeah, well, if he starts smoking during a game, cut him off," Fel said.

Tome gave Fel a sharp look.

"These are my friends, you're my business partner. I've got to watch out for my own." Fel turned to Allie. "Set me up with the rest of that bottle of rotgut, Allie. I've got stories to tell. But first, I've got some business with Tome."

"I was just about to start another game of grum. Can it wait?" Tome said.

Fel stuck his hand in his pocket and jangled the coins within. Tome's eyes brightened, and he turned to the others.

"Count me out for this one, but save my spot. I'll be back."

Fel slipped into the semisecluded booth where the more surreptitious business tended to be done. Tome joined him. When they were certain they had as much privacy as they were going to get, he counted out thirty cenots and dropped them on the table in front of Tome.

"Three thousand duots for a job well done."

Tome narrowed his eyes. "You mean to tell me a family of businesspeople only managed to sell those priceless contraptions for ten thousand duots?"

"We sold one of them for forty thousand."

"I *knew* you weren't going to sell that bag of chains…" Tome hissed. "Fine, then. By my accounting you owe me another nine thousand duots. That's thirty percent of forty thousand."

"If you recall, the deal was for a portion of my *share* of the profit. We split the earnings equally. That means you got thirty percent of my ten thousand."

Tome sneered. "You are a dirty dealer."

"I didn't even twist my words. You just didn't listen."

"Three thousand duots. That's enough to replace the paper and ink, and line my pockets a bit. Barely break even."

"Well, look at the bright side. When we sell the standard goods, you'll be getting another few hundred. And then there's the matter of the next trip."

"Next trip?"

"That vault had a lot more in it." He leaned forward. "And there are plenty more vaults."

"Oh… Oh I see. A longer-term alliance." He jingled the coins and put them in his pocket. "Provided you don't make a pet of half of our potential earnings on the *next* trip, I think this might turn out to be worth my time after all."

Allie walked over and set down the bottle of booze and a glass. Tome stood.

"Allie my dear! Break one of these coins, if you would? And keep five for yourself. I've got more grum to play."

She took the coin, rubbed it with her thumb and tested its weight for a moment before digging through her apron to count out the ninety-five duots he was after. When she was through, Tome took his small change and rushed back to the grum table.

"So… Your sister got you into some trouble, eh?"

"My sister and I collaborated on some trouble. And I guess I shouldn't be surprised you know about it, but how'd you find out?"

"Epiphany and I collaborated on some trouble of our own while you were gone."

Fel poured out a drink and swirled it in its glass. "I don't know if I like the thought of you two working together on anything. She's schemer enough for the whole family. The sort of stuff you two could pull off together is a terrifying thought."

"I wouldn't be too terrified. There was an awful lot of running around, wheeling and dealing, and as far as I can tell it came up empty, since you and your friend here had to deal with the 'griff riders on your own."

"What exactly did you try to do?" He took a sip, then looked at the bottle. "And this isn't rotgut."

"Eh. I felt like you deserved some of the good stuff. Provided you're willing to trade a few stories for it." She pulled a second cup from her apron and poured herself a shot. "Oovay! Take over for a bit."

"I am waiting for Davie to bring me an order from the West Side!" Oovay called back.

"Davie had to take the afternoon off. Now get out here and take over." She sipped at the booze and smiled at Fel. "Now spill it."

Fel savored a bit more of his drink. "If you want the *full* story, you're going to need another bottle."

"We'll just see about that."

He took another sip. "Have you ever been down to the Greater Lands Wall?"

"Can't say I have."

"Well, if you ever do go, you'll want to watch the ground for shadows—"

"Fel!" Tome called. "I know you've got some heavy pockets. Would you like to get in on this game?"

Fel jingled the coins in his pocket and narrowed his eyes. "I think I've pushed my luck enough for a few weeks. And I've got a story to tell."

#

Across town, Cheek and Temple were seething in a cell, staring down the two watchmen assigned to guard the door. Beffshire may not have had the best-equipped watch in Thayn, but along with their wall, they inherited a very sturdy jail. Most of the cells were occupied, if at all, by troublemakers under the influence of strong drink who needed to be locked up until their wits returned. For that purpose, the jail was wildly excessive. But the thick bars, thicker stone walls, and the sequence of locked doors separating cell from hallway from exit to freedom made it perfect for keeping the mercenaries from escaping. Despite the lingering light of day, there were no windows to let the sun in. If not for the flickering oil lanterns on either side of the cell, there would be no light at all.

"It's been hours. How long are you going to keep us here?" Temple asked.

Leonard scoffed. "You're upset about *hours*? It'll be a week before our messenger gets to Teskal to see what's to be done about you. Another week to get back. Plus however long it takes for them to decide, and they aren't quick with their decisions. You'd better get comfortable. You're going to be seeing a lot of this face."

A key turned in the lock to the otherwise empty block of cells. Leonard turned to see a pair of the recent conscripts enter.

"You're done with your shift, Leonard," said the first man.

"We'll take the evening shift," said the second.

"Hah! I guess you're done with my face for today, though." Leonard ran his club along the bars. "See you tomorrow. Bright and early!"

Leonard delivered the keys to one of the guards and marched out the door. One watchman locked the door behind him. The other took a lantern and marched the length of the block of cells, scrutinizing each one. He returned and gave a simple nod to his partner. The first watchman turned to the cell and scowled.

"You worthless idiots. You had hippogriffs. You had the name and location of the people who would have your goods, and you end up disarmed and locked up. It is outright *theft,* the fee you charged for your worthless services."

"No one said there would be a mage," Temple said.

"Or whatever that chain thing was. No one said it would be loyal to the Maskers."

The watchman crossed his arms. "When the Bolivan family hires people of your supposed caliber, we expect the capacity for some degree of improvisation. Fortunately for you, we had the foresight to find a place within the watch. Considering your inadequacy as mercenaries, I highly doubt you would have been able to keep Bolivan secrets under any degree of interrogation."

"Just let us out and we'll see to it that the Maskers aren't a problem any longer."

"The Maskers aren't the problem. And more to the point, they are clearly indispensable for now, as the only people with the degree of expertise necessary to access the vault and secure the final item. You will leave them be until they've outlived their usefulness. Once we have the items we require, we will happily hire you for the brutish work of exterminating them, as it seems the only thing you are capable of doing."

"Keep insulting us and you'll see what we're capable of doing firsthand," Cheek said.

"Here is what is going to happen," the watchman said. "We will wait three hours, perhaps four, until the sun has thoroughly set. We will be midway into our shift. That worthless Leonard will have dozed off like he always does, and Captain Boltt will have gone home for the evening. Then we will unlock the doors and release you. You will steal the horses in the watch's stable and make your escape. We will wait a half hour, then alert Leonard and tell him that you had a hidden weapon, assaulted us, and stole the keys."

A dull thud echoed off the stone walls. The second watchman slumped forward and spilled to the ground.

"What in the—" the remaining watchman yelped.

"Boys, boys, boys," came a voice in the darkness. "You seem so certain you know what's going down, but this isn't your city, is it? The Bolivan belong up north. When you come treading into Beffshire, you're tracking dirt on Donovan Verfessa's carpet."

The watchman grabbed one of the lanterns and held it high. His other hand went to his hip to draw his truncheon.

"I've got to hand it to you Bolivan boys, though," the unseen interloper continued. "You make a decent plan. I've got a few changes in mind, though."

"Where are you!" the watchman shouted. "Show yourself! You can't hide from me. The door is locked. You're trapped in here, and there's three of us and one of you."

"Two of you are unarmed and locked up, though. That leaves it one on one, and considering it was two on one a moment ago and that didn't make a lick of difference, let's say I'm not worried about my chances."

"I am a trained agent of the Bolivan family. I am equipped with contraptions you've never imagined. I could take a man twice my size."

A figure dropped down from above, landing on his shoulders. A leather-wrapped stick came down hard across his face. Two more quick blows and he crumpled as easily as his partner. The lantern fell to the ground. The mercenaries huddled against the far wall of their cell, wary of the still-unidentified foe.

"People always brag about being able to beat someone twice their size," muttered the assailant. "They never consider how tough it will be to beat someone *half* their size."

A hand reached down to grab the lantern and raised it up to reveal Davie, The Fox and Log's runner. He grinned in the light and set about carefully disarming the incapacitated watchmen. As he did, he addressed the mercenaries.

"Like I was saying," he said, gingerly slipping a ticking canister from one of the men's pockets. "They had a good plan. Only takes a couple small changes to be the sort of plan I can get behind. First, I don't think these two fellows will be alerting anyone to your escape. I think they're going to mysteriously vanish. Can't have a couple of trespassers and traitors traipsing about unsupervised. And then there's you. I've got good news and bad news. The good news is, I'm going to need someone to head up north and deliver the message of what happens to Bolivan agents who don't have the common courtesy to ask permission to do business in another man's shop."

He slid a long, gleaming blade from one of the fallen watchmen's equipment.

"The bad news is… I don't see why I need two…"

###

From the Author

Thank you for reading! If you liked this story, or perhaps if you found it lacking, I'd love to hear from you. Leave a review, or contact me directly on social media or via email. You can find the relevant links (as well as my newsletter sign-up) at bookofdeacon.com/contact

Discover other titles by Joseph R. Lallo:

The Book of Deacon Series:

Book 1: *The Book of Deacon*
Book 2: *The Great Convergence*
Book 3: *The Battle of Verril*
Book 4: *The D'Karon Apprentice*
Book 5: *The Crescents*
Book 6: *The Coin of Kenvard*

The Big Sigma Series:

Book 1: *Bypass Gemini*
Book 2: *Unstable Prototypes*
Book 3: *Artificial Evolution*
Book 4: *Temporal Contingency*
Book 5: *Indra Station*
Book 6: *Nova Igniter*

The Free-Wrench Series:

Book 1: *Free-Wrench*
Book 2: *Skykeep*
Book 3: *Ichor Well*
Book 4: *The Calderan Problem*
Book 5: *Cipher Hill*
Book 6: *Contaminant Six*